MW00982314

OLD TOWN

To Jordan & Devi

Thanks!

Bill Vernon

OLD TOWN

BILL VERNON

FIVE STAR

An imprint of Thomson Gale, a part of The Thomson Corporation

THOMSON

GALE

Detroit • New York • San Francisco • New Haven, Conn. • Waterville, Maine • London

LIBRARY OF CONGRESS CATALOGING-IN-PUBLICATION DATA

Vernon, Bill, 1941–
    Old town / Bill Vernon.
      p. cm.
      ISBN-13: 978-1-59414-552-0 (hardcover : alk. paper)
      ISBN-10: 1-59414-552-0 (hardcover : alk. paper)
      I. Title.
    PS3622.E748O43 2007
    813'.6—dc22
                                          2007000440

First Edition. First Printing: June 2007.

Published in 2007 in conjunction with Tekno Books and Ed Gorman.

Printed in the United States of America on permanent paper
10 9 8 7 6 5 4 3 2 1

For my parents who are present in whatever I write, Clarence Moses (Pete) Vernon and Ruth M. Hauser. And for my three best friends, who though also gone continue to influence me now: college roommate Ray Makos, graduate student and poet Karen Torpey, and eccentric writer, teacher, athlete Turnip (Hugh Tom) Smith.

ACKNOWLEDGMENTS

Old Town and I owe much to Rose Vernon, Viki Church and Ed Davis, who read early versions, suggested revisions, and put up with an often erratic personality. And to John Helfers of Tekno Books, his kind professionalism; and especially to Gordon Aalborg, the editor who recommended, greased and oiled and tinkered until a sputtering machine ran more smoothly.

CHAPTER ONE

Even my friends may tell you that I'm frustrating, paranoid, stupid, contradictory, self-righteous, and withdrawn. My ex-wife Angela will enthusiastically concur. Hell, although six adjectives cannot adequately describe anyone, I accept all of them except for paranoid.

It's not paranoia to defend yourself when you know danger is coming. Is a boxer in a ring paranoid for covering up and back-pedaling when opponents viciously attack? If somebody slaps you at every encounter, aren't you smart to step out of that person's reach as he approaches? Aren't you naïve not to?

In other words, damn good reasons had made me defensive long before that April day when something disturbingly odd appeared up ahead near the bike trail I was running on.

Of course I at once looked away, out through the dawn and the trees to a foggy field—my practiced reaction was to ignore disruptions. Plus, jogging had released endorphins and brought me a peacefulness that was easily lost. I was dancing with the moment and wanted to maintain my speed.

So when simple decency made me stop, foul words rattled out as if they might have the power to change what was there.

The incantation didn't work. Wading through the damp grass into high weeds, I already sensed before leaning over the thing that it was human.

A moment later I realized that it was an old man. THE old man. "Sammy!" The word created a cloud of breath that I had to look through. "Sammy, what happened to you?"

A terrible odor and grotesque visual details assaulted me. The gray hair was matted, the head battered in and dark-stained. The body was curled up and looked as rigid as a root, as if it had been dead for hours.

I staggered back onto the bike trail, gasped two lungfuls of clean air, and by habit glanced both ways for bikers, walkers, in-line skaters, other runners. Nobody else was around.

My bare thighs quivered, a warning that immobility would chill and stiffen my muscles. I unwound the nylon windbreaker from my waist, put it back on and zipped up.

What should I do?

My eyes roosted on high bare limbs far enough away from the body to allow me to think—but not about how awful Sammy's death was. Giving in to emotions now could get me into a mess. This thought sparked visions of what could happen: inconveniences, complications, even disasters.

Jesus, the law. I wanted no more entanglement with it. A necessary call to police a few days ago had produced intrusions into my house, uncomfortable interaction with armed bureaucrats, proof of their inefficiency, but so far not the help desired. I could do without any more police in my life.

As for Sammy, if there were anything useful to do for him, anything medical, I'd do it and become involved. Too late for that!

The question was, Could I get away from here cleanly? I looked up and down the old railroad track right of way again, strained my eyes, and confirmed that no one else was about.

I said to the air above the pile of rags: "Nothing I can do for you, Sammy. I'm sorry."

Then I raced back a hundred yards and disappeared from the bike trail, taking a cinder-mud path fifty yards through the trees and brush to State Route 86. There, I resumed my original pace upon the broad shoulder of the highway, heading back to where I'd left the car, concentrating on my physical safety with oncoming traffic roaring past just a few feet away.

Inside my car, I felt confident of a successful escape, but driving did not occupy my mind enough. Atop a plastic torso magnetized to the dashboard, the little round close-up of my daughter's face swayed with the car's momentum as if she were there, berating me—as Laura had done four years ago when her mother and I divorced. That reminded me of Angela, and her voice started harping at me in the silence.

In the seclusion of my living room, Dad's photo glared at me from the fireplace mantel. I knew what he'd say if he were alive. Mom's and Aunt Judy's framed faces joined him in glaring at me. If I called Mom's house, there was no doubt what Aunt Judy would say, or Mom if she could start talking again.

I hurried upstairs into the shower, scrubbed and scrubbed and rinsed, but failed to wash away the last image of Sammy. The distorted features obsessively replayed, and my comment of "Sorry" echoed in my mind like an accusation.

A chorus of voices began insisting that I ought to do something. "It's your duty. Do your duty."

"Duty my ass!" I growled into the bathroom's misty heat.

Naked except for the towel draped around my shoulders, I fled downstairs to the kitchen, filled the water pot, laid it on the largest burner, and switched the burner on high.

Then dictates beyond logic took over. I punched 911 and reported the body. Located it to the nearest half-mile painted in white on the bike trail, drew a map with words, but that of course was not good enough—not for the woman on the phone, not for the laws of Ohio, not for the cosmic forces that had decided to twiddle with me.

"Who is this?" came the demand.

My breath whooshed across the line, conveying my impulse

to disconnect.

"Name, sir? What is your name?"

"You have my phone number, don't you?" I growled, disgusted with myself for creating this awkward position.

"Your name, please?"

"What do you have as my number?"

"Sir, let's not play games."

"So you don't have my number."

"I do, sir, but anyone could be calling from a phone. Please give me your name."

"I don't think so." I hung up.

Fuck 'em. Didn't sound to me like she had my number.

Before the slices of wheat bread I dropped in the toaster popped up, the phone rang.

I sighed, pressing the receiver against an ear.

"It's me, sir. You want to give me your name now?"

I said shit to myself, my name to her, then agreed to meet detectives at the body. There was no other choice.

Naturally I felt bad for Sammy, and I would feel worse when I let myself think about what had happened to him. Sure. But what about me? I had just been forced to play a role, but given no lines, in a drama that might become long and complex. It would definitely screw up my life today. Already had.

Well, I told myself, the plot is in motion, and it won't stop until your part is concluded, maybe in the final act. Therefore, relax. Whatever you do won't make one goddam bit of difference anyway.

CHAPTER TWO

Relaxing was impossible though. I stared through a kitchen window at the brush lining the creek at the back of my property, and reviewed the obvious: I am not good with people, and that may be an understatement. With one person I'm okay, but with more I tend to think and act oddly. With authorities, I'm at my worst. I believed Dad's oft-repeated claim that you can't fight city hall, having seen what city hall did to him, having felt its iron, bruising grip myself. But resisting city hall's corrupting influence was necessary. Ergo, an ordeal was coming. Wonderful.

I chanted one of my credos—Try to control what can be controlled.—and gobbled my toast dry, totally forgetting the new jar of strawberry jam in the fridge. Still standing up I ate a boiled egg. Spilled a teaspoon of instant coffee crystals into a cup, turned off the burner, poured the cup full, suddenly imagined cops pulling up outside—didn't want that—and swallowed the tepid, partially mixed and therefore acrid concoction.

Then I ran upstairs, dressed, and tore away as fast as possible to keep the cops away from home. I parked off Route 86 in a wide space on the shoulder, and hustled over to the bike trail via the same path I'd used earlier.

The police were already there. Two cruisers sat bumper-to-bumper on the other side of the body, and a new white van was on my side. Tied to trees was yellow police tape, blocking off the bike trail behind the van and on the far side of the cruisers.

Two uniformed men seemed to be guarding the scene while three men and a woman in civilian clothes worked around the body.

Also present were two bike trail users, trapped like me behind the van and the tape—a man and a woman in the costumes required for biking these days: aerodynamic plastic helmets and tight yellow, blue and red Gore-tex or spandex or Lycra outfits. An expensive racing bike leaned against each of them. A couple of yuppies . . . yippee!

Cool it, I said to myself, coming up behind the pair. Yuppies are individuals too, not stereotypes.

"Hello," I said, announcing my arrival.

The woman's head snapped around and she nodded. The man looked at me too, but immediately turned back toward the cops.

I said, "Excuse me," and went by them under the tape.

Then the man spoke. "You're not supposed to go any farther."

I raised up on the other side, stared for a moment at his vacant expression, said, "No kidding," and went on.

Don't be rude, I told myself, walking alongside the van. Why not? I answered. First the guy snubbed me, and then he back-handedly insulted me with that phony helpful comment, which implied that I, unlike himself, did not understand the tape's significance.

So what? Forget him, I thought. Don't get riled up. Remember your purpose is to meet the cops and leave. Nothing else.

I focused on the van's passenger door, its large shield-like insignia with "Shawnee County FORENSICS" inside, passed it, looked ahead, and prepared to greet the closer uniformed man.

He threw up a palm and rushed toward me. "Go back!"

"But I—"

"Get back there behind the tape."

He positioned himself in my face, so close his overpowering cologne made me wonder how bad his natural odor was. A short guy in his 20s with something to prove, probably his masculinity.

Rejected by the cops, huh? Okay, fine with me. I had agreed to meet them here, and I'd done it.

I turned around, went back under the tape, and the male biker raised his eyebrows at me as if he'd just won a contest and expected congratulations. Irritating. I raised my eyebrows in response, turned sideways, and edged past.

Behind the bikers, I dawdled, thought of leaving, even started to leave, but fear of the cops visiting my home kept me there. Damn! I should have identified myself even if I'd had to scream the information to the young cop.

After a few minutes I rejoined the bikers, who were arguing about whether to return to wherever they'd started or to wait and see if the police would open the trail so they could get through.

"What is the hold up?" The woman spoke as if the world had pulled a dirty trick on her; the same reaction I'd been having.

One male cop in civilian clothes was taking pictures, circling the body. Soon the other two men in civilian clothes started inspecting the mown grass beside the paved trail, studying the ground, bending forward, moving slowly. One eventually worked his way behind the van, crossed just in front of us inside the tape, and started down the other side.

"What's going on?" the woman biker asked him.

"Police investigation," the man said, continuing on without even looking at her.

The male biker said sarcastically, in a low voice so the cop couldn't hear, "Oh, so that's what it is."

I laughed, thinking, what goes around, comes around. How's it feel to be snubbed? The bikers stared at me and I decided to be nice. "There's a man's body up there. So I think the cops will be here a while."

"Really?" said the woman. She glanced at her companion, then back at me. "What happened?"

"He was murdered."

The man asked, "How do you know?"

I said, "If you want to get around this stretch and keep going on the trail, it's easy. There's a path back there you can take over to the highway. Baumer Road's the first intersection a half-mile north. Hang a right there and you'll get back to the bike trail in twenty yards."

They discussed it, decided to do it, and the woman thanked me. I pointed out the path's location and they left. Good. The sky had cleared, the mist was gone, and my watch said 9:45.

By 10:10, pacing around behind some new trail-users stymied by the tape—an older couple hiking—I'd warmed up enough to remove my jacket and again cursed the insanity of my waiting.

"Hey, you in the Levi's and red hat!"

The couple at the tape looked back at me. Beyond them was the uniformed cop I'd met before. I said, "Me?"

"Anybody else in a red hat?"

What a lovable guy. I passed the hikers and stopped far enough away from him to avoid that cloying smell. "What?"

"Come on."

He didn't ask if I was the one who'd reported the body, didn't explain a thing, just lifted the tape for me to proceed underneath, ordering me around as if a common citizen deserved no explanation. Typical.

I said, "Now you want me to go past the tape. Is that correct?"

With irritation, he jerked the tape an inch higher.

I crouched and bowed going beneath it. At the same time he

grabbed my left arm and pulled, shifting my weight so I stumbled.

I jerked my arm away and straightened up.

His face went red and he reached for me again.

I stepped back and said calmly, "All you have to do is ask," thinking that petty insults by authorities led to abridgment of personal rights.

He frowned, glanced at the couple watching us, and jerked a thumb at the other police. "They wanta talk to you."

Walking along beside him I inquired, "Why me?" but he was pouting and wouldn't answer.

Ahead, the plainclothes people were together on the trail, watching the other uniformed cop approach them from the cruisers.

"Well?" the woman asked that other cop as we arrived.

He said, "This guy told them there'd been a murder and the body was male."

"Uh huh," the woman grunted, and turned to me.

Them? I looked farther down the trail where the uniformed man had come from and spotted two familiar bikers watching from behind the tape beyond the cruisers. The two jerks I'd given directions had ratted me out. Well, at least they'd put me into position to finish my involvement here. I waved at them, though not entirely to express my thanks, but neither waved back.

The woman cop asked, "What do you know about a dead man?"

"I found the body," I said, locking eyes with her.

"You the one who phoned it in?" When I nodded, she asked, "Your name?"

"Clifford Saunders."

She checked her notebook and apparently found me there. "Why so long to get here?"

Put the poor schmo on the defensive, huh? "I've been here a good while. Why didn't you ask for me among the spectators?"

She stared at me, then said, "We were busy, Mr. Saunders."

"Well, Miss, Mrs. Or Ms. Who are you, anyway? I presume you're with the police."

"We are all deputies." From beneath the jacket of her pantsuit she produced a leather case, unfolded and hung it from a breast pocket, displaying a Sheriff's Department badge and a name, Lt. E. Grimes. She said, "Okay? Now, why didn't you tell us you were here?"

I bent my head sideways toward the officer next to me. "The general chased me away when I tried."

"You coulda told me," the cop said.

I said to the woman, "Wasn't he instructed to look for me? Or did he forget? Or was he on a power trip, making himself feel good at my expense?"

"Lieutenant, I didn't—"

"It's all right, Clayton," Grimes said.

"Officer Clayton also manhandled me a minute ago instead of politely asking me to come here the way any civilized person would do."

She smiled. "Officer Jones. Clayton's his first name."

"If you want cooperation, disrespecting people doesn't get it." I could feel Jones's eyes burning into me. "Now, can I tell you what I know and get this over with?"

She swept her eyes over the three plainclothes men, sharing her exasperation, looked back at me, and said, "Please do."

"Thanks. I was jogging by and noticed the body. Then I called 911 and reported it."

"Let's get the times clear. When did you find the body?"

"Well, I started running about 7:15. Let's see. We are over three miles from where I started so, okay. That means I found the body about 7:40 or 45. I didn't check my watch."

Her ballpoint pen jotted in the notebook. "The call came in at 8:30, nearly an hour later."

"Well—" I shrugged.

"Almost any house has a phone."

"I decided to use my own."

"Must have taken a lot of deciding. I'm told Pekin Road where you called from isn't far."

"I had to jog back to my car first, and then drive home."

"Which would take how long?"

I shrugged. "Thirty minutes."

"I understand you didn't want to identify yourself."

"Calling from home was dumb. I could have stayed anonymous on a pay phone."

"Mr. Saunders, the public's help is essential, and time is sometimes very important to an investigation."

"Nobody else was around when I found the body, and he had obviously been dead for a long time."

"Do you know a lot about corpses? You also told the bike riders that the victim was murdered."

"This is too far from the road for a traffic accident. I did see his head, you know."

She glanced at her cohorts again, prompting one of the plainclothes guys to shake his head. She looked back at me and said, "We appreciate your insights. Any more to share with us?"

Just what I needed, condescension from a cop. Well, she was human and doing her job while I was being difficult. Sammy's death should be the subject here, not me.

I sighed, looked past her, glimpsed the body over her shoulder, and knew that saying more could really complicate things. But just saying no and getting away seemed dishonest. I could offer a bit more information and maybe speed up their investigation. I owed Sammy that much.

I shifted my eyes back onto the woman's face. "His name is

Sam. I don't know his last name."

She blinked and her eyes widened with renewed interest. "So you knew the victim."

I mentally sorted my facts, thinking that a little slanting might still get me out of there quickly. "We were acquaintances. We sometimes walked together along the bike trail in the evenings. Walking settled his stomach after supper, or so he told me once."

"Yesterday?" she asked.

"Huh?"

"Were you here with him last evening?"

Her light blue eyes glistened, reminding me of spots on a peacock's tail. "No."

"When was the last time you saw him?"

"The night before last, Monday. We walked for an hour."

"Right here?"

I nodded.

"How often did you walk together?"

"Most evenings the last three or four weeks. One day he happened to be here when I was and we got to talking."

"You didn't know him before that?"

"No."

"Did you pick him up and drive him here? Or vice versa?"

"I don't know where he lives. We'd meet back there." I pointed south down the trail. "See that broken tree limb? There's a path by it that goes over to the road, and maybe he parked over there. That's where my car is right now. No, wait a minute. My car's the only one there so he probably didn't. Unless the killer stole his car. Were keys in his pockets?"

Her forehead wrinkled. "Go on with how you two would meet."

"In the evening I always leave my car a half-mile down the trail at the County Park. Old Town Park it's called. He'd wait at that path, and when I got there, we'd walk on together. He'd leave on the path when we returned, and I'd go back to my car."

"But you don't know where he lived? And you don't know his last name?"

"Nope."

"If you walked an hour almost every evening for several weeks, that adds up to a lot of time together."

I nodded. "I asked him a couple times where he lived, but I guess we got onto other things and Sammy never said."

"You called him Sammy?"

I nodded. "He once said his parents had called him that as a kid so I did it as a joke, then kept on doing it."

"Sounds like the two of you became friends." Her blue eyes widened, urging me to plunge on.

I looked past her again and saw the cuffs of Sammy's blue trousers, his black shoes. "Okay, we were friends."

"Did you touch the bat?" she asked.

"Bat?" Her face revealed nothing. "I didn't see any bat."

"Over here." She led me ten feet north of the body and pointed off trail at rotting, yellow Osage oranges that looked like shrunken heads.

Among them lay a silvery metal softball bat. Its handle was covered by spiraling, dirty white adhesive tape, and soupy redness splotched the black ink of the trademark. The bat was a common toy, but lying there it seemed obscene, out of character and place. It reminded me of a stubby, malformed snake, its big end swollen by a small animal it was digesting.

Half-tripping over somebody's feet, I backed away onto the trail. My imagination had taken over. I heard the bat thunking down as if it were demolishing a pumpkin, and superimposed on top of that was Sammy's voice—telling me he liked our walks.

Poor Sammy. No way he deserved this kind of end.

I cried, and trying to squelch the tears made me choke and

cough. I took the handkerchief from a back pocket and wiped my face. Sucking air helped. When my eyes opened, there was Jones staring at me, flanked by the four other men.

Uh oh. I scanned the row of blank faces, blew my nose and put the hanky back in my pocket. "Sorry."

The woman crowded in front of Jones. "Do you have something else to tell us?" She waited a few seconds. "No? Well, let's go to the station and get your official statement. Frank, you come with us. We'll use the front cruiser. The rest of you wait for the coroner and secure the area. Burt?"

"Yeah," the cop with the camera said, "we'll bag the evidence and check through his clothes."

"Will you move the tape for us, Clayton?"

They put me in the backseat with the plainclothes cop Frank. Wearing a badge and name tag now—F Shepherd—he sat behind Lieutenant Grimes, who drove. Out her open window, she told Jones the two bikers could leave.

As we rolled forward, the bikers stood aside and gawked in at me as if I were a monkey in a cage. Wouldn't they have an exciting tale to embellish for their friends? I pictured them, sipping wine by a gas fireplace in one of those ugly new condominium complexes where they lived together, unmarried of course, biding their time until someone more entertaining came along to sweat and exercise with.

Knock it off, I thought.

As upset as I was by my idiotic performance with the cops, knowing that—Goddam it!—what was coming would not be pleasant, I still felt guilty. I ordered myself to be fair and quit judging the couple. I wasn't really judging them, I countered. I was just relieving tension and reviling the relaxed moral standards of society. That's what I didn't like. Obviously, I didn't know this couple from Adam.

While I mused, our cruiser turned off the bike trail onto

Baumer Road and south off it onto 86. Grimes glanced at my car as we passed it, then told Frank to read me my rights and watched me in the mirror as he did.

How very goddam wonderful! Clearly, it was my right to have to put up with a lot more bullshit, which maybe I deserved. This predicament was almost all my own making.

CHAPTER THREE

I was cutting my own throat and knew it. The rest of our journey into town was silent, allowing me to rummage through dim mental archives and become even more uptight. The problem seemed simple. Police and other people have their own agendas, I have mine, so conflicts occur. Well, I was in charge of my life only, no other lives, so I had to do what felt right to me.

The thought provided little comfort. The prospect of what lay ahead did not elate me.

Make the best of it, I told myself. Learn what you can, be as helpful as possible, but do not sell your soul for a chance to get out of there quickly. As usual, more important things than convenience are at issue, like your personal integrity.

I was plunked down in a typical setting, a small room with a mirror taking up most of one wall, three undersized chairs, a small wooden table. According to movies I'd seen, the Sony tape recorder lying there was redundant because such rooms were now "wired" for picture and sound, capable of broadcasting every utterance and movement to distant observers. And this place was more than modern. We were in the county administration building, a three-story concrete pillbox so new its technological dependence was almost complete. With their computers "down," my hosts were unable to check me out.

"We going to find a record on you, Clifford?" Grimes asked.

"Nothing to brag about," I said, my past being irrelevant to these proceedings.

The interview went on anyway. Properly cued, I said that yes, I had been read my rights and understood them. "I also waive my right to have an attorney present."

Both deputies nodded, and Grimes forced a pseudo-smile.

Coercive responses, I thought, saying, "But do you think that's a wise thing for me to do, Detective Shepherd, or may I call you Frank? I notice both of you using my first name now. Is that because we're becoming more friendly? Or are you deliberately putting me at a disadvantage? If I have to use your job title while you use my first name, then my status is diminished. Or am I just being paranoid?"

Dealing with representatives of institutions always upset me. Now I was babbling. Jesus!

Neither interrogator seemed amused, watching me stone-faced.

Shepherd said, "Settle down."

Grimes said, "What kind of act are you putting on now?"

I said, "Never mind. Don't answer. Excuse me a second. Curiosity is calling." I was hyper and those two were robots so, hell, whatever developed would just have to develop.

I scooted my uncomfortable metal fold-up chair away from the table, stood, and was surprised when neither cop stopped me. I went to the mirror and peered at it up close, then at sharp angles, not straight on, trying to look beneath the surface. Was anyone watching? I let my face light up with sudden, slap-happy recognition, and waved just in case somebody was back there.

Pulling away, I noticed my image and took off my ball cap, but my hair remained in place and didn't need smoothing—what hair I had left, a three-quarter halo of ever-thinning, salt-and-pepper fur around a bald dome.

"I couldn't see through the glass," I admitted, sitting back down without scooting under the table, crossing my legs and arms. "I bet if a light went on in the observation room, a person in here could see it, at least from an angle. Right?"

Directly across from me, Lt. Grimes stared. To my right, Shepherd, who was standing, bent down near me and barked, "Shut the fuck up!"

I leaned away, looking up at him. He reached for my shoulder so I lurched farther away, nearly upsetting my chair, threw my left hand out, caught the table, stopping my momentum, and said, "Don't touch me."

"Take it easy, Frank," the woman said as if to calm a violent comrade and protect me.

The remark seemed scripted and was, as people used to say, too much. I laughed, a diaphragm-propelled explosion that quickly dropped into giggles. I shut them down and said, "Sorry, but this is just like so many movies I've seen. Exactly. Okay, go on. Let's get this over with. I'm ready to talk."

"What were you sorry about before, Clifford?" the woman asked, playing their first-name game. "Out on the trail you said you were sorry, remember? What were you sorry for?"

"Brother. I knew this would happen." I smiled and almost cracked up again, but stifled it.

"Go ahead," she said.

I shook my head. "We're wasting each other's time."

"What were you sorry for?"

"Oh, well, okay then, the truth. I confess—" I paused dramatically, and the energy built up inside so the words finally burst out like air from a deflating balloon. "I was sorry to be crying. I felt ashamed because it wasn't a very impressive performance, though for me, to be honest, it wasn't that unusual and should have been expected. I was sorry because I couldn't control myself better. Mainly, I was sorry because I knew what's going on right now would happen. You'd think I was guilty and concentrate on me. See? I was sorry to throw your investigation off. I mean when I cried I knew you'd think I was the killer.

Very bad timing to bawl like that in front of you."

"Is that all?" Grimes asked softly as if she were comforting a child. "What was your real relationship with Sammy?"

"We were friends, like I told you." I stared into those bright blue eyes uneasily. What was she implying now?

"Weren't you more than that?" She leaned toward me and almost whispered, "Weren't you lovers?"

That startled me. How naïve could I be? This was the 21st century. Any up-to-date cynic would guess first thing that we were male lovers, yet it had not even occurred to me.

"Clifford," Shepherd said. He had also assumed a sympathetic tone, and bent toward me with his hands clasped over his heart. How precious. He said, "There's nothing to be ashamed of. Nowadays, homosexuality is an accepted lifestyle."

The phony bastard. Imagining him with the other deputies in private, joking about the gay crowd, I said, "I'm so glad to hear that, Frank. Are you out of the closet, cutie?"

His cheeks puffed up and his eyes seemed to bulge.

I told him, "I didn't like what YOU said, either."

"Clifford," Grimes said sharply, drawing my attention. "We want the truth. Everyone knows the reputation of Old Town Park where you left your car. When I came aboard here, the first thing I learned was that we routinely arrest homosexuals in that parking lot for solicitation, among other things."

"Okay, I know that too," I said. "It's been in the newspaper and I've even been propositioned there myself. But it just never occurred to me you'd put it together this way. Let me say it straight out. I am not gay. Sammy and I had no sexual relationship. You are way off base accusing me of that."

"Liar! That's a load of shit!" Shepherd roared in my ear.

"Jesus!" I leaned away, wrestled my damp hanky from the back pocket, wiped the ear and that side of my head, and looked at him. "I really don't need a bath in your germs."

"You piece of dirt, who gives a fuck?" He'd brought his face down near me again so more spray struck my ear.

I leaned toward him and yelled, "I do, asshole!"

He jerked away—hopefully, I'd sprayed him back. His hands clenched into fists. "I'd like to kick your ass."

"I'm sure you would like to, Frank, but I'm not so sure you could actually do it. In a fair fight, I mean."

"Oh, I could do it."

"Excuse me, macho men," Grimes said, rapping knuckles on the table, looking from me to Shepherd.

I said, "This escalation into hostile questioning seems too abrupt. After all, I have been cooperating."

"Are you done?" she asked.

I nodded, crossed my limbs again and sat back. "No more spit in the ear, okay? Thank you. And for my part I will admit that Detective Shepherd could very well kick my ass, but he would not be getting a virgin. It's been kicked before."

"Schmuck!" Shepherd brayed.

"Mr. Saunders, do you have an emotional problem? It's one extreme to the other with you."

"Call me Cliff, Lieutenant. Let's start over. What is your first name? Nod if I hit it, okay? Edith? Esther? Emily?"

She slapped her right hand flat on the table and stood. "I think a holding cell for a couple hours might be good for him. While we go to lunch."

Her grinning partner leaned toward me over the back of the empty chair. "Yeah!"

"Wait! I give up," I said. "You got me. Let's end this farce right now. What do you want me to do?"

Grimes said, "Quit smarting off and answer the questions."

"Okay," I said, restraining my right hand, which started to rise as if I were taking an oath. "I have told you the whole truth and nothing but. So really you already know everything that I know about Sammy. Just cool it with the drill instructor approach from now on."

Grimes said, "For the record, describe how and when you found the victim and what you saw."

"All right." I went over the whole thing again, described how I'd gotten to know Sammy, how we'd walked together, how I'd called 911 from home, how I'd seen him the evening before yesterday. "That's it. Really. I don't know anything else."

Grimes asked, "Did the victim think you would be there last night? Or did you tell him you were skipping the walk?"

"He thought I'd be there." I imagined our last time together, our casual goodbye and Sammy disappearing in the shadows on the cinder path. "We both said we'd see each other the next day at 5:15, but something came up so I couldn't make it. Now don't get misled. Sammy went to the trail to walk, period. He wouldn't have waited for me very long before taking off to walk by himself."

At her prodding, I explained that we had never encountered threats of any kind there. I had never seen anyone there who could be considered suspicious, and Sammy had never mentioned being afraid of anyone or having trouble with anyone. "Maybe it was one of those homosexuals you mentioned. Or a gay basher who, like you, thought he might be one."

Grimes said, "Perhaps. Where were you last evening?"

"The village of Red Springs. From 5:00 until 7:30. At a gathering in the college's Student Center. All kinds of people saw me. I signed an attendance sheet, and the meeting's chairperson Betty Schantz, a resident of Red Springs, talked with me for a few minutes just before I left."

"We're going to check," Grimes said.

"Good. Her number's in the phone book."

"Frank, can you think of anything else?"

He told me, "Don't leave the county."

She said, "We don't know the time of death yet, and we'll want to talk to you again."

Keep them away from home if possible, I reminded myself, and said, "Just call me and I'll come in."

Chapter Four

By 4:30 p.m. the Sheriff's Department had me back in the interrogation room. By 5:20 I had convinced Grimes and Shepherd I would not talk to them without making a formal complaint to the sheriff, and they had convinced me that he was unavailable. So I filled out a form, giving times, dates, names, places, details. A routing slip attached said the complaint went to Sheriff Orndorf for action, and then, if necessary, to the Civilian Review Board. Grimes and Shepherd sat, watching, waiting for me to finish.

I detailed every act of incompetence, every denied right and insult connected to Deputy Clayton Jones: our clashes on the bike trail, then the way he'd assaulted me at home, handcuffed, thrown me into a cruiser, and paraded me like a criminal through the parking lot, in full public view, into the county building before uncuffing me—all this even though I had been and was still cooperating with the department. I threw in everything I could think of, asked that Jones be reprimanded and trained better, and the same for Grimes and Shepherd. As his superiors, they had allowed Jones to behave unprofessionally without comment and so had encouraged him. I also threatened a lawsuit if corrective actions were not taken. I signed, tore off a carbon of my two written pages, and gave the originals to Grimes.

She scanned them without expression, then handed them to Shepherd, who did the same.

I felt as if I'd accomplished something positive, but my stomach growled. I hadn't eaten since breakfast.

Make the most of it, I thought. Might as well fast although tomorrow was supposed to be my day for that. If I held off eating until noon tomorrow, that would be over twenty-four hours without food.

Shepherd slid the papers back to Grimes and said, "This is crap. No wonder Clayton jumped you. You'd piss off the Pope."

"Jones jumped me because I wanted to drive myself here."

"You refused his order to get in the cruiser. People like you are ruining law enforcement as a profession."

"The proper word is improving. There need to be changes."

He glared at me, and his fingertips tapped a manila folder on the table before him. In his mid-thirties, he wore a wrinkled blue suit, had brown eyes, light brown hair parted on the left side, and a thick, rectangular mustache so much darker than his other hair it looked dyed.

I wasn't worried about retaliation from him, or any other deputy, because Sheriff Orndorf, during his two decades in office, had revamped the department, set up this complaint procedure, and created the Civilian Review Board.

"You gonna talk now like you agreed to do?" Grimes asked, laying a notebook and a pen on top of my complaint. Her pantsuit was slightly lighter in color than Shepherd's clothes. She was about 5'10", broad shouldered, lanky, in her late 30s, maybe early 40s, with a smudge of red on her lips, a long nose humped in the middle, high cheek bones, and fair skin. Leaning forward, she reached a muscular hand to the recorder and with a thumb on its bottom used the middle finger to depress two buttons on top. I heard the faint whir of tape unwinding.

Good. We needed to get the show on the road. I looked at my watch and said, "Yes, I'm ready to talk. It is Wednesday, April 4, 2001, 6:05 p.m. This is Clifford Saunders with Lt. E. Grimes and Detective Frank Shepherd, the Shawnee County deputy sheriffs conducting this interview. I've been informed of my rights, understand them, and waive my right to have an attorney present."

Shepherd said, "That pisses me off too."

"What more can I tell you?" I asked Grimes. "I did not kill Sammy."

"The Coroner's estimated time of death extends before and after your alibi."

I nodded. "Okay."

"Your alibi doesn't hold up."

"Who's arguing?"

Shepherd said, "You lied about not having a record."

I looked at him. "I did not lie. I've never done anything seriously wrong."

"Serving twenty days in county jail is serious."

"How many felonies on my record? How many assaults and batteries or murders? I never said I'd broken no laws."

"Your record shows a pattern of disrespecting the law."

"Some laws," I admitted.

"That says it all," Shepherd said. "You pick and choose laws to follow as if you're different than everybody else."

"Well isn't that awful? Of course, neither of you ever breaks a law, never jaywalks or double parks."

Grimes said, "Being arrested for destruction of property is relevant."

"That never happened. I was brought in for questioning, just like now. A bulldozer was set on fire with gasoline and destroyed when I happened to be at the site along with three other people, picketing. All four of us were convicted of trespassing, but we were never charged with arson. As far as I know, nobody was ever arrested for that."

Shepherd asked, "What do you do for a living? How do you

support yourself?"

I looked at him. "What's that have to do with anything?"

"I hear there's high vegetation all around your property, odd buildings, signs all over the grounds warning people to keep out. These things indicate possible drug trafficking."

"Yeah? Well, Deputy Jones is really qualified to make that kind of assessment."

Grimes asked, "Do you still teach?"

"I think you know the answer to that."

"Does 'no longer employed at Miami Community College' mean you were fired?"

"I'll save the time it'd take you to find out. I inherited property from my parents and basically retired."

"At forty-seven years old, you're retired?" she asked.

"For five years now, but put it this way. I do not have what most people call gainful employment. I can support myself on dividends from a few investments."

"You have no other family?"

"An ex-wife, who earns more than I ever did. And a daughter with a bachelor's degree and on her own, running around Europe, supposedly looking for a job, but I'll believe that when she gets one. I pay neither of them a penny and have few expenses myself. I lead a very simple life."

Shepherd, on my right, leaned toward me and said, "So why'd you kill him? Why'd you bash in his head? The sight of it turned everybody's stomach. The coroner called it vicious. Overkill. A blow to the back of the head, probably the first, incapacitated the victim, then seven others. Eight solid blows. You were in a real frenzy."

"Open your mind to another possibility," I said. "It was somebody else. Consider that and see where it leads you."

Grimes jumped in. "Oh, the man we have looks pretty good with his emotional extremes and disrespect for the law."

I crossed my arms. "Back to that? If I have no respect for the law, why'd I go to the trouble of complaining about Deputy Jones's behavior?"

Shepherd said, "To get revenge. To get us off your back. To intimidate us."

"Oh, right. I really did that."

Grimes said, "You're a hothead. We've seen it ourselves. You go wild at the drop of a hat."

"I have never gotten violent except in self-defense."

Shepherd jerked my eyes his way. "Verbal abuse leads to physical abuse, and you can't shut your mouth once it opens."

They were ping-ponging me back and forth, from one subject to another, confusing me. I sat back and tried to relax.

Grimes spoke, pulling my attention back to her. "You motor-mouthed in court until a judge put you away. That's out-of-control behavior. Jail time deters most people, but not you."

"It did me too. That was five years ago, the trespassing charge when the bulldozer burned up, and I have not been involved in anything since. Your own records have nothing on me since then. I retired from involvement. The hell with hurting myself over hopeless causes. Yeah, jail time deterred me."

Shepherd said, "Contempt of court shows how you put yourself above the law."

"Contempt of court's a misnomer. Quite clearly during the proceedings I said that I had contempt for the judge, but not for the court. Only a self-centered maniac like Simmons could have misconstrued my meaning. On top of that, he himself had asked me to tell the court my feelings. That Nazi just wanted to punish me. Every day he held court, he'd bring me in and ask me to apologize. I'd refuse and he would lock me up again. Three weeks of punishment for not kissing his ass."

Shepherd snorted. "Victimized by the law. Your own choices had nothing to do with what happened."

"Look up the proceedings. Check with the county ACLU office. Their appeal got me released, and then a lawsuit they filed forced him to settle out of court and pay me off."

Shepherd shook his head. "Bullshit. Judges have immunity from prosecution over something like that. Another judge would dismiss such a lawsuit upon receiving it."

"Unless I had legitimate grounds that would come out in court. A state or federal appeals court would have heard our suit. I can't tell you how much it cost the judge to shut me up because of stipulations in the agreement, but the fact that the lawsuit was dropped at my request is public knowledge. I made money on the deal, the ACLU made money, and even better that son of a bitch left the bench a year later."

I looked at Shepherd and smiled, remembering how proof had surfaced that Simmons owned a large interest in the corporation developing the land. If these cops were smart enough, without more information, they ought to be able to figure out the grounds for my suit had to involve the judge's conflict of interest.

Shepherd said, "You're pathetic."

Nope, he didn't get it. Too negative about me. Oh well. Maybe it would occur to him or Grimes later. I said, "Sometimes a person has to do what's right despite painful consequences. Despite what others might think. Plus, as the only time I've ever been locked up in jail, it was an enlightening experience."

Shepherd said, "You're digging your own grave. None of what you just said can be proven. All you've shown is that you'll do anything to satisfy yourself."

"What would I have wanted from Sammy?"

Grimes said, "Revenge."

I smiled again. "That's ludicrous."

Shepherd said, "Your conviction for trespassing on his property is in the record. Did you forget that? He filed charges against you and got you convicted."

"When?" I looked from him to Grimes and back to him. "What's Sammy's last name?"

He frowned, said, "Like you don't know," and looked toward Grimes.

She said, "Burkhoffer."

"Burkhoffer? Okay, that name's familiar."

"Ought to be," Shepherd said. "He went to a lot of trouble to prove your guilt."

"H. S. Burkhoffer was Sammy?" I remembered Burkhoffer's testimony and the two times he'd confronted and chased me out of his fields. Burkhoffer did not resemble Sammy—except that they were about the same height.

I looked at my inquisitors and focused on Grimes. "I'm sorry. I did know H. S. Burkhoffer. If that's who Sammy was, then I was wrong to say I didn't know him."

"You're sorry." Shepherd laughed.

"Really! I remember H. S. Burkhoffer as bigger than Sammy. Heavier I mean. My contact with him was over ten years ago. He didn't have a goatee then, and his hair was dark too, not gray."

"That's who your friend Sammy was," Grimes said.

"Weird." I shook my head, still trying to connect my memories of the two men, or more exactly the one man at two different periods in his life. "That means Sammy lived right across the road from where I parked my car on 86 today. In that farmhouse on the rise."

"Presumably," Grimes said.

"What it means," Shepherd said, drawing my attention, "is that you have a motive. You wanted to get even for what he cost you, and you got even in the worst possible way."

"I wasn't angry about that. The fine was only three hundred dollars. Hell, I never even fought the charge."

Shepherd said, "How could you fight it? Burkhoffer had videotapes of you in his fields and your car parked nearby, and the videos had dates on them."

"That was a decade ago. Why would I wait so long to get revenge?"

"To hide your involvement," he said.

"I reported the body."

"To throw us off your trail," Shepherd said. "You knew somebody might identify you as Burkhoffer's walking partner."

Grimes said, "Try this scenario. It was a crime of opportunity and passion. Out of the blue Burkhoffer shows up where you are in the habit of walking, gets friendly, and doesn't recognize you. But you recognize him. Strong memories of what he did to you well up in your meetings so your anger grew day after day until suddenly, yesterday, you exploded. I agree that what upset you wasn't the money. It was the public humiliation he subjected you to, something like what you're complaining Deputy Jones did to you today. The kind of person you are, that would bug you forever."

Her argument was cockeyed.

I said, "The whole situation is crazy. I didn't recognize him because he'd changed so much. Besides, he should have recognized me."

"No way! We retrieved your file from the boxes still in the old courthouse and not yet scanned into the digital records." Shepherd opened his manila folder, turned it around on the table so both Grimes and I could see the four pictures he fanned out.

They showed me the way I used to be: chubby, with long, uncombed curly hair on top and full scraggly beard. Shepherd was right. Sammy wouldn't have recognized me. Hell, I barely recognized myself.

CHAPTER FIVE

At my request the sheriff's department dropped me off at the end of my lane on Pekin Road. I was exhausted but keyed up. Going over my story two dozen times had so worn me down, I'd even begun suspecting myself. Could I have slain Sammy without being aware of it? Like in a homicidal sleepwalking state? Stranger things had happened. Don't be stupid, I thought, leaving the cruiser, smelling untainted air, resisting the urge to kiss the ground.

While the deputy turned around, I emptied my mail box—it contained two mass-mailed advertisements—then watched him head back to town. As his red taillights disappeared in the distance, two cars roared up from behind me and zoomed past, racing bumper-to-bumper. Muscle cars, I'd heard them called, the toys of muscle-headed boys and girls. Maybe they'd be surprised, coming up fast enough behind the deputy to receive official recognition for their speeding. They deserved a damn ticket.

I closed my eyes and waited for solitude. The cars' sounds grew faint, but never died out entirely, merging at last with the distant hum of other engines and rubber on roadways. The only true silence anymore was in remote places or soundproof rooms. Motors ruled Nature.

My stomach growled. I felt weak, and God I hated being so negative. What was I anymore, a curmudgeon? Happy about nothing?

My eyes opened on a darkness similar to the incomplete silence. Lights intruded over the ridge behind my home and north and south by other homes, illuminating a faint veil of moisture above the trees. Farther off, above Bethel, the sky itself seemed to glow. Was there no escape from cities?

Four steps took me to the middle of the road, and yes, from there I could actually see Bethel's last street light. Directly above me only a few stars and a slice of moon were visible. As always, though, they looked pure and beautiful.

That's what I should concentrate on. All day my negative mood had been growing so now it had to end. It wasn't healthy.

I unzipped and peed on the center line, taking my time, emptying myself, forcing out and shaking off every drop of waste I could. It brought relief and some vigor.

I loped down my lane, entered the eerie light cast by the large halogen bulb hung on a pipe above the barn doors, went to my car and opened the trunk.

Everything was in there and ready. I removed my loafers, put on the boots, put my shoes in the trunk, grabbed the knapsack, put it on the front seat of the car and drove off, too hyper to sleep despite the hour, anxious for the sedative I'd thought of.

Ten minutes later I was at Old Town, slowing to check out Sammy's farm. Hard to believe Sammy had lived there. I had assumed he'd retired from agriculture and lived in Bethel. Hadn't he mentioned working in town? Well, it was still probable. Many farmers could not support themselves just by farming.

The ubiquitous police tape was at the entrance to his lane, but one end had been unloosened from a fence so the yellow plastic lay across the gravel driveway. Beyond it, from my perspective on the road, every light in the house seemed to be on. The barnyard was dark with a single pole light on the southeastern corner flickering weakly. A car was parked beside a small building. Shadows obscured the automobile's color and make, but its size was clearly a compact model.

Sammy's car? Or did it belong to someone inside the house? A relative? Police? Who? Sammy had told me he'd lost his wife years ago, and my impression was that for years he'd been living alone. Hadn't he expressed sorrow about having no one at home to communicate with?

None of your business, I told myself, accelerating, passing Old Town's five bungalows on my right, the three on the left, then Sammy's north field. I crossed the river and left the car partially hidden in a fisherman's pull-off, the same spot where Sammy had videotaped my car years before. Hadn't fooled him then, but he wasn't around to catch me now.

Wearing the pack, I walked south onto the bridge, stopped to hear the river's tumbling down below, and the moon surprised me, gleaming on the liquid surface like a faint, half-opened eye.

I crossed the bridge, jumped over a drainage ditch, and climbed over Sammy's fence at the field's northeastern corner, being careful the barbed wire strung on top didn't snag me. Three feet of unplowed earth on the field's edge let me walk parallel to the river without making tracks visible from the road.

I hadn't been here in over ten years, not since the Burkhoffer trial when, to avoid jail time, I'd promised not to trespass on the property again. The judge had justified his threat to lock me up by citing my repeated trespassing here and two convictions for trespassing elsewhere. Sammy's death had this one good effect: it freed me from that promise to him. Now I could come here and visit this rich land again.

The budding saplings and brush along the fenceline rustled against my boots and legs. Occasionally, thorns from wild roses and berry vines grabbed me. I forged ahead, jerking my clothes loose from them with a noise like Velcro parting. Farther right, denser vegetation robed the river, hiding its flow.

Ahead of me a doe leaped the fence, gliding high enough to profile against the dimly lit sky, hooves clicking on something hard as she touched down in the field and ran away. The beautiful silhouette stayed with me the few seconds needed to reach the place where she had leaped, at a gate where rutted wheel tracks led through undergrowth toward the water.

Thinking the deer had been a signal, I stopped, pulled off my pack, removed the flashlight, put the pack back on and studied Sammy's dark field. The land was denuded except for roots and stubs of corn partially buried by fall plowing.

How had this place looked two hundred, two hundred fifty years ago? Had the people who lived here then planted maize? Maybe. Probably other crops as well. Unless this had been a natural prairie, the great hardwood forest would have predominated here except where people had burned it back.

The land rose up from me away from the river, rising gently to a hillock in the middle of the field. The Indian village would have been there, on the high ground above the level of most spring floods. I imagined smoke from campfires curling into the air around teepees—no, that wouldn't be right. The last native people who'd lived here had more permanent dwellings, and I amended my vision to square huts covered by long grass. That probably wasn't right either. I'd read years ago about the Shawnee tribe, but forgotten most details.

Beyond the hillock I could see Sammy's silo, several roofs, and three lit, second-floor house windows. A coyote howled on the higher hills lining the western side of the river. Out on the road a car whirred by, heading toward Bethel, and its purring seemed as far away as the little wolf's cry.

I held my flashlight at the waist, aimed the beam directly down just ahead of my feet so it would be hard to see from houses or road, scanned the ground, and started off, following a narrow path the rains had washed out, streaming downhill.

Months of freeze and thaw and precipitation had prepared the ground for this moment, dredging up and uncovering what hundreds of years had buried. Expectation filled me. Not hope, not even belief. For certain, there were valuable things here, and any moment one might appear for a person who was alert and lucky. I was due for some luck.

I bent, examining the earth, and my little circle of light revealed dark topsoil, withered weeds and bits of rock, several of which I tweaked with a finger, flipping them over. All were little more than what had been showing. I went on, searching.

At the base of the hillock, where the ground rose at a steeper angle, the white, cord-like roots of a corn stalk clutched a rock. I lifted the clump, shook off the plant, and the cold stone dropped into my hand.

I turned off the light, put it under an arm, brushed dirt from the rock with my fingers, and felt the rock all over. It was more than two inches thick with smoothed edges and rounded, blunt ends. My fingers could barely circle its girth, and upon my palm it stretched from fingertips to wrist like a petrified Idaho baking potato.

I held the stone in my left hand, turned to face northwest, making my body a shield from the road and the farmhouse, held the light in my right hand and lit the rock. It was brown with dirt. I would clean it better and study it later, but it was clearly altered by humans for a purpose. Not as an ax though. Maybe something to pound or grind with.

Inside a pocket, the stone pulled my jacket down and strained the seams. I turned off the light and climbed to the top of the hill on a level with the farm's buildings a couple hundred yards away. I removed my pack, extracted the ten-foot-square plastic painter's drop cloth, spread it on the ground, and lay the pack down. I stood on the cover, stripped to my undershirt, shorts, and socks, hurried into the insulated long underwear from the pack, and got back into my clothes. I pulled the wool sweater on over my shirt, put the hood over my head, tied it beneath my chin, put my jacket on, and zipped it up.

Rolling the empty pack into a tube, I lay down and used it as a pillow. The ground was rough beneath me, but soft enough so rolling and squirming mashed it into my shape, providing a relatively comfortable bed. I dug the stone from my pocket and held it in both hands on my chest, thinking I would lie there until the cold drove me off.

Warmth engulfed me except where cool air touched my cheeks and nose and fingers, but that was refreshing. I gazed up. The heavenly view spread away as awe-inspiring as it had ever been with uncountable numbers of stars and the moon.

I closed my eyes and released my mind, vowing I would not lose myself again in emotions and petty concerns. I would not let today's events destroy my ability to appreciate life. I would concentrate on now.

I was lying on earth containing the vestiges of forgotten people who'd lived here before. I tightened, then relaxed my muscles, working one by one up from my toes, to my feet, calves, thighs, hips, on up to my head.

I resolved not to blame Grimes or Shepherd or Jones for anything. They were doing their best. Like me, they sometimes overreacted and misunderstood because of weaknesses. Forgive them, respect them, and concentrate on more important things, I instructed myself.

Idiot! I thought. Somebody bashed in Sammy's head.

Not now. Forget it. Feel the air on your skin. Think of yourself lying in the middle of this huge, dark field with the stars overhead and the people asleep in their houses unaware that you are out here. Consider the heavy, ancient rock pressing down on your chest like a holy message from the past.

It was a relic and an amulet.

I heard only a vague groan of machines. Gradually, more distant sounds came to me, the crackle of burning wood, the padding of moccasined feet, voices calling in a language like Chinese, faint laughter. I tried to see the people but couldn't.

I woke up with my legs, arms and back cold where they touched the ground. The glowing hands of my watch said 3:35. I sat up and saw the red taillights of a car leaving Sammy's barnyard. Maybe its engine starting had awakened me.

The stone lay on my right thigh. I picked it up, stood, and it hung heavily in my hand like a weapon.

The house lights were off, and its darkness seemed like an invitation. A compulsion rose in me to go there.

CHAPTER SIX

From the fisherman's pull-off, I U-turned on 86, sweeping my headlights over the bridge, then the field I'd just come from, illuminating mist that had snaked out of the river in long, wispy arms so the land seemed like a giant stage with shifting props and ghostly characters who lurked in the wings, waiting to enter. Odd, I thought, how so little could make ordinary things unusual.

I shook my head to snap myself more awake, and drove on past Sammy's house, vowing to forget about the poor guy's tragedy, confirming my decision to let the experts handle the case. The road took me up out of the valley's mist, and a few miles later Pekin Road led to my driveway, which plunged me back down into a private fog, swirling up from the creek bottom behind my house.

I stumbled up my front steps, across the porch, shoved the door open, stepped inside, and tripped. My shins, knees, and waist lodged against something where nothing should be. What the hell was wrong now?

I pushed myself up, felt behind me for the wall switch, and flipped it on. I'd fallen upon my favorite chair, overturned. I heaved it around, set it upright, and stared with shock. The brown leather arms and cushions had been slashed so badly, the chair resembled a gutted animal.

"Son of a bitch!"

The mess extended throughout the room. I staggered

forward, stepping on picture frames and broken glass, shattered crystal and decorative china plates. In the center of the room, I turned slowly under the light fixture, surveyed the damage, and shook my head. The disarrangement of familiar things made them almost unidentifiable.

It was last Friday all over again, but worse. Nothing in this room had been touched then. Obviously, the police response to my call about that had put the fear of God into no one. The cops had accomplished nothing.

FUCK YOU! said three walls in black paint and capital letters.

"Fuck you too! I ever get my hands on you—" I imagined somebody's neck in my hands and me squeezing.

A spidery crack decorated the big picture window. Below it on the floor lay a sturdy can that had probably been thrown against the glass. I went over, picked up the container, and yes, it rattled. It was the spray can of black paint I'd left on the kitchen counter for touching up the iron railing on the porch.

"Bastards!"

Was the whole house in this bad a shape?

In the kitchen one shelf of one cupboard had been emptied, and its cups, saucers and glasses were on the floor, most of them broken. The other cupboard doors were opened, and two were sprung from their top hinges as if someone had hung on the doors, but nothing had been removed from their shelves.

The water pot and the skillet were gone from the stove top. I guessed they'd been thrown outside because a large pane of glass in a window behind the kitchen table was broken out. Except for the radio smashed on the floor, everything else in the kitchen was untouched. Not too bad here, I thought.

"Worse here than last time, though," I said, and thinking about the places they'd damaged then, I hurried there.

On the way, I checked the bathroom. The doors of the

medicine cabinet and the little closet were wide open so somebody had been in there, but only to snoop.

I hurried into my office. Goddam it, the place was much worse than Friday. This time the three tall bookcases had been toppled, the computer monitor lay busted on the floor along with the keyboard, and the computer tower was also there. When I straightened it up, loose parts bounced around noisily inside the casing.

A moment of intense, inarticulate rage closed my eyes, but the darkness of seeing nothing balanced the anger, allowing me to calm down, and rationalize. If the contents of the hard disk were not salvageable, I had at least saved almost everything on floppies.

But were the floppies okay? My eyelids slapped open. The two boxes of fifty disks each had been on a bookcase shelf. Now they were on the floor, emptied, the disks strewn around in the mess.

I picked up a few, clearing places to step, and the floppies looked all right, but I'd have to check them out on the other computer at Mom's house, later.

On the other side of the room, the steel filing cabinet was emptied again. I righted it, reinserted the drawers, but their contents, the manila folders and pages of printed copy, were scattered around with the other debris.

"Brother, what a damn mess!"

The other downstairs room had also been searched on Friday. Afraid of what I'd find, I hurried there.

Yes, it contained another big mess. The drawers of my father's old black desk were on the floor on top of their spilled contents. That desk was heavy and still upright, but the smaller desk was overturned and its drawers removed and emptied. The two small bookcases near it were also dumped. Books and magazines lay scattered beneath the cases on the floor.

I had a lot of work to do in these two rooms alone, and some things would have to be replaced. Damn!

What else could be wrong? The upstairs!

There I found covers but not springs or mattresses off the beds. Drawers were out of the four dressers and on the floor, but they had already been empty except for the two drawers I used.

In my bedroom closet, clothes that had hung just inside the doorway were on the floor, but the ones on the sides remained hanging on the rod. Sweaters off the shelves were on the floor.

The upstairs bathroom was untouched except for the opened cabinet door. At the end of the hallway I grabbed the rope strand to pull down the ladder to the attic, but the cobwebs were whole and thick around the plywood cover on the ceiling, showing it had not been opened. No need to check up there. I dropped the rope.

Not too bad up here, I thought. Could have been worse. But some nosy bastard had pried into every corner of my home.

A flood of adrenaline sent me stomping down to the living room. I righted the couch, shook debris off the cushions and slammed them back in place.

What the hell was going on? The first vandalism had seemed like invasion for theft, and that was bad enough. But this one seemed malicious. There was more deliberate destruction of property. Was I dealing with a damn nut? People who hated me? Was it liable to happen again and get even worse? Maybe I was in danger. Maybe the next time they'd try to hurt me physically.

Jesus oh Jesus, what a day! Now I was scared.

Enough to lock the front door, the back door, then check and make sure every downstairs window was locked. My wife and I had locked the doors leaving every day, but in four years of bachelorhood I'd grown used to locking up only when I'd be gone for more than a day.

Therefore, maybe stupidly, locking up like this made me feel as secure as if I'd posted armed guards.

I turned off the house lights and scuffed my way through the darkness in the living room, sliding my feet, pushing junk out of the way, until I reached the couch and lay down.

Tomorrow, all that stuff I'd cleaned up on Saturday would have to be picked up again. And I'd have to do a lot more.

Call the cops again? Right. They'd be a big help. No, I had to do something about this myself. Bring a gun here from Mom's house? Get a guard dog? Put up more outside lights? See about surveillance cameras?

There were going to be a lot more complications to go with the ones I already had concerning Sammy's death. Wonderful.

I took the Indian stone from my jacket pocket, laid it on my chest, held it in both hands, and closed my eyes. I couldn't think clearly now. Too tired. Exhausted from stress. Wrung out by emotional extremes. Tomorrow I'd figure out what to do.

CHAPTER SEVEN

The next day the telephone jangling woke me, but I kept my eyes shut, counted the rings, one, two, three, and heard my voice say, "I screen calls to avoid solicitations. Please state your name and purpose and leave your number. Thanks."

After the beep, I heard, "Hello. This is Sheriff Orndorf. You there, Mr. Saunders? I got your complaint right here in front of me. You there?"

The sheriff asked for me twice more, but hell, I didn't want to start this day with another hassle.

"Okay, Mr. Saunders, I got into your complaint first thing this morning. Talked to Deputy Jones and the other people involved. And I want you to know I'm dealing with it. Okay? I'm scheduling more training for all our personnel. Thank you for your input. Let me know if you have any other concerns. Okay? By the way, regarding your comment about the illegal entry of your home last Friday, the deputy who investigated will get back to you shortly. If you like, we could discuss all this sometime."

He hung up, the answering machine beeped, and I laughed, impressed by the speedy response and the good news of everything the sheriff had said. I sat up, caught the Indian rock—it must not have moved at all during my sleep—stood, put it on the fireplace mantel, and noticed the photos were gone.

They lay near my feet, the faces wrinkled underneath shattered glass. I separated the pictures from the debris, lay them without frames back on the mantel, and looked around.

The living room's chaos alerted me to respond more cautiously to the sheriff. His message included no apology and no details of planned corrective actions, just a vague thing about training. He'd thanked me, asked me for other concerns, invited me to discuss things, but left no number. I'd have to go through the dispatcher to reach him. His call could be no more than a public relations ploy.

My stomach spasmed at the thought, reminding me that I was famished and thirsty. I went into the kitchen where the wall clock still loomed moon-like over the table: 1:05.

Past noon. My fast was done an hour ago.

I retrieved the skillet and pot from just outside the broken window, washed them and fixed a quick brunch of four scrambled eggs with cheddar cheese, twelve sausage links with mustard, whole wheat toast with jam, and coffee. I gorged, did the dishes, and despite china shards crushing underfoot, suddenly recognized a familiar anticipation coloring the world: Something good lay ahead if I was alert and open enough to find it.

Slow down, I thought. Feeling so positive was inappropriate. My house wasn't the only thing messed up. Sammy was dead, and cops were making me struggle against their suspicions.

Well, all that was true, but struggling was good. It often produced worthwhile results. Prodded you into creative action and thought. Achievements grew out of struggles. Anyway, if I was optimistic, why kill the mood?

Maybe the meal was its cause, the deep sleep and the sheriff's quick response. I was also stronger than normal because I hadn't completed a full run yesterday.

My energy seemed in fact too potent to harness for the mundane chores in the house. A manic desire rose in me to talk to a friend, meaning Ed Hilliard, the only person I ever spontaneously called or visited. But if I drove to Ed's abode, we might sit and drink beer and bullshit until the day was shot.

In the kitchen I picked up the phone, poked his number, and when he answered on the second ring, said, "Not working today?"

"Just quit and it's snack time. Time to reward myself for working so hard."

"You never need an excuse to eat. Hey, my house was trashed last night."

"Again?!"

"Worse than last time." I described all the damage.

Ed whistled sympathetically.

"I may have lost everything on the computer. All my files were copied on floppies, but they could be damaged too."

"Anything important?"

"Hell yes, but most of that stuff's at Mom's house."

"Could be the people moving into that bunch of new houses just south of you."

"That was my first guess, teenagers with time on their hands, expressing themselves."

"Or somebody mad at you."

"Me . . . get somebody angry?"

"That used to seem like your purpose in life."

"No more. I haven't made anybody really irate since a year before Angela left."

"Not true. Angela and Laura were both mad enough to kill you."

"Yeah, close to it."

"Which reminds me of those obscene calls and threats you got back then. Maybe the people making those calls are the ones."

"Five years afterwards? They did nothing then, except of

course scare my family and alienate them from me. No, it's not whoever that was. I did get some cops' dander up recently, but I doubt they'd tear up my house."

"Who? The police you saw on Saturday?"

"No. I became a homicide suspect yesterday."

"What? You're involved in murder now?"

Describing Sammy's case and the police interrogations of me took some time.

Ed listened quietly, then said, "How do you get into these things? My life's peaceful. Nothing ever happens around here."

"You have a goddam dog so big you could saddle the bastard and ride him. Only a maniac would come to your house."

"That's why Brute's here. You want him? I told you to borrow him Saturday."

"Like I told you before, he'd just be more trouble. Dog shit all over. He might wander away and chew up somebody so I'd have to keep him tied up. He'd tear up everything indoors."

"He's housebroken."

"Brute's potential scares me."

"You got to do something."

"I'm getting a gun from Mom's house. No sense calling the police this time. Cops can't help. I'm too isolated here."

"You'll need a police report for insurance purposes."

"Damn, you're right. Hey, come over and we'll exercise in the barn."

"Can't. I got business to take care of. By the way the crew I brought over last week said they want to dance again."

"Yeah? They like the barn, huh? Well, let's do it this weekend. I'll call you."

We hung up, and I immediately phoned the police, reported the vandalism, mentioned last Friday's incident, but couldn't remember the name of the deputy who'd investigated it. The dispatcher said she'd find out and send over a deputy.

I swept the kitchen, sacked the trash, but kept it inside for the deputy to see. The work was too precise and confining, and thinking about the home invaders had me edgy. I needed a workout to settle down.

Leaving a note on the front door for the deputy, I warmed up with a two-mile jog; lifted weights in the barn, doing three times nine sets of exercises, mainly for the upper body, but adding three to five extra repetitions per exercise; ended, in my wool socks, with slower and slower speed-skater slides right, left, right, left, in time with songs, gliding forward clockwise and circling around—my old cool-down routine.

I skipped the free-style dancing I'd been doing instead of sliding the past few months, planning to invite Ed and his friends for two or three hours of that Saturday. It'd be a nice change. Yeah, Saturday. One of the women with him had called it dancercize. I'd see just how strenuous dancercize could be.

With Ray Coniff's Orchestra echoing in the gables, I turned off the player. My muscles felt tired and used, pumped up and powerful, yet under control now. I leaned on one of the six rough-hewn beams that rose from the ground to the roof, bracketing the barn's central room, the polished tongue-and-groove oak floor that Ed and I had laid last year.

These columns were beautiful, hand-carved from whole trees, studs that supported cross beams, rafters, the barn's entire structure. My palms and fingers dragged over the squared wood, discerning the cut-lines of ax, adz, hatchet and ancient saw.

I left the barn wondering how long the workout had taken. A couple of hours at least because the southwest sky was gleaming red. Evening approacheth. Glancing back inside, shutting the doors, I saw dust motes whirling in the sunlight. Nearly invisible pieces of the past. Pretty. But where was the deputy?

Memories of *Psycho* slashed through my mind, cut my shower time in half, and I resolved to pick up a gun today, yet my optimism persisted. I changed clothes and came back downstairs when feet thudded across the front porch. I opened the door, and my good mood oozed away. It was Lt. Grimes.

Without greeting, she said, "Deputy Eaton questioned six of your neighbors, but no one saw anything suspicious. Eaton also told me you would have heard from him today. Except, of course, now I came instead."

I nodded and stared at her, unprepared for more harassment. She said, "Satisfied?"

"Not really."

"What's your gripe now?"

"If he'd caught somebody, or at least made his interest known to the right party, it might not have happened again."

"That's why I'm here, to see what can be done about the new damage."

"Why you and not a patrolman?"

"Your complaint has gotten all of us on our toes."

Sure, I thought, switching on the light, leaning aside so the light struck her face. When those blue eyes glinted, I said, "You wouldn't normally go on a call about vandalism. You see this as a chance to search my house without a warrant."

"Let's just say I'm willing to resolve my doubts about you." Her eyes glinted again, looking around me inside.

I said, "A quick once-over, okay? The ruined easy chair and computer are the big things. I'll file an insurance claim for at least three thousand dollars to replace them. I don't know how much for the clean up and repainting and other repairs. Please make note of those kinds of things in your report."

I stood aside and let her in.

Head turning, she went to the center of the living room and stopped. "Did you put anything away?"

"Just in the kitchen. Wasn't much wrong in there. See the cracked picture window? See what they did to my chair?"

She wrote in her notebook. "More damage anywhere else?"

"Yeah, the back rooms."

I led her on a tour, told her not to step on the floppy discs in the office, took her upstairs and brought her back down.

In the kitchen, I described what had been done in there and pointed out the smashed window.

She said, "All this happened while you were at the station?"

"Probably."

"Was it like this when you got home?"

"Yes."

"We brought you in about five. Released you about ten. So during that time span."

"Well, I didn't come inside right away."

"When?"

I hesitated. "About 4:00 a.m."

"Six hours later?" She stared at me, waited for more, then asked, "Anything stolen this time?"

"Nothing here to take besides what was ruined."

"VCR? TV? Silver?"

"All gone long ago. My ex-wife took any valuable stuff like that. Well, it was hers anyway. I have no jewelry or antiques."

"Was there forced entry this time?"

"No. The doors were unlocked again."

She shook her head. "You didn't lock up after last time?"

"I didn't think they'd be back."

"Not locking up provides an easy opportunity. It invites prowlers to come in."

She trained those blue lasers on me, and under their pressure I said, "You're right."

She looked down at her notebook. "The last time you said this looked like the work of, and I quote, 'Kids high on testosterone, angry, alienated, after a thrill, wanting to break things.' You thinking the same this time?"

"I don't know. This seems, well, more malicious."

"I'm going to let you in on a secret because it may get you to think of something helpful and we need to discuss it anyway. What happened here is like what happened at Burkhoffer's house."

"At Sammy's farm?" Her eyes were blue cauldrons. "What happened there?"

"Apparent vandalism, but without any damage. Things out of place and thrown around."

"Are you implying that whoever made the mess here also went through Sammy's place?"

"It's one possibility."

"That doesn't make sense."

"Could be they weren't vandalisms per se. They might have been searches for something."

"Besides money, what would they want here?"

"How about written materials? Everywhere Burkhoffer might have put his papers was ransacked. We found no list of addresses or phone numbers or relatives, no canceled checks, no diaries or old letters, none of the important papers everyone has. And I didn't see any of that stuff lying around here either."

"My address book was on the floor over there, but I put it back in a drawer by the phone."

"That printed stuff on the floor of your computer room didn't look like what I'm talking about."

"No, those are mostly handouts for classes I taught."

"You reported nothing was taken from the first illegal entry, and I think that could have been a search for documents too. That's why I'm here. Weren't the desk drawers and filing cabinet emptied then also?"

"Yeah."

"Where are your other papers?"

"I've got them." Those blue eyes were about to drag out an

explanation so I turned away, went to the refrigerator, took out a bottle of beer, twisted off the lid, and threw it into the trash bag. Ed's mention of the obscene phone calls and the threats of five years ago, plus memories of their effects on Laura and Angela, made me leery of getting Mom and Aunt Judy involved. Why upset them? There was no need for the police to invade Mom's household, and they would if they knew of my connection to her place. No reason the cops needed to know about my papers or anything else over there.

I faced Grimes and said, "I just finished working out and need a drink. Want one? I suppose you're on duty, but I can also offer water and pop."

"No thanks. What I'd like is an answer."

"There's wine too." I pointed to the bottles in the refrigerator door. "A white and a red. Both dry."

She shook her head. "Where are your papers?"

"In my possession, but where is private and irrelevant."

She frowned. "All right, I suppose your intruder would, like me, assume they'd be here in your home, in the drawers or in a strong box."

"I guess that's right—if they were what he wanted."

Her staring made me nervous.

I swallowed half of my beer, and it ran coolness down to my belly. "Look, I'm glad you told me about the possible connection to Sammy's vandalism, and I do want you to get Sammy's killer."

"If you're serious, then help." The direct blue gaze again.

What could I say to help, and to distract her from Mom, Aunt Judy and my personal papers? Only one fact I knew might work, but it would also make Grimes suspicious again. Oh well, I had to say something. "Somebody was in Sammy's house until 3:30 last night."

Her eyes narrowed.

I said, "I just happened to be near the house then."

"Driving by?"

I shook my head, thinking, Jerk, keep your mouth shut.

"Where were you?"

"I was on foot, relieving tension from the long grilling that you put me through." That *was* the truth.

"Precisely where?" She put her hands on her hips.

I could say I'd been on the bike trail or roadside, but hell! I was not going to lie just to avoid an awkward situation—or even jail. I would either not answer at all or tell the truth.

The latter. She needed verification that someone had been in the house last night. "I was in one of Sammy's fields. There was a person, maybe more than one, inside his house, and I checked my watch when he left. The car looked small, like a compact."

She stiffened and glared at me. "In a field? You were in one of Burkhoffer's fields last night at 3:30?"

I nodded.

She said, "In a field, not beside a field or on the road?"

I nodded.

She asked, "Doing what?"

"Mostly walking. Look, I think whoever was in the house may have gone there after being here."

She shook her head. "That was me. I was in the house."

"Oh."

"That's all you were doing, walking?"

I nodded. "More or less."

"You were not in any of Burkhoffer's buildings?"

"No."

"Which field were you in?"

"North of the house, the one that borders 86 and the river."

"What could you possibly be doing in that field, if that's where you were?"

"I never lied to you. I couldn't sleep and went there."

"I really don't know what to say at this point. If you are not the strangest person I've ever met, then—" She shook her head as if she lacked the words for what she felt. She stared with darkened eyes, then said, "It's clear we have more talking to do. Will you come in tomorrow morning?"

"Again? Is that necessary?"

"Yes, if only to consider a connection to Burkhoffer." She shook her head so hard, her short brown hair rose, then dropped in a wave. "Will you come into the station tomorrow at eight? See how I'm asking you to come in voluntarily? I won't send Deputy Jones or somebody else unless I have to."

I frowned, balancing my plans with her request, which was actually an order. "I have to do a long run tomorrow morning. So make it ten or eleven."

"All right, 10:30. And don't touch any more things in this house than you have to. I'll send people over to dust for prints tomorrow. Is that all right? Do I have your permission?"

"You think there might be prints? Well, okay. Good idea."

She said, "I don't think there'll be prints. There were none at Burkhoffer's. But we'll check. Hold on. If you go jogging, you won't be here early when I want them to do it."

I sighed, not about to skip my run. "They can come in. I'll leave the front door unlocked."

She scowled. "Don't do that. Give me a key."

I gave her the key hidden under dishtowels in a drawer.

"Fine." Grimes pivoted around and left, squelching a feeble impulse I'd been entertaining, of asking her to stay for dinner. Even if she hadn't been very pleasant, having a woman in the house struck me as civilizing and enjoyable.

CHAPTER EIGHT

I entered the Sheriff's Department at 10:26, four minutes early, eager for once to talk to Grimes. A deputy deposited me in that same small interrogation room, promised that the detectives would be along shortly, and left.

I plopped down, spread my legs out, leaned back, slid forward on the seat, crossed my arms on my chest and tried not to fall asleep—my workout had overcooked me.

It had started sanely, that is slowly, at my normal pace for a 13-miler, a distance I'd been running twice a week for the last two months. But six and a half miles up the bike trail near the edge of Red Springs, I'd turned around, checked my watch, become afraid there wouldn't be time to eat breakfast before meeting Grimes, and sped up coming back.

I knew better than to rush so fast I hurt myself, but the 7.3-minute-per-mile clip returning had taken a lot out of me.

My stomach churned, digesting the big breakfast I'd managed before leaving home, but the rest of my body went dormant.

The run was the one I'd been trying to do on Wednesday. Today, where Sammy's body had been, there was nothing, no yellow tape, no baseball bat, not one sign of the violence there. I'd slowed to look, jogging by on the way out, then settled into a faster, but easy gait that let me think about the case. By the turn-around point, I had remembered something that, despite near exhaustion now, still made me anxious to tell Grimes about.

It was Shepherd, however, who plopped down on the chair across from me while the door clicked shut to my rear. I opened my eyes as wide as I could, stretched my arms, grimaced while stiff back and neck muscles complained, sat straight up, yawned and looked around. "Where's Grimes?"

Shepherd said, "Is that some kind of act? Falling asleep is too calm for a homicide suspect."

I crossed my arms again and snorted, "Forget about me. Did you know Sammy had a son? All your damn questions and we never got into what Sammy and I discussed. If friends and relatives are the usual suspects in a murder, then you better include him."

The door snapped open and I twisted around to see Grimes shutting it. With a hand still on the doorknob, she faced us and said, "Just a minute."

I said, "Hey, I got an idea—"

"Save it!"

"Sammy had a son who—"

"Shut him the fuck up!" she told Shepherd.

"Quiet!" Shepherd said.

She raised an index finger toward us, meaning to hold on, turned, cracked the door open, looked out for a minute, then closed the door, came inside and sat on the chair to my right.

"You must have a serious mad on," I said, still relaxed. "I can't remember you ever cussing before."

"Then you weren't listening very well."

She inserted a cassette into the recorder, turned it on, set it down on the table, and we went through the whole Miranda rights thing again. I agreed to talk without a lawyer, but her hostile attitude put me off enough to say, "What tied your panty-hose in a knot?"

She frowned. "You must enjoy putting your foot in your mouth."

I smiled. The comment seemed like a joke. Hell, I hadn't said anything yet. Then I remembered her bolting from my house last night. "You still upset because I was in Sammy's field?"

"We'll get to that in a minute. Know what? You're guarded in what you tell us, then burst out with things as if you got no worries at all. Is that how you are or what?"

Her lips went rigid and her eyes sparkled. She looked at Shepherd, who shrugged and nodded at the same time, maybe as confused as I was.

She looked at me. "Did you see anyone out there before you came into this room?"

"A couple deputies in uniform. The dispatcher was out there. There were people in the hall and the parking lot too."

"Anyone you recognized."

I shook my head.

"You know Simon Croft?"

Another surprise. "I know he's a bastard."

"Are you personally acquainted? Ever talk to him?"

"Through a microphone a couple times, at County Commission meetings a few years ago. What's going on?"

"Why didn't you ever mention that Burkhoffer had a son?"

"You never asked me. You were trying so hard to nail me for the killing, you never once asked what Sammy and I talked about."

She rolled her eyes. "We asked you that several times."

"No, you asked if Sammy discussed threats or people bothering him and things like that. Go back and check your damn tapes. That's why I didn't mention the son. Don't blame me if you just now learned about him."

"Oh, we've known about him since yesterday afternoon. He heard the victim's name on the news and came in. Croft is the son. You didn't know that?"

"Hell no." I sat up straighter. "Simon Croft's the son?"

"Yes, he confirmed the body's identification."

"Goddam! I can't picture Sammy and him together. What did Croft do, change his name? Well, no wonder they didn't get along. See, Sammy mentioned to me that a long time ago he'd had a falling out with his son, who then moved away."

Shepherd said, "He didn't move far."

"Maybe Sammy said the son moved out, not away. I don't remember exactly, but I got the impression they'd never talked after that. Well, Lieutenant, there you go. A prime suspect. Check him out. Maybe he's your killer."

Grimes said, "Concentrate on clearing yourself. Like explain that midnight jaunt into Burkhoffer's field. What were you doing there? And don't say walking around. Your tracks show you walked to one spot, stopped, then went back the same way."

I gawked at her. While I'd been jogging this morning, she was in the field, checking out my story.

She said, "You were lying down for one thing. I could see that. Were you watching Burkhoffer's house?"

"I admitted being there only because I mentioned that somebody had been in the house. Obviously, I couldn't tell it was you."

"Why were you watching the house?"

"I wasn't. I took a goddam nap. Okay? I found an artifact, lay down and after a long day, conked out and slept for a while."

Grimes stared at me, at Shepherd, at me, and chuckled. "You went out in the middle of that mud field to take a nap?"

Jesus! She thought it was funny. I looked up at the ceiling, crossed my arms, and tried to ignore her.

The two of them laughed—first Grimes. She started slow but the intensity built up. By the time she was full voiced, Shepherd was laughing too. Their laughter reverberated in the little room until it was all I could hear.

It pulled my eyes off the ceiling onto the two clowns, and

gradually it bubbled up in me too. I laughed, but quit when I realized that they were laughing at, not with me. Their laughter was another kind of goddam insult, and my laughter was shameful, full of self-loathing and the desire for approval.

They both had to wipe their eyes when they'd finished, but their smiles hung on.

Grimes said, "Anybody else and I'd think they were lying."

"Were you drunk?" Shepherd asked.

They glanced at each other and smiled at my expense. My jaws clenched tight enough to hurt. I leaned back and sat rigidly.

Grimes finally said, "Tell us, please, why would a supposedly sane individual go out on a chilly night into the middle of an empty field to sleep?"

I sneered. "How about that, an intelligent question."

Shepherd laughed again, but I ignored him. Grimes offended me more because she'd been in my home alone with me. She knew me better than he did. But both had a smugness that no amount of explaining would overcome. Even if I could make them understand, they certainly wouldn't respect my point of view.

I said, "Do you know why the little bunch of houses out there is called Old Town?"

Grimes shook her head. I glanced at Shepherd, and he said, "Tell us." They'd moved to this area for what it provided, their livelihood, but aside from that, it had no intrinsic value worthy of their respect or attention.

I said, "Where you saw my car parked on 86, a state historical sign explains that a large Indian village once existed there. In fact it's where Tecumseh grew up and lived. You have heard of him, I suppose. White settlers destroyed the village several times and eventually drove off the Indians. The land where the village was has been farmed ever since."

Shepherd said, "So what?"

"Visiting there is like going to church. It settles me down. I used to go there before Burkhoffer took me to court."

Grimes said, "Did you say you found something there?"

"An Indian tool, a carved rock that's at my home if you want to see it."

She asked, "Have you found anything there before?"

"No, but a lot more must be buried there."

She asked, "Did you and Burkhoffer talk about that?"

I thought for a second. "It's very weird now that I know who he is. Sammy didn't seem to know about Old Town, and I probably told him everything I know about the Indians."

Grimes asked, "More than what you've just told us?"

"Well, there are also tales of a Shawnee silver mine because the tribe wore silver ornaments. I told him that."

Shepherd scoffed, "There's no silver in Ohio."

"Same thing he said, and I told him there was none we know of, but there is gold in some Ohio creeks, glacial deposits, and there was even a gold mine at one time. So why couldn't there be some silver around here too? That's the thinking of some people. I've read articles about maniacs literally going around, digging up this area, looking for the silver."

Grimes asked, "Are things like what you found valuable?"

"Is that rock I found worth money?" I shook my head. "Arrowheads, stuff like that? Flea markets have them by the hundreds. No, they're not worth much."

Shepherd asked, "Aren't there rarer things, though, that could be worth more?"

Aha, Shepherd could think. "Yeah, pipes or beads, ornaments, effigies, stuff like that would be worth something. Those fields at Old Town have to be rich with relics because archaeologists have never systematically studied them. Nobody knows when the Indians built the village. It may go way back before the Shawnees. Scientists might learn a wealth of information if they excavated. Not that that would sit well with Indians. And they do have a valid point."

"Which is what?" asked Shepherd.

"It's all theirs. Their artifacts, their relics, their bones if burials are ever found. Hell, it's rightfully their land. They should have something to say about what science does."

Shepherd said, "Do Shawnee Indians still live around here?"

"Very few if any. There are Indians here, like my friend Ed Hilliard who lives south of Bethel. He's part Cherokee. I think most of the Shawnees are living on a reservation out west, but I don't know their numbers. Old Town and this area in general is part of their ancestral home. What happened here may not be part of anyone's living memory, but stories about it would have been passed down if the tribe still exists. The Shawnees are a displaced ethnic group, and what happened here would matter to them."

Grimes asked, "Did you tell all this to Burkhoffer?"

"Yes, more than a couple times. It's hard to believe he could own the property and not be aware of the history."

Grimes said, "Oh, I think Burkhoffer knew. A building on his farm is full of Indian stuff."

CHAPTER NINE

My reflex was to ask to see Sammy's collection.

"Why?" Grimes responded.

It was a thrilling prospect, that was why, but my reason had to be pertinent to her.

"To help your investigation," I jabbered. "Maybe I'll see something that'll remind me of other things Sammy said. I might recognize things that you ought to guard. Maybe I'll recognize something that shouldn't be there."

"Nobody's allowed in those buildings," she said, but asked Shepherd, "What do you think?"

He shrugged. "What could it hurt?"

After Shepherd parted from us on other business, I went out to a cruiser with Grimes and automatically reached for the passenger door handle.

She said, "I don't think so," and opened the back door.

Damn her negative instincts. Was she afraid I might grab the shotgun off the rack up there?

She parked in the center of the circular barnyard, let me out, and went directly to the barn.

I caught up with her and asked, "Sammy filled this huge building with Indian things?"

"I'm just checking it out. There's no lock on these doors." With both hands she slid the doors open a body's width, revealing a dusty, two-year-old Buick and an older car parked ahead of it.

"Sammy's cars?" I asked.

"Yes, still here and they look undisturbed."

"Any clues in them?"

"Nothing."

"Nice barn," I said, opening the door on her left and edging inside. "Very similar to mine but bigger, and look at this floor." I kicked aside straw, hay and dirt so the planks showed. "Old timber. This barn itself is a relic."

I stood and looked into the upper reaches. "The mow on the right is half full of hay bales. Looks like straw on the left. Can't see much else. Where's his equipment?"

"There's some over here." She passed me and went fifteen feet inside to the left.

Coming up beside her, eyes adjusting to the darkness, I saw two cutting bars, a small Ferguson tractor, a wagon, and a snow plow or grader blade.

"That's all? Nothing else?"

"There are things in the other buildings too."

She led me out, and I pulled one side of the door shut while she pulled the other. When they banged together, I dropped the big L latch into place. Then she led me across the yard past the cruiser to a long, narrow, one-story building. At the door on the end near the house, she tried inserting keys from a key ring into a heavy Yale lock.

"This is an old chicken coop," I said.

"I thought it was built special for what he put in it."

"Where you from?"

"Chicago."

"At one time there was probably a high wire fence around part of it so the chickens could get outside. Earlier, they probably ranged free over the barnyard and came inside at night. Imagine twenty or thirty of them out here clucking at our feet, running around pecking in the dirt and grass, eating bugs and fallen grain. It'd be neat."

"Dirty and smelly, I'd guess."

She tried other keys. When the lock opened, Grimes removed it, pushed the door in, stepped inside and flipped a switch.

Lights flickered, erupting brightly as I entered. "My God!"

There were hundreds of Indian things. Thousands! And the room had been arranged to show them off. There were no roosts or perches, no nesting boxes, no feeding trays, nothing for chickens. No stench or filth. The place was immaculate.

And totally remodeled. About seven feet up, suspended from the peak of the ceiling, were three metal box mountings holding long florescent tubes end-to-end underneath. Two other such lights hung perpendicular from them at both ends of the building. With seven lights in all, there were no shadows.

The floor and the underside of the roof gleamed with dark varnish. A three-foot wide table was attached to each side wall, and the surface of each table shone with transparent varnish, maybe shellac, that showed off the wood's grain beneath and the natural color of the artifacts on top.

What a collection! "Okay to touch them?"

"Go ahead."

"I've never seen arrowheads like these before."

In my right palm, the milky-white flint looked lethal, three inches long, thin, tapering down from a notched back to a point, which was very fine considering that it had been chipped into that shape with another rock. Proportioned in width and depth too, I thought, flipping it over.

I put it back among five others like it and said, "Sammy grouped these by color. There's this white flint, which has to be rare, then these larger groups of brown and red and black ones. A geologist might be able to tell you where the Indians got the flint. Maybe trace their travels that way. Look how well made these arrowheads are. Took a lot of skill to flake the rock into these perfect shapes."

Grimes nodded, and her blue eyes glistened in the light.

"These are spear points," I said, going farther in along that side. "Heavier and bigger. Boy, they're all in great shape. Not a broken one."

"Broken pieces are under the tables," Grimes said.

"Yeah?" Now I noticed long, not very wide or deep cardboard cartons on the floor between two-by-four braces that angled, every three feet, from beneath the tables' front edge down and back to the wall just above the floor.

I went to the wall's end. "Hatchet heads and ax heads here. All stone. I suppose steel would have totally rusted away by now. Look, there's more of them on the other side."

I went along touching, lifting, admiring them. "Over here Sammy put things like household tools. This one's like what I found in the field. Something to grind or mash with."

"I don't see any pots. Didn't Indians use clay?"

"I don't know. Are there any chunks of pottery in the boxes?"

"I didn't see any," she said.

"Maybe they used wood pots and wove natural fibers for baskets. I suppose any of that would have rotted away."

"I've seen nothing made of wood or woven."

"I'm ignorant about how the Indians lived. Look here at the end. Beads and trinkets. Some look like baked clay. The rest are stone, carved bones, teeth. Hundreds of these things alone."

"There's a box of them underneath too."

I bent over, pulled out a box of things several inches deep, shoved the box rattling back under the table, straightened up and walked around the room, gazing in amazement at the objects.

"It's a museum. I mean it ought to be a museum. Experts need to look over this stuff. I bet Sammy picked all this up off the surface, didn't deliberately dig it out. Think what a systematic archeological dig might uncover."

"Is all this valuable?"

"It's the largest collection I ever saw, but its value lies in historical and archeological significance. Would people kill to get this? I doubt it. Doesn't look like the killer was in here to take anything either."

"And he had access to Burkhoffer's keys."

"Are there more Indian artifacts in the house or the other buildings?"

"No."

"Maybe the Indian things were stolen out of them?"

"No sign of it."

I looked around again. "God, this place excites me."

"Yeah, interesting," Grimes said, but without enthusiasm.

She went out the door, held it open for me until I also left, and then she locked up.

I walked to the nearest small building. Its door was four connected top-to-bottom panels hung overhead by rollers on a metal track. The panels accordioned open, revealing a simple one-car garage, a wooden box on top of a concrete slab. Inside was a work table and electric tools, including drills, saws and a grinder. On shelves were brushes, small tubs, cans of paint and solvents, and on one wall hung two wooden extension ladders. I pointed to brushes, whet stones and mower blades. "Here's where Sammy cleaned the Indian things he found. Also sharpened things."

Beside this building was another the same size. It contained a self-propelled rotary mower, rototiller, hoes, shovels, rakes, bags of fertilizer, insecticide, some carpentry tools, old buckets, and two wheelbarrows—deep, heavy steel ones, not the plastic or shallow aluminum types sold in hardware stores now.

Leaving, closing the door behind us, I said, "Gardening equipment mostly," and pictured a young Sammy bustling around, fixing up the buildings, maintaining the grounds.

A minute later as Grimes and I reached the cruiser, awareness overwhelmed me: of Sammy's death, my presence on his property, his apparent interest in Indians, and the rich mysteries of his life as well as of the place itself.

I looked around. Sammy's buildings surrounded us, and the open fields surrounded them. Farther off, the treeline by the river to the north curved straight west for over a half-mile, then turned back south, passing a 200-foot-high ridge that ran from it to the east. That hill was heavily wooded also, too steep to allow development or agricultural use, but at its foot near Route 86 was another old white farmhouse. Across the road, running south to north, were the trees along the bike trail, and nearer us were the buildings of Old Town along the road.

"It's a miracle, but this place is still a lot like it was a couple centuries ago, and we're standing right where part of the Indian village was. I can't help but imagine Indians, dwellings, a great hardwood forest surrounding us. That's why I was in the field the other night. This is a sacred place."

"Ripe for development," Grimes said.

Shaking my head, wondering if I had detected displeasure or indifference in her voice, I said, "Yeah, development will happen. It'll be a disaster, but there's no way to stop it."

"That's progress," she said, and again I could not tell if approval, simple acceptance, regret, or irony was in her voice.

She was staring at Sammy's house or maybe beyond it into the distance at the road where cars were zipping past. Heavy traffic. Always heavy traffic.

"Peaceful back here," I said.

"Not for me. I have to get going on this case. Anything you notice might help."

"I wonder if Sammy collected even more Indian things. If his house was torn up like mine was, how could you tell that something besides documents hadn't been taken?"

"Drawers were on the floor along with what had been in them. That was it. Nothing was smashed or broken. So I don't think anything but documents was taken. No indications of it. Anyway, in terms of your involvement, does visiting here remind you of anything the victim said or was concerned about?"

"Nothing comes to mind."

"Notice anything odd?"

"Well, do you realize somebody must be leasing this land and the barn? Sammy doesn't have the equipment and was too old to farm. That person probably talked with Sammy and might know something, especially if he's leased the land a few years."

"Good thinking."

"The neighbors along the road might know who he is. If they don't, there are county and state agricultural agents in the courthouse, like at the conservation district office. And how about people that show up at the funeral?"

"Got that covered." Grimes went around the cruiser to the driver's side. "I have to get back."

I quickly opened the other front door, sat in the passenger seat, and smiled at her when she slid inside behind the wheel.

She said, "You're like a kid. Don't touch anything up here."

"Before you start, I have another idea that might help. If Sammy's intruder took documents, you better check Sammy's mail and put a stop-delivery hold on—"

She held up a hand. "That's already done. And you better stop your mail delivery too. Yesterday, I didn't see any personal documents in your house, and you said they weren't taken. Well, whatever your explanation for that, and I haven't heard it yet, your illegal entry may have been effected for the same reason documents were taken here. The contents of your desk drawers were underneath the other stuff thrown on the floor. Remember? In your computer room and that other room?"

"Yes."

"So the desk drawers were searched first, perhaps for papers. That also was what your first intruder searched, right?"

I nodded.

"Okay, if the intruder was looking for documents, he may think something's been mailed to you. In that case, he might try to intercept your mail?"

"That assumes Sammy knew who I was."

"Don't you think he did?"

"Maybe. I never told Sammy my last name, just Cliff, but how many Cliffs could he know? There aren't that many around. So maybe he'd have figured out who I was. He'd have remembered Cliff the trespasser's name for sure. Sammy was sharp."

"That's right. Another thing. Why'd he listen to you talk about Old Town and the Indians and not admit what he knew?"

"Maybe it was a game. He knew I didn't realize who he was and thought it was funny hearing me ramble on about his property. Maybe he wanted to understand my thinking." I shrugged. "Hell, to be honest, I can't figure it out. Maybe he wanted to see if I knew something he didn't know about the subject."

"Think about this." She swiveled in the seat, scooting her knees onto it, one on top of the other, facing me. "Maybe he knew who you were from the start. Maybe he didn't meet you on the bike trail by accident. What if he sought you out?"

I shook my head. "Why not just call? I'm in the phone book. Or he could have come over."

"You don't exactly welcome strangers. Ever read the signs you put up out by the road at your house? Besides, Burkhoffer may have wanted to remain anonymous to you."

"For what purpose?"

"That's right. He would have had a purpose. He was up to something." Grimes looked excited. She leaned my way and jabbed the seat between us. "What was that purpose? You're connected to his death. I'm sure of it."

I turned in the seat too. "Are you finally convinced that I'm not the killer?"

"That's a possibility."

"About time!"

"Well, this connection I'm proposing between you and Burkhoffer's death may not be accurate."

"But it is worth pursuing. Something to start on. Congratulations, Lieutenant. You've got a new lead."

She said, "What was Burkhoffer's purpose? Think about that and we'll discuss it, but not now. I have things to do. Later."

"I have errands too. How about if we talk over dinner at my house? I'll make something nice, and we can relax and talk things over while we eat."

"Buckle up," she said, squaring herself in the seat in one fluid movement, turning on the ignition, shifting into drive, easing ahead, circling around the barnyard.

I said, "Look, bring Shepherd. Hell, bring the sheriff too. I'm serious. Just let me know they're coming. We both have to eat anyway so let's talk in a relaxed atmosphere that might foster creative thinking. What do you say? I eat about five."

She hit the gas hard, and we roared down the lane fast enough to make me straighten around and brace my feet against the floor. She lurched to a stop at the road and got out to put up the police tape again, or so I thought, buckling my seat belt. She also went to the mailbox and checked it for mail. Then she came back inside the car and took us onto 86 toward Bethel.

"Empty," she said to the windshield. "I'll ask the postman what he remembers delivering the last few days."

We roared up the incline out of the valley, leaving Old Town behind us. I sank back into the seat, wondering, What next? and prepared to submit to whatever inevitable thing would occur.

Halfway to the station she finally said, "Okay. Make it at six. We can do dinner and talk at your house if you want to. Maybe being there will help you think more clearly."

"I need all the help I can get in that department." I grinned, but that was no joke.

CHAPTER TEN

Because Grimes said she liked salmon, and Megastore had fresh fish, I fought a Friday afternoon frenzy of housewives in SUVs, all of us milling about, repulsed and attracted simultaneously. Purchases complete, I rushed home, set up the meal, and made the living room livable, kitchen and downstairs bathroom acceptable, then myself presentable, donning my best slacks, loafers and favorite shirt. When a car entered the lane, I was out on the porch before Grimes could park.

You're pathetic, acting as if meeting Grimes is romantic, I told myself. Her first name is Lieutenant to you. What the hell is your problem?

I'm lonely, I thought.

You'd better cool it, you self-destructive dumbass.

As she walked to the porch, I pulled on an aloof mask, swallowed a bug-eyed greeting, and said, "That powder your people put down is hard to get up."

She stopped before the steps. "Been straightening up?"

"Had to get ready for you."

"Our techie called your place 'Extraordinarily clean.'"

"Clean? The place was a wreck."

"Clean of prints," Grimes said. "He found only three different sets. Do you obsessively wipe off your furniture?"

"I can't remember the last time I dusted."

"You must have very few visitors then."

Feeling no need to go there, I said, "One set of prints would be Ed Hilliard. One is mine. Who could the other one be? Maybe the electric meter reader."

"Or the vandal? Did you remember anything useful?"

"Not yet."

Inside the front door, I tingled at her nearness, quickly handed her a glass of chilled white wine, hoisted my bottle of lite beer toward her, and forced a near shattering collision.

Embarrassing. "Well, we found out the wine glass is strong. I just bought a couple of them special for today."

"It's nice." She swallowed a bit of her drink. "Good wine too. Should I tell you something?"

I shrugged and drank and admired her eyes.

"This is a brandy snifter."

"Well, damn. There's never anybody to wait on you in Megastore so I just grabbed what looked good."

"I wasn't criticizing. It's fine."

"It's better than jelly jars, which was all I had before."

She dropped onto the couch while I went to the kitchen, put the salmon in the oven (preheated to 325 degrees), set the timer, and zapped the bowl of rice in the microwave for four minutes, planning another zap just before serving. I emptied my beer, grabbed another, went back to her, poured her more wine, set the wine bottle on the end table, sat on the wooden rocker facing her, and scooted closer.

"The food will be done in half an hour," I said.

"What would Burkhoffer want from you? Any idea?"

"Look, I've been thinking, and I'm afraid your theory's wrong. Meeting Sammy could very well have been a coincidence."

"And the intrusions in both homes?" Grimes asked.

"They could be coincidences too."

"How many people know your exercise schedule?"

"Nobody. It varies too much."

I explained that I alternated two long and five short runs per week, but where I ran was unpredictable. Each long run, I took the bike trail in any direction from any point where I could park and safely leave my car. The bike trail went on for many miles in east–west as well as north–south routes, which crossed at the restored railroad depot south of downtown Bethel. I simply parked wherever I felt like it at the time, and did my mileage from there. Only the evening walk was predictable, always about an hour before dark on the same stretch near Old Town. "Sammy wouldn't have to know I'd be there, though. He could have met me by coincidence because his home is so close."

"Do many 82-year-olds walk on the bike trail?"

"A few."

"Out there in the country?"

"Well, mostly in town."

"Burkhoffer had cancer, underwent chemotherapy, and he'd lost a lot of weight."

"So that's why Sammy seemed smaller than he was ten years ago. He seemed weak, too. We never walked fast or far, and we stopped and rested sometimes. Which didn't bother me. The walks were just a stroll. But that's too bad. So Sammy had cancer."

She said, "For a sick person, wasn't that a pretty long way from his house to the bike trail?"

"Yeah," I admitted. "He had to walk down a long lane."

"Maybe he drove across the road to get there, but why go to the trouble? He had over four hundred acres of his own land to walk on."

"Maybe he wanted company."

"He wouldn't know he'd have company the first time he went to the bike trail. That is unless he knew you were there at a certain time every day. Meeting you there was no coincidence."

"Okay, let's say he was there to meet me."

"Two things then. First, how did he find you? And second, what did he want?"

"Yeah, that's the thing. Why would he want to talk to me?"

"First things first. How'd he find you, or learn your schedule? Maybe with a private detective."

"Somebody followed me? That's creepy as hell!"

"I'll contact all agencies around here and Dayton, and I'm contacting banks to find Burkhoffer's checking accounts. Canceled checks could lead me to a detective."

"To other people that knew him too." I didn't know if Sammy would have hired a detective, but obviously the checking account could be useful.

She said, "As to why he contacted you, what he talked about should indicate his purpose."

"Let me think about that a little more." Rocking furiously, my chair creaked and squeaked, leading me away from her subject to fond memories. Having a woman here was nice—the first one in my living room in months. No, years. "I bought this chair when my daughter was born, and used it hundreds of times to quiet Laura when she was sick or upset or eating. The first light of dawn broke through that window many a time just as she was going back to sleep. I'm glad my ex-wife left this chair. The stuff she took meant nothing to me."

"What did Burkhoffer ask you about?"

"Hmm," I mused, miffed at her insisting on business.

"Huh?" Grimes asked, bending forward, untying her shoes, pulling them off, dropping them aside, lying back, sliding forward on the cushion, setting her goblet against her stomach with the fingers of both hands splayed around the stem.

"Tired?" I stared at those heretofore hidden extremities, her bare feet, and excitement surged through me as intensely as if she had unbuttoned her blouse. Her pale arches glowed in the light from the end table's lamp, her toes curved out as discreet elongations of flesh, and I fought an urge to kneel and knead their undersides—as I'd often done for my wife in the evenings.

"Very tired," she sighed, letting her head fall back. "I have to get a handle on this case."

"I'm surprised you paint your toenails."

She shook her head, raised the goblet and drained it.

"I just meant you're so down to earth and natural otherwise. You don't wear jewelry or make-up, you have a sensible, plain, practical haircut, and your fingernails are bare."

She held up her right hand and turned its fingernails toward me. "Clear enamel."

"No perfume either."

"I dye my hair."

"Really!"

"It's actually dark brown."

"Dark brown hair would look good."

"I was tired of it."

"Let me get you some more." I stepped over her feet and that bright red polish, took her glass, filled it, and handed it back. "Now help yourself."

"This'll be it for me. Three's my limit." She rested the glass on her stomach again. "Let's get to the matter at hand. What did you two talk about exactly?"

I sat back down, sipped my beer, gazed at her feet, and said, "It must cost a lot to wear a suit every day. Do you get a clothing or laundry allowance?"

She frowned. "No, and dry cleaners charge a fortune."

"I haven't worn a suit in ten years. I go entire summers without wearing trousers."

"You can get arrested for that."

I laughed. "I meant when the temperature stays in the 60s, I go into shorts until the fall. What's your first name?"

"Eden."

Repeating the name in my mind bathed her in a Biblical context. I raised my bottle to hide a reddening face. Good name, I thought. Perfect name. Without meaning to, I said it, "Eden."

"What?" Her eyes turned to me again. "Think of something?"

"I better check the food. It must be about ready."

We ate, and when she asked again about my conversations with Sammy, I observed that the much-publicized upgrading of the county's legal services must have been what brought her here.

"I was hired to organize a detectives unit. And make assignments, and so on. With six years investigating homicides in Chicago, this murder case is mine."

"Yeah, a chance to establish yourself in a new job," I guessed. "Where's Shepherd from?"

"Detroit, worked mainly in burglary. He's downtown at a business break-in or he'd be here too. Our other two detectives were the ones who checked for prints. They're our best trained in crime scene investigations so they'll do our forensics work."

"How long you been in town?"

"Two weeks, two days longer than Shepherd. You think of anything Burkhoffer asked you about?"

"Let's talk about that after supper, okay? How's a sheriff go about finding people to hire? I'm curious."

She ate faster than I did. I passed her the remaining fillet, told her to go ahead, I didn't want more, and she took it. That'd be at least twelve fishy ounces for her. Good appetite.

She said, "I interviewed with Sheriff Orndorf at a sheriffs' convention in DeKalb, and was offered the job. Shepherd saw a jobs-opening ad in a law enforcement magazine, applied, and eventually came here that way. Pay and benefits are pretty good. The quiet life of Shawnee County's the main attraction for Shepherd. He's married with two children."

"Life used to be a lot better here," I told her.

Spooning another mound of rice onto her plate, she said, "A lot's going on all right. This area's bulging at the seams."

"Is the Department going to hire more people?"

"Two more detectives I'm helping the sheriff interview for. The sheriff's a busy man. In constant meetings. He's forced to delegate responsibilities."

I said, "I've always respected him. In 1973, he was at a job fair with other professionals speaking to us high school seniors about careers in their fields. He'd been in the news for being the youngest sheriff in the state. Plus, almost being killed in a murder case. I raised my hand and asked about going into the Marine Corps and said something about maybe winning a Silver Star the way he had. Know what he said?"

With a mouthful of Chinook, she shook her head.

"That I made it sound like winning a medal in the Olympics. He said that he wasn't a hero, and such medals were misleading anyway. He told me I should go to college and get educated. Nobody should want to go to war."

She swallowed and looked at me down the length of her crooked nose. "I didn't know about the Silver Star."

"I remember exactly what he said because it influenced my life. Your boss has some brains, Eden. His heart's in the right place, and he's efficient. Look how quickly he dealt with my Clayton Jones complaint."

"Yeah, yeah." Her lips tightened into a smile more like a grimace. "We were already setting up a training program to establish policies and practices. Now can we get back to our real topic of conversation?"

So he had scheduled some training. That pleased me. What didn't was Eden's attitude. Her remark implied that my thinking and my complaint were inconsequential.

All I said was, "You want more rice? Green beans? I bought some vanilla ice cream for dessert, and there's chocolate or strawberry topping."

We ended up back in the living room. She stretched out as before, note pad replacing wine glass, and I sprawled on the other end of the couch with my right hand holding a beer bottle on the cushion between us. The picture window reflected the *Fuck You* behind us on the wall.

"So what'd Burkhoffer want to talk about?" she asked.

"I'm not sure Sammy steered our conversations." I drank some beer and concentrated. "Seems to me we talked about everything, what was on television, movies, sports, news, politics, the weather. We hit many subjects, but nothing stands out."

"What subject came up most often? What seemed to be his major interest?"

I shook my head. "All I can think of is the past. We talked about how things used to be, how people used to live."

"Like?"

"He'd wax nostalgic the way you expect old people to do, describing how bad the winters used to be, how hard the rains fell, how bad the floods were, how much hotter it got then." I chuckled. "Sammy tended to exaggerate more than I do. He mentioned membership in a Grange that used to exist around there. He talked about coal furnaces and problems he had with them. Things like that. Really, nothing specific stands out in my mind except the past in general. Well, maybe Old Town itself and the Indians. That came up more than once."

"How many times? A lot?"

"Five or ten times, maybe more, but I brought it up. The nature of that area was my reason for being there so it was on my mind. Sometimes I jump on a high horse and rave. Well, raving's not the right word."

"Raving sounds right to me."

A smile implied her caustic tone wasn't intended.

It still made me defensive. "Certain likes and dislikes get me excited so I run my mouth and tell whoever will listen what's wrong with the world and what ought to be done."

"What did Burkhoffer do?"

"When I preached? Well, he didn't take notes. I don't know if he even paid attention. We never argued. Never disagreed. He seemed to be a quiet guy so I did most of the talking, and usually he'd just make a noise to show he was listening."

"Like he was pumping you?"

"Didn't seem like it."

"Let's go day by day. From the first time you talked to him to the last time."

"Gawd! All those times with Sammy?" In my mind they ran together, forming an impenetrable tangle of noise and sights and feelings too difficult to separate. I yawned and glanced at my watch. "Jesus, after 9:00 already. It's my bedtime."

"It's early," she contradicted.

In the picture window, her reflection straightened up alertly, ready to forge on, staring at me.

"Let's figure this out," she coaxed.

"Sorry, I've had it." I could be stubborn too.

My fatigue was genuine. I needed sleep to recover from my workout, and by now Eden's negativity toward me was obvious. Her interest extended only to her case. I had overreacted to her, for sure, and she'd shown no real interest in me.

She gabbed on while I sorted through my feelings. She had not apologized for being late, and she had not inquired about my ex-wife or daughter or other family members when I'd mentioned them. She had not said the food tasted good. She had asked for no explanation of anything except what pertained to the case. She had also offered no details about her life in Chicago or her family. Even though I had inquired and opened the doors, she had stepped less than halfway through, offering little more than professional disclosures. Conclusion: she was on duty, I was her source, and this situation bored me.

My grunted non-replies to her questions and prodding finally convinced her to stop. I escorted her out to what I saw now was a new mid-size Toyota with deep red paint. Eden opened the door and slid inside. Actually, I was back to thinking of her as Lieutenant. Her handsome feet and toes were distant memories, and her first name produced no magic.

"Think about it," she said, grabbing hold of her door handle. "You can remember more specifics than you've told me."

I said flippantly, "Maybe hypnosis would help."

"Yes, we can try that."

I guffawed. Shouldn't she know by now that I wouldn't let anybody pick around in my brain that way?

She said, "Talk to you tomorrow?"

"I'll be around."

"Thanks for the meal," she said, and then smiled.

I was shocked.

This polite friendliness instantly rejuvenated my vague hopes. "Let's do it again sometime."

She seemed to squint—trying to see my face clearly?—then said, "Yeah, maybe," slammed her door and left.

Yeah, maybe? What a hedging response.

I listened while her car crunched over the gravel out of sight. When that noise stopped, her motor whined, accelerating, telling me she had turned south on Pekin Road toward Bethel. Heading back to the station? Off to wherever she lived? She'd never said where she'd found a home.

I stared up, found the Big Dipper and felt like a big dipshit. My breath was visible. The air was colder than yesterday. It would get down near freezing tonight.

"Yeah, maybe," she'd said.

Well, hell, that was okay. It meant there were possibilities. My pulse quickened and I told myself, Concentrate on the good that can develop out of this.

I opened the trunk of my car, grabbed the backpack and boots, took them inside, shut the front door and locked it, trying to be content with what I had.

There were dishes to wash. She hadn't offered to help clean up. I turned off all the interior lights, thinking, Do the dishes tomorrow and quit finding fault. You rushed Eden away from the kitchen table back onto the couch before she could offer.

Admit it. Eden is okay. She's emerging, and you're beginning to understand her.

CHAPTER ELEVEN

The roar of detonation, the rush of air on my face, the tremor of the ground, all seemed to be imagined, a dream, but my eyes opened to a fleeting illumination of my house, and then I heard debris raining down, striking earth and brush and trees.

I blinked and sat up as several lights flared, then erupted, billowing in red, yellow and white waves inside a huge, dark hole, allowing me to see that half the outer wall of my office/computer room and my bedroom above it was gone. This light was from fires that spread like the burner on a gas stove, its circle of individual flames merging into one large flame. The fire rose on the ground level floors and walls, struck ceilings, curled back down upon itself, climbed back up through the gaping hole into the second floor and began burning there.

The sight stunned me as if an irate, overpowering giant were strangling me with one hand and slapping my face with the other. I felt as catatonic as I'd felt when told that my Dad had suddenly died. I saw what was happening, but the events wouldn't process into understandable meaning.

Caught in brightness, the inside of my kitchen appeared through the windows and the backdoor, which was standing wide open. Then black smoke swirled outside, obscuring my view, and the flames followed, chasing the smoke upwards toward the roof.

What had exploded? That couldn't have been fuel oil from the furnace. Not where those flames were. My fuel oil tank was in the little half-basement beneath the kitchen.

Trying to rub my eyes, finding my hands strapped down, I panicked and clawed for freedom, then realized that a sleeping bag encased me. I found the zipper's tab beneath my chin, pulled it down to my knees, untied the sleeping bag's hood, shed my cocoon, lifted my pack from the ground, stood, removed my clothes from it, put them on, and sat back down.

I reached to my right and retrieved my ball cap and boots. I'd forgotten to place them under the plastic ground-cover sheet so they were damp, but I barely noticed, putting them on. I stood, took my jacket from beneath the bag, placed there for cushioning, put it on, and with my right foot folded the head of the sleeping bag down over the foot end, sandwiching the open center between the water resistant outer layer, protecting its insides from dew and ashes. All this was done by habit, without conscious direction.

From two hundred yards away, I thought I heard the fire growling and roaring, gorging on my home. It was Change personified, an Inferno. It paralyzed me. The rocking chair was gone—I thought of it above everything else.

And watched the house burning. I stood rooted like a dumb tree and simply stared until a siren screamed somewhere off by the Pekin Road intersection with 86. The siren's volume increased, approaching, crescendoed down my lane, then shut off.

Firefighters, I presumed, were on the other side of the house, but they would never be able to save it. The entire house was blazing, and all they had to spray was what their tanks held. There were no hydrants, no city water lines installed beyond the developments south of my property, and hydrants would have been out on the road anyway, not back a long lane.

But the firemen had gotten here very fast, considering the Township fire station was over three miles away.

The explosion must have alerted someone. Perhaps the burning was visible from the road or another vantage point. From the hillside across the creek looking back at my property before lying down, I had been able to see lights in the new housing developments east and south, but nothing north and west. No lights anywhere were visible now because of smoke.

I think this clinical inspection of facts released my logic so it finally could conclude: Someone had done this, had blown up and burned down my house. Had tried to kill me! ME!

He would have come on foot so he wouldn't be seen. He might have stayed long enough to see the results of his work, maybe until he heard the siren. Where would he have come from? North or south or east, I decided. If he'd come from the west, where I was, I would have seen or heard him. Maybe he was still nearby.

I grabbed the flashlight and leaped straight down the slope as if I could reach the bottom in one huge step. My heels dug into the leaves and soft soil, and I grabbed limbs and saplings and brush, slowing myself. I descended to the creek, teetered on a large rock in its middle, and tried to decide where to go.

My flashlight lit enough of the rugged creek bed to show that I could run downstream and north. But the arsonist could have left in the other directions as well.

Hell, the truth was he could've even passed me on the west side while I'd slept. He could have come from anywhere, and by now he was long gone. Looking for him was hopeless. Even if I were to see someone, what then? What could I do?

Nothing, I thought, and my feet simultaneously slid off the rock into ankle-deep water. When the leather boots allowed an icy trickle inside, I stepped out onto rocks again, sat on the twisted roots of a familiar sycamore on the bank behind me, and shined the flashlight toward the house. Ashes fluttered down; farther away, smoke obscured the backyard.

I was still stunned. The house was lost. Everything in it was lost. There was nothing I could do.

Eventually, I wandered downstream, pushed through chest-high willows at an old wagon track, followed its path of matted grass east, hiked through a field past the barn, circled south onto my lane, and stopped to gape downhill at my burning house.

After a lengthy time of jumbled contemplation, I walked closer, stopping at the fire truck parked by the hut, my little sweat lodge, my little hogan. Two firemen holding a hose they'd dragged from the truck were facing the wet front of the barn. Off to the left, my car was wet too. Thirty yards behind my car were three other vehicles, the nearest one an ambulance.

The fire truck's engine churned. I went around it and joined the five men standing shoulder to shoulder, facing the house.

We stared at the fire together. It was roaring all right, as I had imagined earlier, but there were also snapping, cracking sounds, and something big collapsed with a crash.

"The whole thing's gettin' ready to go," the man farthest away said. He looked around, saw me and pointed.

I told them who I was.

One of the men—the badge on his blue uniform read "Chief"—said, "Mister, it's forty minutes since we got here and there was an explosion first so we just figured the worst."

I nodded.

"We thought you were in there, but it was too far gone for a rescue attempt."

"I didn't think you could save the house," I said. "But thanks for getting here so fast and saving the barn and the car."

"Credit for that belongs to him," he said, nodding toward a man in civilian clothes. "He alerted the firehouse, and before we arrived, he put out anything burning near the barn."

I shook the man's hand and said, "Thank you." He was Burt,

the deputy who'd photographed Sammy's body.

Burt said, "That big tree caught almost everything blown out of the house in that direction. So I didn't do much."

The hidden truth of his presence seemed so sad, I barely managed to say, "Oh no, you did a lot. Thanks again."

I think I mentioned the 150-gallon fuel oil tank, and the fire chief said something, and I nodded without understanding him. But the tears had started by then, and they poured out, disturbing my comprehension. I stumbled around the truck and hesitated at the entrance to my sweat lodge, thinking about sitting down in its cramped interior, rejected the idea, and fled to the barn. When I slid open a door to go inside, a fireman on the hose stopped me. Embers might drift over, and even the dust was combustible in there.

I closed, latched the door, and crossed the backyard far out on the edge away from the heat. At the path to the creek, I sat down on the swing. Its chains always creaked and squeaked, rubbing against themselves and the steel eye-bolts in the wood frame and the wood seat, but the fire absorbed the sound so I seemed to be suspended in a warm sea of white noise such as a radio makes on empty frequencies.

I sobbed so hard for so long, bent over with my elbows on my knees, that my back began to ache. Tears ran off my palms, down my wrists and forearms, and formed a sticky, half-dry paste. What the hell was going on? I kept wondering. Why was I the victim?

Somebody sat down beside me. A leg pressed against my left, and a hand twice patted my shoulder.

I dug the handkerchief out of my back pocket, sat back, and wiped my face.

A familiar voice said, "It's only a house. You only lost things, not your life. Being alive is the important thing."

Lieutenant Eden Grimes, trying to sound sympathetic.

I sniffled. Blew my nose. And tried to see some light ahead besides what came from flames.

She said, "Where were you when this started? Where've you been?"

The fire reddened her cheeks. Her hands were bunched on her lap. She wore a short, down-filled coat and pull-over rubber boots. I noticed that she had not called me Cliff or Saunders, names she had also avoided during our evening together. Addressing me, she used the second person pronoun or nothing. I looked back at the fire. Oh yes, I understood her role now.

"Where were you," she repeated, "when this happened?"

"You know what gets me the most is that someone tried to kill me. ME. Picked me out of everyone else on the earth. Blew up and then burned up my home. It's like society declared that I am not worthy to exist and sent its executioner. It's so goddam deliberate and personal. I get no more respect than a goddam cockroach you'd squash if it got in your way."

My legs tightened, pushed the swing backwards, then slowly let us glide forward again into the rest position.

I looked at her and said, "You were right, connecting me to Sammy's death. No doubt about it. I don't suppose Burt saw anyone sneaking onto my property. He didn't mention it when I thanked him for calling the firemen here. Did he see anyone?"

"No."

"He was on stakeout, right? Watching me?"

She looked away toward the fire. "That's police business."

"Parking at any nearby turnoff he'd be too noticeable. Where was he? Can you be honest enough to tell me that?"

She took a deep breath and blew it back out. "Behind trees across the road from your driveway."

"In what's left of that pasture? Was he on foot?"

"The Department owns that four-wheel-drive out front."

"I didn't notice it."

Part of the roof collapsed, crashing down, blowing out a shower of sparks and a gust of heat.

"I'm sorry this happened," she said.

"Were you wired when you were here this evening? Were you recording everything we said?"

"Does it matter?"

"I tried to be friendly and helpful, but you used my good intentions against me. Does that matter?"

She shook her head and looked away.

I said, "Does Simon Croft have an alibi for when Sammy died? Are you investigating him at all? Or anyone else besides me?"

She formed a pinched smile. "You know I can't give you information about our investigation."

"You told me I'm not under suspicion any longer and then—"

"I never said that."

"I can't trust you at all. You have me under surveillance when my house blows up, but see no one come onto my property. I cooperate with you, but you won't even admit Croft is a suspect."

"Mr. Croft has been open and helpful in this case."

"Does he know I'm a suspect? Did you discuss me with him?"

"He said your name was familiar. When I asked you about him, you said you'd spoken to him years ago at a public meeting."

"I don't suppose my face was familiar to him either. The old pictures in my police file do not depict my current looks, as you yourself pointed out to me. So showing him those would not be good enough, right? You had to get him to actually see me."

"He didn't recognize you."

"When exactly did he see me?"

She stood up abruptly, throwing the seat sideways so my armrest struck the frame.

I stood beside her. "This morning, right? You put him behind the one-way glass to see me when I was at the station."

I turned my back to the fire and faced her. Over her shoulder I could see the path to the creek. My shadow fell on her face. The fire's heat started baking the back of my head.

I remembered us in the interrogation room. What I'd said and her angry responses and actions could mean only one thing.

I moved my head so the firelight touched her face and said, "You let Croft observe me this morning, and that gave him a good reason to kill me tonight. He heard me call him a suspect and urge you to investigate him. You ought to be proud of yourself, Eden. You and Frank set me up. The only good thing is that finally, after what happened here, you must know the killer has to be Croft."

She looked up at me as if to say something. Her mouth moved but nothing came out, and then she looked away.

That meant no. That meant I was wrong again. Okay, I understood. From her perspective, I was still not cleared of suspicion. I was still the odd man out. Jesus Fucking Christ!

I said, "Lieutenant, you want to see where I was when this happened, come on. I have to go there and pick some things up."

I started down the wide, bush-hogged path toward the creek, knowing that Grimes had to be thinking that I had burned down my own house to divert suspicions away from myself.

I went a good twenty yards along, then glanced back.

She was still at the swing, on a radio, telling someone where she was going, but slowly coming after me, sniffing at my heels like a dog—a bloodhound with a head cold.

No, it was not laughable. In fact, I had to protect myself from her. She could not only lock me up, but also get me killed.

The best defense was a good offense. I had to get proactive.

I snorted at the stupid word. What I meant was that I myself had to do whatever was necessary to resolve this goddam case.

Chapter Twelve

Grimes dogged me, demanding every detail of my movements before and after the fire, increasing my desire to get away from her. After rolling up the sleeping bag, packing my other gear, putting on the knapsack, I shined my flashlight downhill and told her what the dark trail of leaves and dirt dug up by my heels in the lighter duff was.

I led her back down the worn, easier trail to the creek, pointed my light downstream, refused the request to accompany her where I'd gone, described the route I had taken, and said she could find it herself. She had a flashlight and boots on and there would be clear tracks in the field.

Then I left her and didn't look back, circled around the house, circled around the firemen, hurled the camping stuff into the trunk of my car, and dropped onto the driver's seat, ready to go. But the car was so hot, the steering wheel so scorching, I worried the motor might be damaged. It started on a turn of the key, however, and propelled me back beside the three vehicles in the grass. I opened doors, let cooler air pour through for a couple of minutes, and listened. The motor sounded okay to me.

I shut the doors, shifted into drive and fled from the turmoil. Nobody followed me as far as I could see. A deputy at the end of the lane waved me around his cruiser, and I was gone.

A sense of release overtook me, euphoria and exhilaration. The open road lay ahead, the houses I was passing were dark, the ruins of my home were behind me, and I was free—free to drive right on south to the bypass of Bethel, and continue on in any direction: to wooded lakes in Canada, beaches in Florida, eastern mountains. All were accessible with a few hours' ride, all mysterious and inviting.

Bullshit pipe dreams! My daughter's face bobbed on the dashboard, a penlight shining in a dark shadow. She'd grown up in that house with me and her Mom.

I had to get down to business. What could I do to reveal Sammy's killer?

I was too hyper for the subject. My attention shifted to the confined space in the car. It smelled, and so did I. Everything bore the stench of smoke. I cracked a window for fresher air.

What time was it? The clock on the dashboard read 6:24.

I stared out at the road, steered on without conscious thought, approached Megastore, open twenty-four hours a day, put the blinkers on to turn in, said, "No way!" and drove on downtown.

The question came again: How to resolve the case? What could I do? I had no idea. Not one! Talking over what to do would help, but it was too early to go to Mom's house.

I wouldn't be working out today, would I? It was Saturday so a two-mile jog and weight-lifting were scheduled, and oh yes, I'd been going to invite Ed and his friends to join me. Well, the barn was intact, but people were out there so the workout would have to be later and alone if at all.

Right now? To breakfast. I was starving.

I drove past the courthouse and parked on the south edge of the three-by-four-block business district, which was half empty nowadays. The number of store fronts with for-rent and for-sale signs had steadily increased since the shopping mall opened west of town ten years earlier.

The Diner was still operating. I'd patronized it habitually

afternoons during high school, and weekend mornings for breakfasts when I'd been teaching, but I hadn't been in the place in years. It was homey, with four square Formica-topped tables, a counter with eight stools, and three red-padded booths against the back wall. Ed Hilliard frequented the place, and I looked hopefully for him as I entered.

He wasn't present this morning. In fact only two tables were taken and one stool—seven customers counting me. The place had always been much more crowded on Saturdays. Customers must be at the chain restaurants, I guessed, choosing the counter.

I ordered coffee and my favorite Diner breakfast—blueberry pancakes, bacon and two whole-wheat muffins with strawberry jam. The waitress was in her fifties, black, energetic, and friendly, but a stranger. I spun on my stool and noticed a back booth where newspapers were piled on the table.

Had something subconscious brought me here for them? Truly, I had forgotten that the Diner let the papers accumulate through the week before throwing them out every Monday.

I searched through the stack and collected the relevant issues. The Dayton daily newspaper mentioned my name in a Thursday and a Friday article about Sammy's murder, but only as the jogger who had found the body, not as a suspect. Friday's article also mentioned Simon Croft as the victim's son. But there were few other details.

Sammy's obituary appeared in today's edition. Among a full page of obits, his was the shortest, mentioning only date of death, survivors (son and three grandchildren), Sammy's birth in 1919, his graduation from Gordon Plains School in 1938, his US Army service in France and Germany during the Second World War, and his profession as farmer and retired NCR employee (1979). "Visitation Saturday at the Denver Funeral Home 6:00–8:00 p.m. Memorial Service at the Restfield

Cemetery Memorial Chapel 10:00 a.m. on Sunday."

That seemed like a very fast release of a murder victim's body. Croft had probably used political clout to get it. And a Sunday funeral? Unusual. I checked all the obituaries. No other funeral was on Sunday. Croft apparently wanted to dispose of his father as soon as he could. In fact the obituary's shortness implied that Croft was giving only a perfunctory nod to the social practice of an obit. He wasn't about to bother supplying specifics about Sammy.

I turned to Bethel's biweekly paper. Today's edition had a front page article that recapped everything from the body's discovery on Wednesday. It quoted the sheriff saying that leads were being followed, but asking anyone who knew Mr. Burkhoffer's movements and habits to contact his office. Sheriff Orndorf would rule out neither a random act of violence nor a deliberately planned attack.

This article also mentioned Mr. Burkhoffer's farm in Old Town, called him a lifetime resident, a veteran, a member of the VFW, and the father of County Commissioner Simon Croft. The article quoted Croft, " 'In recent days my father and I grew closer than we've ever been. During his illness, we often reminisced about my mother, who passed away eleven years ago. She was on my father's mind to the end. I will really miss him.' "

"What bullshit!" I said aloud, remembering Sammy's comment about an estrangement from his son. I dropped the paper and looked up into the dark eyes of the waitress.

"Never any good news in that," she said. "More coffee?"

My plate was empty. I'd eaten everything while reading. I couldn't even remember if the food had been any good.

I took the refill, thanked the lady, and stewed. Croft killed Sammy, vandalized and burned down my house, and tried to kill me, the lying bastard. I was sure. There was no doubt.

I drank the cup of coffee, and by then wasn't sure. There were in fact many doubts. Thousands of them. I really didn't know anything for sure. What would be Croft's motive? What other people knew Sammy? Damn my ignorance!

I paid and drove into the town's southern residential area, a trip that usually was like time-traveling to me. These were the streets where I'd grown up, where I'd delivered the Dayton newspapers on my Schwinn three-speed bicycle, where I'd known everyone, played every day, soaped windows for Halloween and begged for treats. Almost every bush and tree and house could stimulate memories—but not today, not with a mind trapped by questions. Was Croft the killer? What could I do to be sure? What could I do to resolve the case?

I turned down the gravel alley off Mulberry Street, parked by the garage on a wide bare spot, walked under the metal arch supporting grape vines, crossed Mom's back porch, opened the back door, thrust my head inside, and yelled that I was there.

"Come in!" Aunt Judy's voice called from the living room. "I've been wondering when you'd show up."

The kitchen was neat and clean and good-smelling as usual: aromas of cinnamon and toast, probably from Aunt Judy's meal. And coffee? Yes, half a pot of coffee was on the stove. A red light was on, a dial was set on simmer, and the star-shaped wire guard lay between the Pyrex container and a metal burner.

"Want some coffee?" I yelled, taking a mug from a peg on the wall and filling it.

"I've got some," she called.

In the living room, my mother's older sister had risen from the couch where she'd been reading a book, which lay on a cushion. *Joshua* was the title on the rainbow-colored cover. On one end of the coffee table lay the Holy Bible and *The Daily Breviary*. On the other end were three months of *St. Anthony's Messenger* and *Maryknoll Magazine* in two separate piles. Aunt

Judy's reading material. The town paper, which would be on the front porch, would end up unread if I didn't get to it.

"Where've you been?" she asked.

"Sorry I didn't call," I said, going to her.

"You should be sorry. Haven't seen you since Tuesday, you big lug. Did you forget about us?"

Before I could bend to kiss her, she stood on tiptoe, pulled my head down and pecked my cheek.

I tried our normal hug, but holding my empty hand in hers, she pulled away with a gasp and studied me. "What's the matter? What happened?"

I'd forgotten my appearance. The mirror on the back wall showed what she was reacting to. There was soot on my forehead, cheeks and white hat. There were cockle burrs on the sleeves of my jacket and pants, which also were wet and mud-stained. Plus I needed a shave. "I'm a mess, and it's been hell the last few days, but I'm okay. How's Mom?"

"The same. Go see her. Say hello."

I went down the hall into Mom's room. She was a shrunken, twisted hump beneath a sheet and a pale blue blanket. Her eyes were perpetually closed, her forehead and cheeks as unwrinkled as a baby's, her arms and hands as unmoving as the bed. She had degenerated into a fetal state. If pneumonia or infection from bed sores didn't get her, the prediction was that one day Mom's brain would simply stop an autonomic response. The heart or the lungs or something else would cease operating because its switch to work shut off. She had lost all functions but the autonomic.

Mom was Aunt Judy's ward, and I was their main connection to the rest of the world. Supplier of groceries, mender of what needed mending, tree trimmer, shoveler of snow, flower planter, mower, payer of bills, driver when transportation was needed. Daily, Aunt Judy walked to St. Francis of Assisi Church four blocks away for 6:45 a.m. mass, then walked home. She could leave Mom alone for an hour.

"Hi, Mom. How you doing?" I kissed her forehead, brushed her hair back with a palm, and suppressed the images of how she'd once been, the memories that seeing her always evoked.

"Not much longer," Aunt Judy said.

"We've been saying that for two years now."

"When the Lord wants her, he'll take her. Do you have bad problems?"

"Yeah, and I don't know what to do."

"Go clean up and we'll talk."

As I left the room, Aunt Judy was checking the IV bag.

God, Aunt Judy inspired me. She was a registered nurse, had been for fifty years, the same length of time she'd been a member of the Caritas Sisters of Saint Augustine. Retired at seventy-six, she'd had artificial hip operations, rehabilitated herself, and now, spurning crutches or canes, all by herself bathed Mom, turned her, and changed the bed.

Upstairs in my dormer, I threw my clothes into the plastic clothes hamper for washing, shaved, brushed my teeth, turned the water on, and showered until the water cooled. I got out, started drying off, and thought I heard a dog bark.

A dog? I went to the door and opened it to check.

Ed Hilliard's voice and Aunt Judy's laughter rose up the stairs, then the deep thrum of Brute.

Aunt Judy must have called Ed. What a woman. And Ed had come right over. What a friend. But Brute?

"Pretty boy!" Aunt Judy said, certainly not about Ed.

I yelled down the stairs, "Don't let that damn dog in!"

Large paws immediately pounded across the carpet and upstairs, reaching the door as I closed it, but not completely. I was afraid he might run back down to my aunt. What the hell was Ed thinking? The dog was so big, his weight pushed the door farther open although I braced both hands against it. The hell with it. I let him in.

"You big dumb animal. You're glad to see me, huh?"

He stood on his hind legs so his front paws rested on my shoulders. His drool slopped onto my chest; a few drops hit my thighs. I rubbed his head, his shoulders and back with my left hand, then twisted sideways, trying to get him down onto all fours. His muscles vibrated with energy beneath my palm. Part St. Bernard, part Great Dane, part other big dogs even Ed didn't know because Brute had come to him as an abandoned pup from a dog pound.

I slapped my right thigh and he sat. "Stay," I said, and laughed the way he watched me, his head and eyes jerking with any movement I made. He was very excited, but so well trained he wouldn't move again until he was called or told to move.

"Stay," I repeated, dressing, keeping him with me, thinking about what to do with the behemoth.

CHAPTER THIRTEEN

I told Ed that my aunt was vulnerable if the dog were to bump her hard or jump on her the way he'd jumped on me.

"Nonsense," Aunt Judy said. "Brute and I are old friends."

"He could knock you on your keister and break some bones."

"Cliff's right. I'm sorry, Sister. It never occurred to me."

I took Brute outside, returned, and joined them at the kitchen table, munching hunks of sweet banana bread zapped in the microwave oven, drinking coffee from the Ed-fashioned mugs.

We must have looked like an odd group, a nun in the passé, blue-gray habit with white headpiece; me in shiny yellow, blue and white nylon jogging outfit; Ed in tan bib overalls, black leather boots, and long sleeved blue shirt rolled up to the elbows. Of course Ed stood out anywhere anytime, with reddish-brown beard and shoulder-length hair like a Viking.

He said, "Friend of yours came to see me yesterday. Lieutenant Grimes took my fingerprints and asked about you."

"I'll be damned." She'd been with me last evening and this morning and hadn't mentioned Ed. "What'd you think of her?"

"Feisty, and the lady has taste. My house appealed to her, and she liked my stuff."

"Oh sure. What did she buy?"

He shrugged. "She's a potential client."

"Yeah, her flattery fooled you. How'd she react to Brute?"

"Went right up and petted him."

"She was checking on me," I said. "They dusted my house

107

for prints yesterday."

"What about this dead man Edward told me about?" Aunt Judy asked. "When did you find him?"

"Wednesday." I sat back, looked at a canary-yellow wall I'd painted two years before, and narrated unstopped the whole sequence of events. Neither Ed nor Aunt Judy had been aware of the explosion and fire so that was the big revelation. I went over everything, answering questions, clarifying facts for them.

My final thoughts emphasized how the police had questioned me three times and how Grimes had probably secretly recorded our conversation while I fed her and was friendly. "I'm still under suspicion even after my own house was destroyed. Grimes is probably out there right now, searching through the ashes. The goddam house is gone and everything that was in it."

"The barn too?" Ed asked.

"Not the barn."

"A blessing," Aunt Judy said.

"Yeah, I love that barn."

"You couldn't replace it," Ed said.

Aunt Judy said, "Why do the police suspect you? Explain that again."

I stared at the ceiling and once more described the interrogations. "They don't trust me because I'm too odd for them. And too convenient a suspect."

Ed slapped my right arm. "Grimes couldn't find documents in your house, but you said none was missing and never explained. You're hiding things about yourself, like this place, and she knows you're doing it. You got to level with her."

Aunt Judy said, "Yes, you have to help stop the killer."

Remembering what revealing all would subject Mom and Aunt Judy to, I said, "My private life is irrelevant."

Ed shook his head. "Not when hiding it makes you a suspect. You have to tell the truth."

"I AM telling her the truth!"

"All the truth!"

I glared at him. This hippie look-alike was as conservative as the Republicans from whom he made a good profit, selling variously sized gold or silver elephants that he specifically cast for them to subsidize his real art.

Aunt Judy said, "Your moral responsibility is the most important thing, Clifford. You're involved in this affair whether you like it or not, and that is God's will."

"I'll find out who did it myself."

"What you better do, buddy," advised Ed, "is talk to the cops. Tell the pretty lady everything. Then hide somewhere until they sort it all out. They're professionals. You mess in their work, and you'll get hurt one way or another."

"Bullshit!" I told him. "The goddam cops almost got me killed last night."

"I do not appreciate that language!" Aunt Judy roared.

I said, "It's just that—"

"I've had quite enough foulness and blasphemy. You're going through an ordeal, but Lord, enough is enough. Even a gorilla like you can control your tongue."

I glanced at Ed, who grinned so wide, delighted at this attack, that I could see his lips and teeth, which were normally hidden beneath his heavy beard.

Aunt Judy saw him. "Edward, don't laugh. Your mouth is as filthy as his."

"Worse," I said standing, stretching, looking outside at low, gray clouds building up, seeing Brute, roped with clothesline to a grapevine stanchion, guarding the concrete slab back porch like a huge gargoyle that had dropped from the eaves.

I sat again and told them, "Okay, we all agree that I have to do something, but it won't be talking to the cops. I wouldn't trust them to shine my shoes."

"Shithead!" Ed said, and we glanced at Aunt Judy.

She frowned at Ed's indecent word and said, "You must act in some way to control the killer and protect people."

"Which is the cops' job, not yours." Ed crossed his arms on his chest and sat back.

I told Aunt Judy, "The question is, obviously, how to find out who the killer is."

"You know who it probably is. That man you mentioned."

"Croft?"

"Who else could it be?" she asked.

"Anyone. That's my point."

"Name somebody else that fits the facts."

"I don't have enough information to do that."

"You never will, either," Ed insisted. "If you told the cops all the truth about yourself, they'd consider other suspects."

I said to him, "Look, if that was the only way, I'd do it, but I'm going to try other things first."

Aunt Judy said, "Then, let's figure it out. Logic indicates the miscreant is Croft, and the logic is this—"

"Miscreant?" Ed interrupted, grinning.

She ignored him. "The woman detective thinks there is a connection between Sammy's death and you, between the theft at Sammy's house and the intrusions at yours. Correct?"

"Yes."

"The attempt on your life has convinced you of the connection, and you think it involves the land he owned because the subject came up so often in your discussions with your dead friend. And wouldn't the only child apparently be the heir?"

I nodded. "I suppose that's right."

Aunt Judy said, "Now, if no one except Croft fits the facts we know, limited though they are, then odds are it's him."

"And you think I ought to do what?"

She said, "Test the idea. Confront him in public. You

mentioned your friend's showing. I think the funeral home this evening is perfect. There'll be witnesses."

I liked the way she simply assumed that I had her courage. From sheer cowardice, I imagined such a scene and objected, "Being among people would inhibit what he'd say."

She answered, "Or the opposite. He might get emotional and blurt something out. Anything he says or does could be useful."

"He'd sue me for slander."

"Morally speaking, you have to take the chance."

"I guess I wouldn't have to accuse him point blank. Just insinuate or ask a question. In fact just being there might be enough to get him to do or say something incriminating."

Ed leaned forward between us. "Talk to the cops."

"No, I'll be safe in public," I said, and Ed sat back.

Aunt Judy said, "Nonviolent, direct action is the best approach. It has worked before, if you recall."

Recall? I'd grown up reading about her and listening to her tales: civil rights and anti-war sit-ins and marches in Cleveland, Cincinnati and Columbus. She had been arrested several times while her male religious colleagues cowered in church and from pulpits criticized her and other nun-activists.

She stood, fished inside the folds of her habit, and came out with a string of clear crystal beads. "I'm going to say the rosary, and both of you should join me."

She tugged at my left arm with the hand holding the rosary, and tugged at Ed with the other.

Pulled up onto my feet, I shook my head. "You know how I feel about Catholic rituals."

"Don't blame the church for what one priest or one bishop did. They are not the church."

"Aunt Judy, you know the church's annulment policy makes me boil. The very priest who married me and Angela declared that we were not married, and he knew that she and I had lived together for eighteen years and raised a daughter. It's so absurd and hypocritical, it turns me off all the Catholic hoopla."

She said, "Well Angela was very devout and she raised Laura that way too. You never went to church after your wedding."

"And my example is what led Laura away from the church?"

"Oh no, and I'm not defending the annulment, but I think Angela had her concerns and you're overreacting."

"I don't think so, but I have other things to do besides praying right now."

"Prayer is not the invention of the church, you know. Talking with God will help us figure out exactly what to do. I have no doubts whatsoever."

"I do," I said. "I'm going to wash the dishes, then go to the farm and lift weights. Working out is the way I pray anymore."

Ed said, "I'll go there too. I want to see the damage and maybe there'll be some things that need to be done."

While Ed helped me clean up the kitchen, Aunt Judy droned Pater Nosters and Aves in the living room.

Our kitchen work completed, Ed and I looked in on her. She was kneeling on two small pillows by an arm of the couch, but not leaning on it or anything else. She was telephone-pole stiff and straight, staring at a large brass crucifix on the wall.

I said goodbye.

Ed told her that we would be back in a couple hours to make final plans with her then.

She didn't look around or say one word—to us.

CHAPTER FOURTEEN

In the 7:30 p.m. darkness on the western edge of Bethel, in a cold drizzle that had been falling for three hours, the new house of death, the Denver Funeral Home, resembled a posh resort, an island in a large, black lake, which was the tarred and sodden parking lot. What the business lacked was a catchy neon sign out front, THE MILE-HIGH BODIES-R-US.

To check out the inside of the charnel house before exposing myself, I shunned the group of twenty bunched cars, parked on the opposite side of the building, and walked to an unlit entrance.

A window showed the lobby was empty so I started in, but stopped with the door a few inches open because just then someone appeared, entering on the other side.

Two someones, Aunt Judy with a black shawl over her habit, then Ed with a dark blue raincoat hanging down to his knees.

How very goddam nice! I had ordered them not to come and, of course, that had guaranteed they would.

Well, fuck it. Maybe they would help. My agenda was fluid. I'd pay my respects to Sammy and see how Croft reacted. If he did nothing, I would say something directly to him.

I waited several minutes after my allies had disappeared, then entered and crossed the lobby, passing an empty alcove on the left, the front door. Ahead of me, a man appeared in the alcove around the door used by Aunt Judy and Ed, extending an arm toward the proper room. The gesture was dramatic but unnecessary. The three other rooms that I passed on my right were closed-off with accordion walls, and so were several other rooms I could see along a hallway to the building's rear.

Conclusion: Sammy's was the only body on display, perhaps the first ever here, but the owners obviously expected a lot of business.

I stopped in front of a podium that held a large, opened book. The left page was filled with ten signatures, and the opposite page contained eight more. The fancy, thick, yellowish-white paper had ethereal blue garlands around the edges and thick lines centered down each page between wide left and right margins. The top of each page bore oversized, black, Gothic print: IN MEMORY OF HAROLD SAMUEL BURKHOFFER.

The book was probably a Megastore special, and that thought gave me a strong desire to sign Mickey Mouse.

Instead, I picked up the pen and wrote my name slowly and carefully, thus managing to scrawl it worse than usual. I should have just signed with a goddam flourish.

Over the top of the podium I could see there were about twenty wooden chairs in the room. Their padded seats aimed away from me toward an open area where the bronze coffin stood before a wall of off-white cloth, the inside of the moveable walls. My lobby-side of the walls was a folded, hard gray plastic.

To the coffin's left were an American flag on a wooden pole angled out of a floor stand, and a pyramidal stand containing a dozen bouquets of flowers. On the right was one large bouquet.

The thirty or so people present raised a buzz of conversation that reached the lobby. With some slow milling around, most were in clumps on the left side, jammed together in front of the chairs. Five of these seats held two children and three white-haired women. Frank Shepherd sat two chairs behind them.

Apart from everyone, Lieutenant Grimes stood in the right corner with her arms crossed, watching.

I thought I recognized Croft, but I'd last seen him years ago half-hidden behind a table. If that was Croft, he'd lost weight and his hair was different, pitch black, not graying the way I remembered it. He also wore no eyeglasses now. In a dark blue suit, the man seemed movie-star handsome. Could anyone looking like that invade my house three times and destroy it? The man's appearance raised doubts, and therefore depressed me.

When I entered the room down the right side, Grimes instantly started toward me. I veered left among people, angling away from her toward the casket. She cut behind a group of four and touched my right arm.

I stopped. "Hello."

"I was afraid you'd show up."

"Why shouldn't I say goodbye to my friend?"

"Because you're not wanted by the Crofts?"

"There's no sign posted that it's a private viewing."

"I'm warning you. The Crofts are angry and shouldn't be fooled with."

"Really? They gonna keep me off the social register? They gonna blackball me with the nonexistent elite in this town?"

"We need to talk." She pointed back where she'd been.

I nodded, said, "Okay, later," and before she could answer went to the closed end of the casket right of three people side by side facing it. The two by Sammy's head were Aunt Judy and Ed.

My aunt swiveled her eyes, noticed me, made the sign of the cross, and walked away. Ed, with raincoat buttoned to his chin to hide his clothes, crossed himself and followed her off. Good. At least they were acting as if we were unacquainted.

But Grimes would recognize Ed, notice I'd not greeted him and think it odd. Oh well. Nothing I could do about that now.

The remaining person on my left moved over to Aunt Judy's position so I took Ed's. This was a woman in her 60s, carrying an umbrella and wearing a light brown, knee-length coat and a red, totally useless crescent hat with a black veil that hung down over her forehead.

I looked down at Sammy.

My God! What had the ghouls done to him? His cheeks were sallow and sunken in, and his teeth were outlined beneath taut, almost transparent lips. The face looked like a rubber Halloween mask stretched near the breaking point over a too-large skull. The thin gray thatches of hair looked glued on. Where were his injuries? Aha. The head was turned on the pillow to hide them. I would never have recognized Sammy.

But of course that wasn't Sammy. It was only his mangled, discarded vessel. Sammy was a free spirit now. I had glimpsed the real Sammy a number of times in his humor and his nostalgic stories. In retrospect, I now saw the real Sammy in the insistent way he had come every day to meet me on the bike trail, overcoming the weakness from his cancer, never once complaining. He'd wanted to meet me and talk, and he had succeeded. That was Sammy.

"What the hell did you want from me?" I muttered, and for the umpteenth time that week, I wept. Tears trickled out of my eyes slowly this time, the way rain was dribbling from the clouds outside, and anger swept through me, resolving my doubts about coming here, arousing anger at the killer for what he had done to Sammy and me.

Something nudged my left elbow. I looked down into the face of the woman. She looked up at me through her veil and smiled.

I smiled back, dug a hanky from my back pocket, wiped my eyes and looked back at the carcass.

The woman hummed something, and thinking she'd spoken, I leaned down toward her. She glanced at me again, her lips moved, and I heard, *"Amazing grace! (how sweet the sound)—"*

I think my sorrow made me join in: *"That sav'd a wretch like me!/I once was lost, but now am found,/Was blind, but now I see."*

My outpouring was self-protective and instinctive, and I think it strengthened both of us. Upon my first word, our voices paired and became louder, making me feel as if my tears had become words. I vaguely was aware of the people around us, aware enough to think that I didn't care what they thought. Fuck 'em if they didn't like it, and if Croft didn't like it, then let him do something. That's what I was there for.

By the end of the verse, we were very loud. Somehow the woman's right and my left hand clasped. We squeezed each other's flesh, her warmth streaked up my arm, poured into my chest, and we blared, *" 'Twas grace that taught my heart to fear,/ And grace my fears reliev'd;/How precious did that grace appear,/ The hour I first believ'd!"*

I noticed others were singing with us. Someone grabbed my right hand, a man, one of the four people I'd passed. His palm and fingers were softer than the woman's. Others came up beside him. Everybody was singing. The voices filled my ears and washed across me in waves of heat, stoked, I think, by a sense of shared mutual caring.

I prepared to stumble on the third verse, being unsure of it, but the man beside me launched right back into the first, and everyone joined in again, repeating the first and second verse louder than we'd done them originally.

There was consolation in the lyrics, melody, and voices. The lights seemed to dim, and as sometimes happened when I played recorded music and cooled down by dancing after lifting weights, what was before my eyes, in this case the blank wall, seemed to thin out as clouds do, revealing beyond them limitless space and unexpected beauty, taking me into almost perfect tranquility.

When the singing stopped, a hush fell as if we were unable to believe the harmony we had spontaneously created together.

The woman squeezed my hand once, then released me, her actions as natural as a breeze lifting a few strands of hair. The man released me too, but immediately offered his right hand and said he was the Reverend Walter Armstrong, who would deliver the eulogy tomorrow. After I gave him my name, the Reverend reached in front of me, shook the woman's hand, and repeated his name.

"Ethel Creech," she said.

"Lovely singing," the minister said, and turned away as someone behind us spoke to him.

"That was nice, Mrs. Creech," I told her.

She stared at me, then asked, "Are you the one who met Sam in the evenings? He mentioned the name Cliff."

I nodded. "Yes. You must be a good friend of his."

"Well, I s'pose we got to be something like friends this last year. I worked for him, and heard him talk about you a time or two. Followed his car out the lane several times, and seen him park over 'cross the road where he'd walk on to meet you."

"Were you at his house every day?"

"Pert near. Wasn't too many days I missed. Cooked and cleaned and did what-not for him."

"You were his housekeeper?"

"For the last eight years, and I'd of been there a while longer, too. But no complaints. Could be the way Sam went was a blessing in disguise."

"Because of his illness?"

"Doctors wanted to start him on chemo and radiation again, but he said he didn't want no more of that. It was his time to go and he was ready. My sister died of stomach cancer so I can tell you that he would of suffered a lot."

"Sammy never even mentioned his illness to me."

"Sammy?" She smiled. "He said you called him that. Poor, lonely man. Memories were all he had."

"Sammy talked a lot about his childhood."

"Didn't rightly have no relatives left. The son and his family never did visit. Well, the girl stopped once. Said she had an urge to see her grandpa. But she never came back that I know of. Her brothers the twins never once came. Neither did that high-falutin' man over there or his wife."

She jerked her head sharply toward the left, at Croft.

I looked in that direction. "Which one's the wife?"

"Don't know. I never met her."

Croft was speaking to people at his elbows but looking at me. Our eyes locked and his face darkened, perhaps just now recognizing me. I had on a tie and dark suit—my only suit—and a fedora, which I'd found among remnants of Dad's clothes and worn on impulse. Croft spoke to the people beside him, broke contact, and stepped toward us, but another person stopped him to talk.

Good. The time to confront him was approaching, but not yet. Mrs. Creech knew things that might hang that oh-so-handsome man. I said to her, "The son claimed in the paper that he and Sammy had grown close during Sammy's illness."

"Hah!" She looked directly at my eyes. "If that one ever saw Sam, I never heard about it."

Croft was glad-handing a couple, talking to them now, but he glanced over, saw me and again tried to edge away toward us.

That lying sack of shit, I thought.

I looked down at the woman again. "Mrs. Creech, will you come with me a second? I want you to meet someone."

"Well, I s'pose I got a minute."

I looked around, amazed at how Fate worked. I had done nothing more than enter the room, yet Fate interceded and brought me to the exact person who had information I'd been

119

seeking. Mrs. Creech could set the police straight. Where the hell was Grimes?

She was behind us, among the chairs, talking to Shepherd.

"Over here," I said, and led Mrs. Creech through the crowd, then in between chairs. A glance at Croft told me he'd broken away from the couple who'd had him cornered, but three other people had claimed his attention.

"Excuse me," I said, arriving in front of Shepherd.

He and Grimes looked at us.

"This is Mrs. Ethel Creech, Sammy's housekeeper."

I looked down at the lady and said, "These are the police detectives looking for Sammy's killer. They need to hear what you've been telling me."

The cops nodded to her.

"Hi there," Mrs. Creech said to them.

The aged face beneath that silly veil turned up toward me. "They done heard all I got to say a couple days ago."

The meaning of her words slapped my consciousness like a hard palm against my face.

CHAPTER FIFTEEN

Another misinterpretation. Another misunderstanding.

I gaped at Mrs. Creech, at Grimes and Shepherd, back at Mrs. Creech, then mumbled, "Oh."

"Think of something new?" Grimes asked Mrs. Creech.

"No ma'am." Mrs. Creech looked from them to me, back to them and said, "Well, I got to be going then."

Looked back at me and said, "Nice to meet you, son."

"Nice to meet you too."

She patted my arm, turned and walked out of the room.

Sometimes my stupidity revealed itself like a bottomless cavity opening up in the earth at my feet where I found myself teetering and liable to fall in. What anchored me in place this time was a resurgence of anger, which extended beyond the killer to those who should be my protectors and allies.

My eyes stayed on the space Mrs. Creech had just vacated while my mind considered the police. How much did they know about Sammy and his life, the people he knew and the motives he had? A great deal more than had been shared with me. In fact police deceit had kept me from learning more facts about Sammy.

What did such pervasive dishonesty mean? That they were determined to use whatever I said to incriminate me. Nothing they said or implied could be accepted at face value. In fact, this new understanding of their duplicity undercut my every contact with the Sheriff's Department, including the sheriff's gracious response to my complaint about Deputy Jones.

My focus swiveled down from the lobby onto the two people before me. Grimes in yet another dark, off-the-rack pantsuit, Shepherd in a solid navy blue suit. Instead of collaborators attempting to solve a crime, instead of being simply incompetents who might get me killed, they were my active antagonists.

Grimes said, "Let's go to the lobby."

"For what, to lie some more? No thanks." Contempt hardened my voice so it sounded screechy to my ears.

I looked around and spotted Aunt Judy and Ed on the edge of the crowd. They looked back with quizzical expressions, prodding me to do something.

Where was Croft? Between them and me, with people offering condolences. The woman beside him was probably his wife.

Grimes asked, "Anything come to you in the mail?"

My eyes returned to her and Shepherd. They were staring at me as if I were an insignificant piece of slime that they would deal with any goddam way they wanted. These two had lied to me and almost gotten me killed. Meantime, they ignored the probable killer, who was twenty feet away receiving good wishes from an admiring throng.

I said in a calm, measured tone, "If you want to talk to me, make arrangements with my lawyer, Tyrone Gibson. He's in the phone book. Now, excuse me."

I spun around and made my way among chairs and people to a place directly behind a tall man speaking with the woman I'd guessed was Croft's wife. When the man moved from her to Croft, I stepped forward, and thrust my right hand out. "Mrs. Croft?"

"Yes."

"I'm sorry about your father-in-law's death."

She took my hand. "Thank you."

"I'm Clifford Saunders, the one who found Sammy."

Her plucked eyebrows rose, her brown eyes widened, her hand pulled out of my grasp, and she looked sideways at Croft.

His eyes flicked our way, then refocused on the man to my left. I held my ground waiting for Croft to free up. During the minute this took, Mrs. Croft continued staring at her husband.

When the man left, I stepped over and extended my right hand to the grieving son.

His eyes knifed into mine. "You have a lot of gall coming here."

"I'm sorry—" I said, beginning an expression of sympathy over Sammy's death.

"You've been on my back seems like forever. Accusing me of outrageous things at County Commission meetings like you're some kind of certified public defender."

"Twice I spoke up. It's called free speech!"

"We had to cut you off to shut you up. Then embarrassing Letters to the Editor in the paper."

"Ditto. Free speech. Politicians are supposed to listen to voters."

"I was appointed to the Regional Planning Commission, not elected."

"So why didn't you protect the land like you're supposed to do?"

The conversation was odd because we were both speaking in a calm, conversational tone, as if discussing the weather.

He said, "You burned up my equipment at a job site."

"I burned nothing. I was picketing there, and you had a conflict of interest. You voted on the Commission to approve that development?"

"You arrogant bastard! Showing up here, acting sorry."

"Sammy was my friend. I am sorry."

"Your friend. You killed him."

His right hand took mine. It had been hanging there between

us like a wish. And he gently pulled my hand, and me, forward.

I leaned toward him automatically, not yet perceiving a threat from this handsome person.

He leaned toward me also, but fast, jerking his head forward so the top of his head hit my brow.

For a moment I was aware of only the soundlessness that comes with shock, and the sensation of falling. My legs buckled and I would have gone down except that Croft clutched my right wrist in his left hand and my upper arm with his right. As consciousness returned, I tightened my legs and struggled to regain balance.

My eyes refocused. He was sneering. I half fell, half leaned forward so my head touched his chest.

He said something in my ear.

"Huh?" Gaining strength but still dazed, I leaned back.

His eyes were icy black rocks. "You're not going to get away with THIS insult. I'm not as ineffective as the law dealing with you."

His right hand released its grip, shot up and forward, and the pain was instantaneous. He'd jabbed my cheek below my left eye, snapping my head back. His fist withdrew and hovered menacingly before me.

I twisted sideways, trying to break his grip.

His left hand still held my wrist, and his right drew back to hammer my flesh again.

A collage of faces surrounded us, only a few of them watching. No one moved to stop him. The assault was happening too fast for others to have noticed. Our conversation had been too low in volume, too matter of fact to attract attention in the hubbub of other voices.

I tucked my head against my chest so this jab only grazed an ear.

Fear pumped energy through me. My left hand clawed at his

grip on my right wrist, dug beneath his index finger, seized it and yanked it back.

Croft screamed, released me, and twisted his body around to relieve the pressure on his finger.

I increased the pressure, bent the finger farther, moved up against him, forced his whole body to bend down lower and lower beneath me. As he collapsed onto his knees, then sank onto his haunches, I held the hand and finger level with his eyes, and pushed down, keeping the pressure constant.

He screamed, "Stop! Stop!"

"Shut up!" My right hand slapped his right hand away when he tried to reach my grip.

His wife yelled behind me, "Help!"

"I'll kill him!" A younger version of the man beneath me stood at my left, his right arm and fist cocked back. "Dad, one punch and it's over."

"I'll break it!" I screamed.

"No!" Dad said.

The clone looked uncertain and lowered his fist.

I looked around and yelled, "Everybody, listen!"

"God!" shouted Croft.

"Cliff, don't!" Grimes crowded in front of the young man and reached for my hand.

"Stay back or I'll break his goddam finger like a pretzel!"

Croft whimpered.

I bent the finger back until Croft's elbow swiveled forward and the back of the hand I held touched his shoulder.

He wasn't pretty now. Tears and snot coursed along the ridge of his grimacing upper lip. Ugly. Sub-human, I thought.

And noticed caps. Looking down into his mouth revealed that all of his lower front teeth were probably dental crowns, and the sight instantly associated with worries about my own receding gums around caps and subsequent sensitivity to cold and hot stimuli.

For whatever reason, I felt a surge of sympathy, but fought it, thinking, Facades! There was nothing but snags of real teeth below those shining surfaces. What a false front this man projected.

I shouted, "Croft killed his father! Tell 'em!"

"You're crazy. Please!"

"You killed Sammy! You blew up my house! Tell them!"

"Clifford. Clifford." Aunt Judy brushed against me and lay an arm around my back. "This is wrong. It's torture."

She laid her free hand over my grip on Croft's finger.

I looked from Croft into her eyes and back at him. Aunt Judy was right. Of course. Aunt Judy was always fucking right.

I spat down at Croft's distorted face, "Goddam you!" dropped his hand and straightened up.

Croft collapsed backwards flat on the floor, clutching his sore finger to his chest, holding the hand loosely in his other.

He was defenseless and disgusting.

"Darling! Simon!" Mrs. Croft knelt and ministered to her husband. Even this man was loved.

"Stay back!" Grimes said, and I saw her shoving away the two young men who looked like young versions of Croft. They glared at me but didn't try to get around Grimes.

Aunt Judy bent over Croft. "I'm a nurse. Let me see."

I panted, my fists clenched and unclenched, and I felt like jumping up and down and running in place.

Croft flexed his index finger several times. He was all right, the bastard.

Then the pain fully hit and my head felt awful. I softly fingered the sore places, and the touch made them hurt worse. I groaned, and my fingertips came away with blood.

"Here." A handkerchief touched my cheek.

I held the cloth loosely in place, and looked at the person

who'd offered it. Grimes.

"There's not much blood," she said. "Let's go out to the washroom and clean it."

She led me off with a hand on an elbow. As I walked, my forehead throbbed with each footfall, and in between steps, my left ear hurt with a burning sensation.

We went into a bathroom off the hallway. I rinsed my face while Grimes soaked a paper towel, which I took from her and dabbed on the broken skin. The ear damage looked minor, but the whole ear was red.

Two spots were swelling, the one on my forehead the larger. I dried my face, held the hanky against the cut cheek, thanked Grimes for the hanky, said I'd clean it and get it back to her.

"Don't bother. Throw it away."

I looked at her and said, "I'm surprised you and Shepherd didn't hold my arms and let Croft beat me to death."

"We thought about it." She smiled. "I warned you about the Crofts. He and his three children have all studied martial arts."

"Why didn't you tell me that before?"

Aunt Judy appeared on my left in the mirror, glanced at me, but spoke to Grimes. "The other one's okay. How's this one?"

"I think he'll live," Grimes said.

"He's got a hard head."

"I noticed."

"You must be the woman detective."

"Eden Grimes. You must be Sister Judith Merced, his aunt."

Wonderful. Grimes already knew about Aunt Judy. What else did Grimes and her buddies know?

When the women shook hands in the mirror, they seemed as if they were one person, meeting herself at two different stages of life, in two distinct but strangely similar costumes.

CHAPTER SIXTEEN

Oh what fun lay ahead, I thought, driving to Mom's house alone, following Ed and Aunt Judy in his pick-up, Grimes and Shepherd leading all three of us there in a cruiser.

What a merry group were we. Aunt Judy was beside herself, cutting a crumb cake she took from a Tupperware container, dredging up chocolate chip and raisin/oatmeal cookies from the big crock, brewing yet another pot of coffee, which she assured Grimes and Shepherd was decaffeinated because it was so late in the day she didn't want them to have trouble sleeping. Sometimes saintliness was a very big pain in the ass.

The clock on the wall ticked loudly, 8:25. I wrapped a towel around ice cubes and applied them awkwardly, shifting the cold from one sore to another. A heavy dose of ibuprofen eventually masked the pain, but nothing could stop two bluish-red Ping-Pong balls from popping up, making my face feel and look lopsided.

Oh, no, I assured my wonderful police friends, no need to call the barrister Gibson and ask for his presence. What did I need an attorney for? I didn't care if they locked me up. A cage would be safer than freedom. I held the ice to my throbbing head and led them off on an exploration of my life.

Ed stayed with Aunt Judy, helping her prepare a coffee klatch while I showed the officers my mother and explained her condition; then Aunt Judy's room; the spare bedroom; and finally upstairs, my bedroom, bathroom, and the southern end of the house where I opened the door to and put the light on in my workroom: two walls solid with books, one with the computer and its accessories.

"Cozy," Grimes said. "May we go in?"

I hesitated. Why let the bastards delve that far into my life? "Look, if you can use multiple deceptions to protect your work, why can't you understand that I don't want to disclose some irrelevant, personal details?"

"What are you pissed off at us for?" Shepherd asked.

He was serious. Such sweet innocence. I stared at him for a second, changed the ice to my left hand because my right had gone numb with cold, managed a fake smile, and said, "Come on. Time to pig out on Aunt Judy's snack."

Following them downstairs, I considered Shepherd's question seriously. I wasn't as angry at them as at myself. My attempts to control anything pertaining to Sammy's death had been in vain. Everything I tried was thwarted in some way, swept aside in a stream of events that carried me along no matter how hard I fought to go forward. Maybe I should flip over onto my back and float down-current until I reached shallows where I could wade out and dry off.

Hang in there, I thought. Shut up for as long as you can.

Aunt Judy, Ed and I, sitting on the couch, used religious magazines on the coffee table as coasters. The two police were put on chairs and provided with metal TV trays by the distaff clergy—wouldn't Aunt Judy hate that phrase?

While we sipped and munched, Aunt Judy badgered "Eden"—not asking for whys, whos or hows about what in the hell they were trying to do to her nephew—asking if "Eden" found her work rewarding. Was she growing in it? How high up the organizational ladder could she climb? How dangerous was her work? Jesus!

"Eden" emoted about doing good and helping people and

working her way up the ladder without disclosing one real piece of information. She was without a doubt shifty. Nausea threatened to empty my stomach.

"I've never heard of a woman sheriff," Aunt Judy said, accepting the vacuity of Eden's discourse at face value.

"You will. There are a few." Grimes smiled. "Chief hospital administrators who are women were unheard of until recently, yet you were one at two big hospitals."

Aunt Judy smiled. "Well, my order owned the institutions."

Grimes said, "Still, that was quite an achievement."

The point to me was clear, and not very subtle, that Grimes was showing off her investigative prowess. It evoked sarcastic praise from me. "Bravo. You've dug up a lot about my family."

Grimes said, "Your aunt was easy. The priest at the church gave us some background and her convent's name."

"Good old Father Gable. He's a real helpful guy."

Grimes said, "Neighbors told us about your mother."

"How'd you find this place to start with?"

Shepherd said, "The County Treasurer's Office lists you as the owner of this and the Pekin Road residence."

Grimes said, "The post office has dual addresses for you with a stop-delivery notice at the other one. By the way, I am glad to see that you did that. Also, both the phone lines, here and out there, are in your name although the phone book lists your mother's name here."

Ed said, "Now you know all about Cliff."

Grimes frowned. "Not quite. He wouldn't let us in the room where the computer is."

Ed elbowed me. "Buddy boy, now is the time."

I grumbled, "Where'd you get that ugly blue raincoat?" and looked pointedly at the hall tree on which it drooped.

"It's yours," he said, but I couldn't remember it.

Aunt Judy said, "Clifford, Eden and her friend can keep a secret."

Wasn't that the truth? They could certainly hide things behind euphemisms and omissions if not out-and-out lies.

I barked, "Honesty is an important value," which of course meant nothing to them. I was protesting to the air, stalling.

Ed said, "They need to know your source of income. Right?"

Grimes nodded. "That might answer some questions."

Well, they'd proven their goddam competence in researching. They'd soon dig up the information themselves.

I took them back upstairs, ushered them into my workroom, sat down on the seat before the computer, and watched them look around. There wasn't much to see but printed matter.

"Those are copies of his books," Ed explained from the doorway where he and Aunt Judy stood, overseeing this operation.

Grimes said, "So you write. Is that it?"

I nodded.

Grimes inspected the bookcase nearest her, saw my name, pulled out three slim volumes, one off each of the top three shelves, handed one to Shepherd, and they flipped pages.

"Poetry!" Shepherd concluded, and looked at me.

"Guilty as charged," I said.

Grimes asked, "Can you make a living with this?"

"Hell no. Poetry's been dead for fifty years in America. You can make money doing workshops, teaching and receiving grants, but that's it. Rod McKuen was the last great American poet to make money writing poems." They'd never get my sarcasm, but I enjoyed it. "Look at the publication dates on those."

I stood up, took the book from Shepherd, and showed them the publishing data. "See? 1980. The other two came out in '79 and '78. Those shelves are full of copies. I can't give them away.

There's a box of them in the garage."

Grimes said, "I'd like a copy."

"Help yourself."

"Me too. I read a lot," Shepherd said, and when I nodded, he also took a copy of each of my three chapbooks. These collections were so slim, the three together fit in one jacket pocket without distorting it: ten or so short poems per book.

Grimes thanked me.

"Yeah, thanks," said Shepherd. "I'll read them."

Bet you won't, I thought, but said, "You're welcome. Enjoy."

"I can't read them myself," Aunt Judy said from the doorway. "Modern poetry is over my head."

Which was the same stupid thing Mom had always told me even though the goddam poems were as transparent as the frigging air on a cold, clear day. Hell, a lot of the poems were about them, Aunt Judy and Mom. Well, I'd given up being disappointed about that a long time ago.

I told Shepherd and Grimes that the rest of that bookcase contained copies of literary magazines in which some of my poems first appeared, but that I had written very few poems since the early 1980s. Waste of time and money and effort, I explained. "Writing poetry is metric masturbation—to be more precise, 'un-metric' masturbation since metering verse is another discipline nobody believes in anymore."

Lurching toward a tirade against academia and "poets" and cliques and phonies, I stopped and looked around. Everyone was staring at me as if I were a lunatic.

Jesus! No normal people cared about that crap.

I turned to the other wall-to-ceiling bookcase. "The top three shelves are mine. The other shelves hold odds and ends."

The detectives bent, inspecting spines in the bookcase.

Shepherd said, "Your name's not on any of these."

"Pen names," I said. "Those pseudonyms are my secret. It's a professional thing so I'm asking you not to tell anyone. Nobody in town but Ed and Aunt Judy know. Plus my lawyer and accountant. Plus an agent in New York. See, I make money on this stuff and have been for almost two decades. Copies of all twenty-one of my prose books are there."

Shepherd said, "Most of these names are female."

"Yeah, right. I do my best writing as a woman."

The remark wasn't funny to them.

"What kind of books ARE these?" Grimes asked.

"Novels—more romances than anything, a couple westerns and fantasy, three mysteries. No mainstream literary junk."

Grimes said, "We need the names of the people you mentioned. That lawyer, accountant and agent."

"With addresses and phone numbers," Shepherd said.

"Why the hell not!" Christ. Might as well give them whatever they wanted.

I sat down and resentfully snapped on the computer. Perversely, though, I also felt good. They had recognized not one title or pseudonym, but my ego loved the attention. They'd know what I could do now. They might respect and admire me. In fact, there were already signs of that from both of them.

Idiot, I thought. Remember the downside. Publicity!

I spun around and said, "Will this information get into my file? I can't let it circulate and people find out who I am."

"It'll be secure," Grimes said. "You going to print it out for us?"

I nodded.

She said, "Okay, I'll give it back to you when we've checked things out and are satisfied."

Satisfied? Those blue eyes twinkled at me? Grimes had outsmarted me time after time already. I had to trust her.

I opened files, copied, pasted and printed off one sheet containing not only the people information, but also book titles, publication dates and pen names for each. I held up the sheet and said, "Promise not to make a copy?"

"Yes," Grimes said.

I handed it over.

Shepherd said, "Excuse me, but I don't get it. Why hide what you do? Are you ashamed of these books?"

"No."

"Well, they'd sell like hot cakes around here if people knew that you wrote them. I mean, it's a novelty. You'd be on the radio and TV and in the newspapers."

I shuddered at the thought.

"You'd be famous," he said. "You're not shy. You'd do good on talk shows."

"Please, I want neighbors to talk to me naturally. I want to remain a part of this community, such as it is anymore."

Grimes smiled at that and shook her head.

"What?" I asked her.

"If anybody acted like he wanted nothing to do with society, it's you."

I almost repeated my old argument, that everything I wrote and did was devoted to society. To criticize was to seek to improve. To entertain was to please. To give information was to educate. To behave morally was to set an example.

But I was smart enough to remember that this had not convinced my ex-wife Angela. In fact, it had infuriated her. She'd hated what she called my antisocial tendency, which she swore was worsening with age.

Well, maybe she'd been right.

Memories of her bloody attacks tossed me in bed all night— her face mixed in with visions of Croft and his sons throwing punches at me as if I were a dummy they used for practice in a gym. And behind them stood Shepherd and Grimes, their eyes squinting as if to discern something hidden in my struggles.

CHAPTER SEVENTEEN

The next morning, I called the funeral home, retrieved my father's fedora from a troll beneath the canopy at the front door, then drove to the Restfield Cemetery. Didn't wear the hat, though, because it hurt the bump on my forehead. Leaving the car at the cemetery, therefore, I had to suffer and run as the low gray clouds pelted my head, hurling ice on a north wind.

I escaped into the Memorial Chapel, bursting through its doors so the small limestone-and-cement structure welcomed me by rattling its windows, crosses, candles, and whatnots. So much for an unobtrusive entrance. I didn't look around, concentrated instead on brushing off my coat, unbuttoning.

When someone grabbed my right arm, I looked up. It was Grimes. She said, "Over here," and pulled me into the last pew.

On the altar, Croft, his wife, a younger woman, and the two young men I recognized from the funeral home crowd, all dressed in dark colors, looked back at us and scowled. Reverend Armstrong said something to them, patted Croft's back, and they all turned away, concentrating on something besides me.

We were among about fifty people, all but a couple in pews ahead of us. I took off my coat, held it on my lap, sat beside her, and spoke softly into her left ear, "Those the three Croft kids?" When she nodded, I said, "It's a sacrilege to have Croft presiding over his victim's funeral ceremony."

Her head turned toward me so close her words smelled of Doublemint gum. "Mr. Croft was in a well-attended County

Commission meeting when Burkhoffer was killed."

"Really?!" I stared at her, back at the altar, then back at her. "Then it's a sacrilege for him to be acting so sincerely grieved when he gave Sammy no attention in life."

"The day he learned of his father's death, Croft was so upset, he drank a bottle of vodka, threw up and passed out."

"I don't believe it."

"The sheriff, the mayor, and another man were there. It was some kind of weekly poker-playing session they have. That's also Croft's ironclad alibi for the night your house burned down."

I thought over these bytes of police information, surprised by them as well as her candor, then whispered, "Even if that's true, he could've gotten his kids to burn my house and kill Sammy. You told me all three were lethal."

"Will you hush up?"

"Hell, look at those two boys. Immaculately tailored, expensive suits, swept-back, oily hair."

"That's a popular style," she said.

"I'm sure growing up they received only the best of everything. Probably spoiled from conception. And conditioned to act violently. Sleek! By God they remind me of Doberman pinschers or long-legged Rottweilers. They're Croft's attack dogs."

She leaned close enough for her nose to brush my ear. "Leave them alone! They all wanted you kept out of here, but I got you in. Keep your feelings to yourself."

"I'm not the villain. That bastard Croft attacked me."

"After you provoked him. He has unbreakable alibis. You don't."

"I still say he could've conspired to kill Sammy and hit my house. Look at his little boys at their grandfather's funeral, strutting around, making a spectacle. Do they have alibis?"

She whispered, "They are just as hostile about you. All the

Crofts have been urging the sheriff to lock you up."

"Goddam villains. The twins have to be suspects."

"Who isn't? Last night you promised no more confrontations with the Crofts."

"Yeah, yeah."

"No words to them at all."

"Sure. I'm only here to wish Sammy bon voyage."

I could think of some things I'd like to tell the twins. They were improved versions of Croft, an inch or so taller, in their 20s, and indistinguishable from where I sat.

Fuck it. I'd promised not to get involved. Grimes had been irate to learn I'd gone to the funeral home to confront Croft and see what would happen. It was her investigation, and I had agreed to stay out of it. Okay, she could be right. Croft could be innocent. I had no way to collect information on suspects, and I had failed miserably trying to do so.

I acted as if I were looking around to my right, dipped my head slightly, inhaled her faint lilac aroma, and spotted just beneath her short brown hair a tiny silver horse romping on a stud in her earlobe. No, the horse's rear legs hid a clasp. The earring was a clip-on.

Grimes lifted her shoulder, hit my chin and chased me off.

Reverend Armstrong began solemnities, launching into the usual platitudes, followed by Psalm 23: "The LORD is my shepherd; I shall not want. He maketh me to lie down in green pastures: he leadeth me beside the still waters."

The Elizabethan formality, the expressions of faith, the pastoral imagery, the hope the prayer conveyed, surged through me like infusions of blood. I silently recited the remaining part: "Thou preparest a table before me in the presence of mine enemies: thou anointest my head with oil; my cup runneth over. Surely goodness and mercy shall follow me all the days of my life: and I will dwell in the house of the LORD for ever."

Led by Armstrong's tenor voice, we stood and sang two hymns *a capella,* reading the lyrics and melody from books stored in metal frames screwed onto the pew's back in front of us. He called for a minute of silent prayer, asked us to sit, then introduced Reverend Harvey Cranepool, who would provide a few personal observations about Sam Burkhoffer.

Cranepool stood up and faced us by his seat on the front pew. He had sandy, curly hair, a walrus mustache, a pale, anemic complexion, a nearly anorexic build lost in a blue- and red-striped sweater, but a surprisingly deep bass voice.

"Thank you so much. It's very good of Reverend Armstrong to invite my participation, having met me only yesterday evening. I want you all, especially Sam Burkhoffer's family, to know that I feel lucky to have made Sam's acquaintance, which occurred while I was visiting a church member sequestered in the same hospital room as Sam's. After that, I daily sought out Sam on purpose. Getting to know the man was a privilege and a lesson.

"Sam seemed troubled to me, and my first impression of the cause was the loss of his wife Dorothy some years ago. However, in subsequent discussions, Sam admitted being near despair many times before her death. I want you to know that even though he was prone to melancholia, it did not manifest itself during Sam's painful therapy, and there was a good reason why it didn't. Sam reconciled with the Lord. Sam was saved.

"I hope knowing that will comfort Sam's family. I hope it will also comfort them to learn that Sam blamed himself for the breach in their contact. Sam rued not providing his young son with more love and understanding and just plain old basic attention. The main thing he regretted, and Sam repeated this several times, was spending so much time working in the city and on his farm while ignoring his son. He expressed this regret to me with great feeling.

"My impression was that Sam, in those early days of his marriage, had been driven by fears that he might lose his home. Sam told me that it had almost been lost during the Depression. When Sam had been a youngster, he struggled alongside his own parents to save the farm. Then, when they expired, the farm, the responsibility, and the worry became his, and his alone.

"Thus, from my point of view, Sam became overly anxious to preserve the property. He became tyrannical with his wife and his son, and distrustful of his neighbors. Sam used those exact words, tyrannical and distrustful, and as he explored his shortcomings with me, I sensed something near paranoia in Sam's fears. I say this because if that is true, I hope Sam's family can understand that his behavior may have stemmed from emotional distress, a hard-to-control illness.

"I cannot say that Sam attended religious services regularly. In fact Sam did not attend even one at my church. But Sam achieved something precious. I can assure family and friends that Sam died in the arms of the Almighty, having accepted Christ into his life and built a personal relationship with our Savior. Amen and Alleluia!"

As Cranepool sat, I whispered to Grimes, "Did you know about him? Ever talk to him?"

She shook her head.

"He might know what was on Sammy's mind."

Grimes turned her face to me and whispered, "Be quiet."

"I think he might know—"

"Shut up?" She whispered it like a question, and turned her head back around.

Meantime, Armstrong had thanked Cranepool and was inviting anyone at this time to share with all of us whatever we would like to say about Sam Burkhoffer—our feelings and thoughts and stories of Sam. We could come up front to speak or sit or stand where we were, whatever we preferred.

"Who would like to say something?" Armstrong looked out into the congregation directly in front of his pulpit, then strolled to the other side of the altar where his gaze darted from face to face. "Anybody want to share a story?"

People shifted in their seats and looked away from Armstrong. My impression was that most of them were friends of Croft and hadn't actually known Sammy. Mrs. Creech was two pews ahead, but she wasn't moving. The silence stretched out and suggested that nothing more would be said about Sammy. That didn't seem right.

I started to stand and half up was jerked back down by Grimes, who'd grabbed my suit coat and yanked.

"Stay out of it," she whispered, and pointed over the shoulders ahead of us.

Croft had been standing up too. When he faced us, his wife took his right hand. He held a hymnal in his left, clutched against his chest, and looked around the chapel, over at Armstrong, who nodded, then at Cranepool.

Armstrong nodded again, signaling Croft to go ahead.

Croft said, "It was very nice to hear those comments. Thank you, Doctor, aah—"

"Cranepool," said the deep voice.

"Yes, of course, Dr. Cranepool. I'm sorry I'm so forgetful." Croft snorted and grunted, cleared his throat, and said, "Your remarks were comforting, but—"

Croft shook his head and looked down. His wife thumbed the back of his hand, massaging. He spoke to the floor so I barely heard, "My father was my torment. I'll never get over it. Never."

He sniffled and looked sideways as if he were studying the stained glass windows. "As Dr. Cranepool mentioned, Father was tyrannical. But that's neither here nor there. I wanted to say something good about him. I think Father inspired me despite himself. Sometimes I think that everything I've ever accomplished was done to impress him. Not that anything did. Well, what can I say? We just didn't get along."

He sobbed. His wife stood, hugged him, and gave him a tissue. He wiped his face, blew his nose, and she sat back down.

"Father and I were just getting acquainted. We were talking, and I'd been to his house and hoped to go there some more when he, but he, I don't know, died." He shook his head and dabbed at his eyes again. "We were mending our relationship, but now he's gone and so is the chance we had. It's very sad to me. I suppose I should be thankful we exchanged a few pleasant words."

He turned and sat, then abruptly stood back up, turned around and gave the congregation his closest scrutiny yet. "It would be nice if any of you who knew Father personally would tell us something about him. His habits or whatever. I mean it. I never knew my own father."

He dropped down onto his seat, slumped forward, and his back heaved. Dramatic sorrow if sincere—and it seemed to be.

"Thank you, Simon," Armstrong said, stepping nearer the front pew. "Now, someone else? Anybody with a story no matter how insignificant you may think it."

Mrs. Creech finally raised a hand and, when acknowledged by Armstrong, without standing, said she'd been Sam's housekeeper and agreed with the other minister over there that her employer had changed during his illness. She told a few tales about Sam, how he'd eaten and dressed and didn't go out very often. How he'd occupied himself doing jigsaw puzzles and watching television.

Croft's grief surprised, but also stirred me. I understood it and felt it and, yes, perhaps it was real and honest. His appraisal of his father was far different from my experience of the man, but it seemed corroborated by Cranepool and Mrs. Creech.

When Mrs. Creech finished, Armstrong hovered over the exact center of the front pew and asked, "Anyone else?"

He looked right at me. "You? I believe you were about to speak a moment ago."

Grimes turned her head toward me and whispered, "Don't."

I looked into those deep blue eyes, thought about only the one lay person witnessing for Sammy, and started up.

Grimes bolted up herself, and acting as if she'd been going to leave the pew, said, "Excuse me," turned her back to the altar, and slowly edged past, facing me.

I had to lean back to give her room.

As she passed in front of me, her knees jabbed mine, and hidden from the altar, she said, "Talking's not a good idea."

Then she was past and in the aisle.

I suddenly felt marooned, standing there, watching her go. I could have left with her, and now I wished I had.

"Yes, sir?" Armstrong said, drawing my attention up front. He nodded, urging me to speak.

Peripherally, I saw that all heads had turned my way. Croft and his wife and the twins had half turned in their seats and were looking back. Glaring at me. Shit!

"I don't want to cause any more pain," I said.

"Don't worry," Armstrong said. "Go ahead."

Short and sweet, I told myself, and said, "Well, Mr. Croft asked for personal details about his father. I can only give a few because I only knew Sam the last month of his life. Sam and I would walk together in the evenings and talk, and I'm very sorry Mr. Croft didn't experience Sam as I did. I lost my father when I was a child so I know how a father's death affects a son.

"Anyway, I can tell you this. Sam never complained to me about his illness. I didn't even learn about it until after he was gone. My point is, he was a gutsy sort of person.

"Also, he talked a lot about the old days, mostly about his childhood years, about working hard and how living conditions have changed over the years. He was nostalgic and sentimental. He did mention to me his wife's death and his separation from his son as things he regretted. I thought he was a very nice man, but then I never saw the negative side we've been hearing about. Maybe that's why I liked him so much."

I sat without looking around, glad I'd said something because it was important to testify to another person's goodness, but afraid I'd offended Croft. Even if grief could be easily faked, no one could judge his soul, and I certainly wouldn't try.

When no one else volunteered to speak, Armstrong said there would be a private interment following this service for the immediate family only, and glanced right, toward an alcove that contained an 18-inch high, fat metallic urn.

Observant me. For the first time I realized there was no casket present and Sammy had been cremated. I had noticed the silvery vase before and thought it out of place with the decor, but assumed it was from a preceding service, forgotten and left empty of flowers in the rush for this ceremony. That Sammy had already been reduced to ashes shocked me.

Armstrong announced there would be a luncheon somewhere in an hour, and everyone was invited to that. He gave directions, then said, "Let us now close with Hymn Number 136."

We sang, and slowly the words sank in. I left the chapel with the hymn's refrain tumbling through my head: *"Yes, we shall gather at the river,/The beautiful, the beautiful river;/Gather with the saints at the river/That flows by the throne of God."*

Outside, I leaned against a bare maple, chanting the refrain in my mind. The wind had died down, the clouds were thinning out, blue patches of sky showed, and sunlight strobed across the jagged lines of tombstones arrayed east of us.

Within this panorama, the Croft family walked over to the

mausoleum, fifty yards away, with Armstrong following behind. Croft carried the urn the way acolytes carry candles. One of the undertakers opened the black steel double doors, and the twins said something to the parents, then hurried off to the parking lot. Too indifferent to stay for grandpa's interment? Was Sammy their victim? The parents, the daughter, Armstrong, and the undertaker disappeared into the building.

The rest of the crowd, along with the twins, was piling into cars. I looked back at the chapel. A door was swinging closed, and I saw Lieutenant Grimes inside, talking to Cranepool.

Damn. How had I lost track of them?

By reflex, I started back toward the chapel, wanting to join that conversation and learn more about Sammy's troubled side.

I stopped. No, I would remember Sammy as I'd known him. Grimes was doing her job, and she did not want me involved. Fine. I would concentrate on getting myself back to normal. That's all I'd ever wanted anyway.

Right! That was my final decision. I drove back to Mom's house convinced I would never interfere in the case again.

CHAPTER EIGHTEEN

Therefore, at 1:00 p.m., soon after that decision, how did I end up back in the middle of the mess, on my way to the Crofts'?

"You sure this is a good idea?" I asked Grimes as she drove us over a bridge a half-mile from the city limits and three miles downriver from Old Town.

"I told you Mr. Croft asked me to ask you to come. Your comments at the chapel impressed him and all he wants is for you to tell him more about his father. Yes, I now think that you meeting him is a good idea."

"And I won't get beat up again?"

"Not unless you antagonize the family—which is, knowing you, quite possible."

I smiled as we climbed the steep hillside, remembering that she'd convinced me to come because she said it might help her investigation, also because she had agreed to bicycle with me afterwards so I could jog without safety concerns on the bike trail—where I'd been headed when she suddenly appeared at Mom's house to get me. Whether to come had been a big decision. I had to change back into my business suit for this.

Topping the hill we passed a huge gilded BCCC on an ornate black metal gate, and I recognized our destination. "The Big Chief Country Club! You know what? This was the old Stegmuller place. I baled hay here during my high school days. Look at that phony-ass mansion. It's like a plantation house along the Mississippi River. See the wide verandahs. I guess we're lucky it's not a Disneyland imitation of a goddam Alpine castle."

Going inside, I thought of meals I'd had at the Stegmuller home, the sweaty, good-natured men and boys I'd worked with, the table with bowls of mashed potatoes, noodles with gravy, tossed salad, ears of corn, string beans, tomatoes, iced tea, lemonade, pie. Meat courses alternating by day among ham, fried chicken, roast beef and sausage. Old fashioned country cooking. I didn't know whether to feel angry or sad.

The lobby matched the artificiality of the building outside. There were five tall tropical plants in large black pots, one wall of shelves holding large silver trophies, and two walls hanging bronze plaques with two crossed golf clubs forming a vee above the raised image of a man's head.

We hiked around a large dining area of oval tables, each with eight padded chairs. Six crystal chandeliers dominated the ceiling but only three were lit because light flooded in from southern-facing floor-to-ceiling windows. Small groups of white people were eating brunch while the omelet-and-waffle maker waited nearby, Old Black Joe in a chef's costume.

"They're on the second floor," Grimes said.

Croft's private luncheon room had purple drapery lashed with golden cords around cantilevered windows. A big chandelier. Ornate flower arrangements on each of four tables. Buffet tables where glass platters with floral etchings supported artfully arranged piles of cold cuts, breads and raw vegetables. Many choices of sauces, hot foods, desserts and drinks.

Grimes took a plate, and I followed her while she selected potato salad, baked beans, slaw, slices of turkey and roast beef.

With our backs to the Crofts, I told her, "This is the inner sanctum of the fat cats. We're in the belly of the beast."

She said, "Simmer down. Get something to eat."

"The goddam new construction spreads out from here almost

146

solid into Dayton's suburbs. Big so-called manors, condominiums, small ranches, shit like that."

"So what?"

"All the agricultural land is being destroyed."

"Are you ever happy? We're not here to buy a house."

"Croft is one of the main culprits on the county commission and the regional planning commission. Hell, he promotes urban sprawl as progress. I've heard him do it."

"Pipe down. Try to be pleasant. Remember your promise to tell Croft what he wants to hear, and get him to talk. Nothing more. If you're not going to eat, can you get me a cola?"

Be pleasant. Be nice. How many times had I heard that? I believed in cooperation and politeness, but indiscriminately being nice allowed evil to happen. It could imply approval, and draw you into supporting, even perpetrating bad things yourself. There were more important considerations than being nice.

I also felt like a barefoot boy, tiptoeing across a scorching beach toward a scary, raging surf. The guy I was going to meet had accused me of killing his father. Had urged my arrest. Had pounded and disfigured my head.

Part of me drew away and observed from a distance as if I were watching a movie. As a performer in the action, though, I had to maintain control. Therefore, I tried to ignore the situation's bizarre nature, concentrating instead on simple things like fetching drinks for Grimes and myself.

Croft had two chairs ready for us, having pushed everyone away from his left around the table and closer together. I set our drinks down, returned to the buffet, and came back with a plate holding nine carrot sticks. I put the plate by my coffee, renewed my pledge to behave, but reminded myself there were limits, and they sure as hell weren't far away.

Before we could sit, Croft introduced Mrs. Creech, to whom we nodded, then Cranepool, who was next to Grimes so I leaned in front of her and shook his hand.

Croft started introducing his sons, and their hostile looks invited response. I watched myself walk behind Croft around the table, stick my right paw down over the left shoulder of one, and say, "Nice to meet you, Richard."

His face turned up, focusing razor-eyes upon me, and his hot grip seemed to challenge mine. The same exact behavior from Jason, along with their identical looks, caused me to do a double take and pull my hand loose. Yes, lethal, I thought.

"How can I tell you apart?" I asked both taut faces.

"That takes practice," Croft said behind me, and introduced his daughter Penny. I turned left of the twins to her, and she shook my hand without hesitation, but she too didn't speak.

"Is your name short for Penelope?" I asked.

"No," she whinnied with no explanation. Her rather flat, long facial features, which like the heavy makeup resembled her Mama's, contrasted the aquiline contours of the males, but she had inherited Papa's tall, strong body.

Mrs. Croft, left of Penny, mumbled something and touched my hand, but her eyes flitted across my face without pause as if to avoid noticing the dark knots from her husband's attack.

As Grimes and I sat, Croft told everyone about my house fire, inducing expressions of sympathy from the minister and Mrs. Creech. I thanked them but watched the Croft children, who maintained dour mugs, averted eyes, and silence.

Croft said that before our arrival, Mrs. Creech and Dr. Cranepool had been regaling the table with details about his father, and Croft hoped I could supply some particulars too.

I said, "Particulars? Okay." Sat back, imagined my times with Sammy, and launched into a rambling monologue, dredging up details that might interest Croft. They were no more than what I'd told the police, things Sammy had mentioned to me: like comments about the Grange, the coal furnace, the canning of vegetables and fruit, the simpler life in the old days, the severe winters, the little and big jobs he'd done, etc.

There were no surprise memories, but I went on for a long time, then took a deep breath to gather myself, looked around, and noticed that Grimes had already cleaned off her plate.

What else might Croft want to know? How about things that I had observed about Sammy?

I described to Croft how his father had dressed, how we had met at a certain time and place, how we had walked and talked, and how his father would tire quickly so we never walked far. I mentioned that Sam had driven from his house and parked on Route 86 as close as he could get to the bike trail, but he'd had to walk to the bike trail and then back from it to his car.

"That's right," Mrs. Creech said. "Late every afternoon the last few weeks like clockwork, he'd go park on the road."

I said, "That was very determined behavior for a man in his condition, and he never asked me for help either. Of course, at the time I thought he was just old."

I thought back for other facts and recalled only one more. "If I remember right, Sam said his parents died before he was twenty."

This cued Cranepool. "He told me that too."

"Some kind of influenza," Croft said. "It got both of my grandparents in 1938."

Cranepool said, "That must have shocked Sam, and taking over the farm was a huge responsibility for a youngster."

"I don't know about that," Croft said. "He could've inherited the land and equipment free and clear, and it's possible the place was never mortgaged. He married Mother a month after my grandparents died and I've always believed he married her to get help with the farm. She worked with him side by side, and when the war came and took him away, she worked like a dog all alone. It must've got better when he returned, but then I came along and aggravated things."

Cranepool said, "Sam was troubled before you were born."

Croft looked at him. "Father was a taskmaster. He had me working as soon as I could walk. I worked all day, every day, never had a playmate, and didn't resent it either. Not until I started school."

His wife patted his right forearm, which lay on the table beside her.

Croft said, "Once or twice a child came to visit with a grown-up, but Father kept me on a short leash. I never went to visit anyone. Mother occasionally took me to town, but Father kept me with him most of the time. Called me his little helper."

Cranepool said, "A difficult way to grow up."

Croft shook his head. "When I rode off on the bus to school and learned how other children lived, then I rebelled. Even ran off a couple times."

"There, there," his wife said as if to quiet him.

But Croft shook his head, then continued.

"I worked with Father in the fields, worked with animals, worked with equipment. Worked, worked, worked. When Father was at his factory job, I had morning and evening chores, and when I wasn't at school, I had other duties. Mother supervised me, and was lenient and sympathetic, but she let it go on, didn't she? She wouldn't stand up to Father. He was the boss. He got his way. I've come to believe that what he did to me was a kind of child abuse. I felt abandoned yet exploited too."

Mrs. Croft held his hand on the tabletop. "Simon, that's enough. This isn't the place."

Croft's face flushed and cords popped out on his neck. "I'm not ashamed of this. I'm proud of it. It made me a man." He blew his nose with a long honking sound.

"I rebelled, okay? I worked poorly and slow. Broke things. Father threw fits and cursed. That could be all I wanted, you know, to get his attention and stop my laboring. If so, I was successful. It didn't get me more freedom, though. When I couldn't be relied on, Father made me sit or stand there and watch him do my work. I'll give him his due. He never punished me physically. Of course, if he had, I might not have gotten so vocal or gone so far."

He dabbed at his eyes, and looked around with a kind of defiance. When his wife said his name again and squeezed his hand, he said, "It's all right, Honey. Like I said, I'm proud of how I took charge of my life. In the sixth grade I was packed off to St. Alban's Military Academy to learn discipline. My behavior had deteriorated in the public school as well as at home, and I was labeled incorrigible. The boarding school was also an orphanage, and going home during holidays and vacations was optional, so I usually chose to stay there, especially later in my high school years. My parents insisted I come home the first few years, but eventually they let me do what I wanted. I was as much an orphan as my playmates."

Croft gasped, caught his breath, and said firmly, "After graduating from the academy, I never once stayed in Father's house. I never asked for a cent from him either. I went through Miami University on an NROTC scholarship. My father! I tell you he alienated me. As soon as I could, I took my mother's maiden name and got rid of his."

The twins looked at each other and exchanged glances with their sister. Mrs. Croft leaned against her husband and hugged his right arm in her left. I looked at Grimes to read her reaction, but she wouldn't lift her face toward me. Cranepool met my eyes, and shook his head sadly. Mrs. Creech sipped coffee.

Croft started off again. "During Father's illness, I did seek reconciliation, as Dr. Cranepool might call it. My childhood was on my mind, but it seemed like a touchy area to him so I put off discussing it, hoping we could work our way into it sometime. We talked about his interests and stayed on a superficial level. I asked to visit him at the house and did go there a few times. Well, just twice to be accurate. Short visits. Both times he acted sick or in need of rest."

He looked directly at me and I nodded sympathetically.

He said, "Hearing how he walked with you, I'm thinking those were excuses to get rid of me. Well, getting together was stressful for both of us so I was ready to leave."

Croft looked at Cranepool. "Like you said, Dr. Cranepool, Father was kind of paranoid. He didn't trust people and probably not me. He always hated the government so he probably saw me as a government agent."

Cranepool asked, "What'd Sam have against the government?"

"Oh, it drafted him and took him away to the war, which left the farm in my mother's care, nearly defenseless from his point of view. The government also levied taxes he couldn't afford, and I assume it restricted what he could grow."

Cranepool said, "Those complaints could be a sign of a clinical condition. Those things happen to everyone."

Croft said, "Well, he did have other reasons. There were rumors the government wanted to make the farm into a park or Indian reservation. Supposedly, an Indian village was there before the settlers came. Once I heard Father tell Mother there was a conspiracy. The government wanted the farm and had people—he didn't know who—waiting around like vultures to pick him clean. I don't know how crazy that thinking was."

Cranepool nodded. "I see."

Croft said, "He had this real strong sense of possession to start with. The farm came down to him in a line of Burkhoffers from the first ones who settled there. That was 1803. Believe me, I heard that year repeated *ad nauseam*. He claimed there were records surviving in the courthouse to prove it, but I could never bring myself to go there and check."

Cranepool said, "The farm's family history may explain why owning the farm weighed so heavily on him."

The disengaged part of me hovered above and appraised this new information. I bet there had been talk over the years of making Sammy's land into a park or a reservation. Hell, I knew there had been because I myself had advocated both ideas to many people on many occasions. I'd never heard of any actual government interest in the farm, but there could have been over the years. For sure, decades ago somebody connected to the state had put up that historical marker on Route 86.

The other, the public part of me identified with Croft's emotions. What an upbringing he'd had. What suffering he'd had to endure, separated from his parents, rejected by his father. What twisting of his personality had to have happened. His warped values were perfectly understandable. None of that, however, made him innocent of Sammy's murder or the destruction of my house.

But Croft was obviously another suffering human being, like the rest of us, so when he looked at me, I said, "I'm surprised about your father. He never mentioned any of that to me so I just didn't know. I didn't even know where Sammy lived."

Did one of the twins cough? Did they glance at Penny?

Those might have been false impressions. My attention remained on Croft.

He had turned so his left knee touched my right. "I don't think you knew Father well, but thank you for sharing your experiences with us."

"You're welcome." He had not apologized for his violent attack on me and must still suspect me. Well, his suspicion of me matched my own of him.

He did reach for my hand, and I hesitated, remembering, then took his. As we shook, I looked along the table. Wearing a

Mona Lisa smile, his wife was resting her left hand on his right shoulder, but his children were not so calm, staring at each other with such intensity, I felt a cutting edge slice across my face when they swung their eyes on me.

CHAPTER NINETEEN

Grimes and I left the Croft group up to their asses in BCCC's fake elegance, but I remained a creature of two minds. My body crawled onto the cruiser's front seat, but another part of me slouched on a cloud and watched the action down below.

"You did good," Grimes said three times, driving us toward town. Eventually, she added, "Real good. You said your piece and shut up and let the others spout off."

"Croft had a lot to say." My circadian rhythms were so low, I slurred, and wished I'd eaten something while at the table.

"You got him going." She was peppy, pumped up with calories.

We passed the fairgrounds and turned on 86 toward downtown before I asked, "Did you learn something worthwhile?"

"Definitely."

"What?"

"I have to think about that some more." She glanced across the seat at me. "Sometimes you got to go slow and let the good stuff ooze out on its own."

At the new county administration building she parked where Jones had parked before parading me handcuffed inside. This time my captor lobbed a set of keys over the hood and said to unlock her car while she checked the cruiser in. Soon after, she dropped me off at Mom's house to change, gave me her address and phone number, and said she'd be ready as soon as I got there. Her place was on Mom's side of town and close.

A half hour later, she greeted me by saying to go ahead and call her Eden. "Be discreet, okay, when deputies are around."

"Sure. You'll be Lt. Eden in their presence. Or Sir." Obviously, she'd learned enough about my life to trust me now.

Her mood influenced mine, and the day had become very nice too, with steady sun and temperatures risen to the upper-40s. I shed my long pants and jacket, threw them into my car, jogged in place, and said, "Let's go!" Then in shorts, insulated, long sleeve undershirt, and ski mask rolled up on top of my head like a turban, I led her to the street and on toward the trail.

I'd offered her the use of the bike in Mom's garage, but she owned a ten-speed with scratched paint and worn tires. Inquiries produced a nice surprise. She used to ride it along Chicago's lakefront, and her descriptions made the city seem attractive.

Discovering she liked the out-of-doors and exercise further inspired my emotional side and made her attractive. Her tight bicycling clothes also helped. She looked good. Very good.

On the trail by then, shielded from housing developments by trees and a narrowing, steep-sided valley, she complained that biking slow was uncomfortable.

"I can go faster," I said.

"Not necessary," she said, and raced ahead to the next half-mile marker, waited there for me, then repeated the maneuver as I thumped up. The serious way she sprinted made her seem as frisky as a child just released from school—an image far different from her professional image.

The dissociated part of me watched her rush ahead and told me not to be so stupid. She was scouting for an ambush.

Nonsense, I argued. No one knew where we were, and there were so many others on the trail, potential witnesses, an assault was unlikely. She was simply enjoying herself.

At the four-mile mark I yelled and asked if that was far

enough for her. Could we go back? I was anticipating a good talk after the run. She had already invited me to dinner.

After a couple miles of retracing our route, she coasted beside me and said, "Croft really put on a performance."

"I think he told us the truth."

"Perhaps. As he sees the truth."

"The guy has suffered so much, it got to me."

"I'm sure he suffered, but—"

"Can you imagine being raised like that? It'd mess you up for life. Croft was about eight when his troubles started, and he had no closure for his grief. Sammy really harmed his son."

"I thought you liked Burkhoffer."

"I must've idealized him and demonized Croft."

"You changed your opinion of them awful easy."

"Not really. I just understand both of them better now."

"You bought that whole sad story?"

"To a point. I'm not as angry at Croft as I was because I understand where he's coming from, but I still think he could've had Sammy killed."

"Croft showed us a good motive. Hatred."

"I don't know about hatred. He expressed anger and sadness."

"For sure."

"But his strongest anger occurred a long time ago and has mostly changed into regret now. Hatred's a lot stronger emotion than anger."

"Since when?"

"Well, right, of course anger can be as strong as hatred."

I glanced sideways at her. She was sitting straight up, wearing a wide, blue, fluffy elastic headband, ski gloves, jogging shoes, and a multi-colored, form-fitting Gore-tex outfit, which must have been warm because she'd removed her jacket and tied its sleeves around her neck.

She said, "Croft's hatred for his father is just under the surface. All of his feelings were extreme?"

She bent forward over the handlebars and pedaled away so the jacket flapped up off her back like Superwoman's cape. Pretty, but I didn't want her to stop confiding in me. When I neared her again, I called out ahead, "What are you thinking then? That his alibis are too good, like he set them up and arranged for the killing? And the attempt to kill me?"

She waited, then coasted beside me again. "It's got to be considered. His feelings go beyond reason. I've never heard such whining from a grown man. Even you don't whine like that."

"Hey, I don't whine. I criticize to improve things."

"Croft blamed his father for everything."

"So you do think he lied."

"He's irrational. I think he can't face the truth. Good God, all parents call their children little helpers. Normal kids crave the attention Burkhoffer gave Croft. Burkhoffer was a farmer so he was teaching his son how to farm."

"By making him work all the time."

"Really? Do you believe Croft never played as a boy? Come on. Where was he deprived? He never went anywhere? Please. Croft's account was totally exaggerated and one-sided."

"Child labor laws were made because exploiting children was so common. If Croft was too little and too young to work so hard, no wonder he rebelled."

"Croft acted that way by choice. He deliberately rebelled. In fact, he bragged about it. Then blamed his father, remember? He said punishment would have stopped his bad behavior. Croft said that he chose not to come home on vacations."

"Yeah, he did."

"He changed his name as soon as he legally could."

"And refused to take money from his father," I reminded her.

"He actually said he didn't ASK for any money, but I'm sure he got some from Burkhoffer. Croft couldn't have paid his bills without it."

Her interpretations were valid, part of me said. Children did embellish stories about their parents, and when egos were involved, memory distorted. Without more information, I really shouldn't blame Sammy nor accept Croft's account at face value.

Exiting the bike trail onto a *cul-de-sac*, I told Eden, "Croft's sorrow was genuine. That's what I empathize with. He still has a lot of old pain along with the new to cope with."

"He's going to have a lot more too. If he's not the one I'm looking for, well then—"

Our eyes met, and I finished her thought, "Then it's someone in his family."

"Odds are."

"Will Croft inherit the farm?"

"If there's no will, and we haven't located one so far, the court will decide, but Croft is Burkhoffer's closest relative."

"And you think somebody stole all of Sammy's documents from his house."

"Yes, and we think his lawyer's office was burglarized too."

"Really? Who's that?"

"Benjamin Brook."

"I've heard of him. What'd he say?"

"He's incommunicado, on a trip abroad, but he's expected back this week. His office was ransacked, but there's no one to ask about it because Brook is retired and has no secretary anymore. Just a little room adjacent to the suite he used before selling his practice. The new owners are in there now."

"Didn't you tell me Shepherd was investigating a downtown break-in?"

"That's it."

159

"I'll be damned."

"Locked files in Brook's office were broken open and emptied. Shepherd found nothing in the office pertaining to Burkhoffer."

We were approaching a through street.

She said, "There could be something at his home, but nobody's there to let us check right now."

"What about the guy in his old office?"

"It's two young attorneys who know nothing about what Brook was doing except that he advises them when necessary and handles a few long-time clients. We think that includes Burkhoffer because a canceled check to Brook is in Burkhoffer's bank."

I said, "This case is all about Sammy's land."

"I think so too. And/or his son's hatred."

She rolled ahead so her shapely hips under the tight black fabric led me on past BOSTON HARBOR, condos designed like New England waterfront buildings. Wrist-sized ropes curled over pilings that held up the sign. Then we took her driveway, which horseshoed around behind four L-shaped, two-story, red brick buildings, which bracketed a commons, swimming pool and tennis court. Eden's townhouse was on the site's northwest corner.

I volunteered to carry her bike inside.

"It's no problem," she said.

I left my ski mask and sweat shirt in my car, grabbed my jacket and long pants, and followed her in.

There was an alcove just inside that let her store the bike out of the way. She wheeled it over the sill into the space.

"What sells these places," she said, "is convenience. Not much upkeep inside, none at all outside. You may not like them, but they save their owners time and work."

"Very upscale," I said, being nice.

"They're comfortable, and if they use up farm land, you got to remember that people have to live somewhere."

"Looks real comfortable." I took my shoes off, left them outside the front door, pulled on my long pants and slipped on the jacket. "Ever find a safety deposit box for Sammy?"

"Not in the banks in Bethel."

"He worked for a factory in Dayton."

"We're contacting all Dayton-area banks, but his checking account is with Landis Savings here in town."

I thanked her for going with me on the run.

She said the ride was fun, took me to the kitchen, gave me a beer, said she had to clean up, and left me with the phone.

In her absence, my jaundiced eyes found prefabricated cabinets and a cramped washer and dryer room whose sliding doors had so much play they would flip off their track easily. It all looked cheap to me, in materials and workmanship.

The living room, though, felt spacious. The high ceiling had exposed roof beams, a sky light, and a second-floor balcony along the back wall where bedrooms probably were. The builders were selling style here—for the busy, distracted and rootless.

It was the first time I'd ever been in one of these places, having despised them from a distance before. This was the queen bee's nest. But was it the heart of Eden's existence? No, there had to be a lot more to Eden than indicated by her choice of home.

One part of me was full of her, and the other struggled to make sense of Sammy's case.

Concentrating on neither very well, I went to the hearth, stared at the gas flames, and telephoned Mom's house.

The cell phone began to jangle with that distant telephone's ringing just as Eden appeared beside me—transformed. Obviously, she'd taken a shower.

The gas flames that licked around three fake logs reddened

her face as well as the white robe belted at her waist in a single loop. Her hair was damp and her eyes gleamed with the fire. She held her hands out toward the burning. Her bare feet shuffled a few inches back from the heat and left outlines of her damp toes on the tiles in front of the hearth.

She stared at the flames and said, "You can wash up now. I'll fix some food."

I swallowed the last gulp of expensive beer she'd given me and said, "This Mexican brand is good."

"I'll get you another."

The phone's ringing stopped and a voice said, "Hello?"

"Hi," I answered without shifting my eyes.

"Where are you, Clifford? I'm waiting."

Eden stepped closer, said, "Here," and extended a hand.

I hesitated, then held out the phone.

"The bottle," she said.

"Oh." I gave her the bottle.

She took it, pivoted in a swirl of terrycloth, revealing a leg from the knee down, and went off to the kitchen, her toes disappearing in the nap of a fur-like, dark gray rug.

The phone went back to my ear and I heard, "Are you there?"

"Sorry, Aunt Judy. Go ahead and eat."

Aunt Judy said, "Aren't you coming?"

"I'll be here at Eden's a while."

"I'll put supper in the oven and keep it hot for you."

"Don't bother. Eden asked me to eat here with her."

Aunt Judy said something as Eden reappeared in the light from the fireplace and handed me another beer.

I said, "Thanks."

"What?" asked Aunt Judy.

In the middle of the tile in front of the hearth, Eden lifted her beer toward mine.

We clinked bottles and I said, "Cheers."

"Clifford," Aunt Judy said.

I downed a mouthful and watched Eden drink. Her chin lifted slightly as she swallowed, and firelight caught her throat so it blushed. The wet hair was pulled back, baring an earlobe, a small, delicate crescent.

"Clifford!" Aunt Judy said again, louder.

Her summons failed to grab my attention. I was stirred by Eden's beauty and this sudden intimacy.

"Clifford! Clifford!"

Aunt Judy's voice dragged the phone back against the side of my head but didn't drag my eyes away from Eden. "I'm here."

"You going to listen now."

"Yeah, sure."

"I want to tell you something that many young people needed to hear at the hospitals where I worked. So I told them."

"What?"

"Use protection."

"What?"

"When you have sex, use protection."

"Jesus!"

"There is no reason to take the Lord's name in vain."

"Damn!"

I glanced at Eden, whose smile faded. Had she heard Aunt Judy? Surely not. I stared into Eden's eyes.

Aunt Judy said, "Unwanted children who come into this world because of lust create great suffering. So use protection."

Like a hard slap to the face, that was enough. Aunt Judy brought me back together in a way I hadn't been in hours.

I smelled the talcum powder Eden had sprinkled on herself, and I understood the truth. Lust? Yes! And maybe it was true for both of us. Why else would Eden be in a robe, standing so close, drinking beer with me?

"Goodbye," I told Aunt Judy, clicked off, and handed the

phone to Eden.

Our hands touched as she took it, her eyes bored into mine, and she stepped even closer. "What's wrong? What's the problem?"

CHAPTER TWENTY

Hell, the problem was simple. I was moonstruck. Infatuated. In lust. Rutting. Whatever you wanted to call it.

Aunt Judy had removed the blinders. Before her comment, I'd let my feelings for Eden intensify, even played the flirting swain, but maybe because of our adversarial relationship, police versus suspect, I'd never imagined her naked and the two of us making the beast with two backs.

Fucking, it was called. Fucking.

I imagined it now, smelling her cleanliness, which the talcum's aroma enhanced with an aura of innocence. My turgid member rose and prepared to address our assemblage of two.

I fought the desire to reach out and crush her against me. I imagined the robe falling off, my lips moving over her body, her mouth chanting poems of ecstasy and encouragement.

"What's the problem?" she asked. "Your mother?"

Fucking? Making love? Having intercourse. Screwing. Doing it. Doing the old in-out, in-out.

The synonyms rattled in my mind.

I hesitated, nodded, shook my head, and finally said, "It may not be that serious, but Mom could die at any moment."

Well, hell, that WAS the goddam truth.

Eden said, "Oh. Too bad."

"I'm sorry. Can we do this another time?"

"You got a rain check, Cliff."

Use of my shortened first name evoked a desire to kiss her,

and I started toward her for that purpose.

But she added, "Leave the bottle. It's illegal in Ohio to drive with an open container of alcohol in your possession. Is there anything I can do?"

"I doubt it, but thanks again."

I gave her the bottle, and skedaddled.

Skedaddled was the right word. I ran home as if some wild thing was chasing me, snarling and biting my ass.

Well, hell, okay, I ran away, but for good reason. I didn't want to hurt Eden. If I wanted a punching bag, a pin cushion, a sex toy, I could do the job myself and not bother anyone. I could dance the five-fingered waltz as well as any man or boy alive.

Of course, rushing off to Mom's house, I caught Aunt Judy at the kitchen table, eating.

"That was a hell of a thing to tell me," I said, stopping my flight by the stove.

She quickly emptied her mouth to create important repartee. "It was the truth."

"You couldn't know what we were doing, or thinking."

"I may be hard of hearing, but I'm not blind or senile."

"You had better go to confession."

"I'm not the one with lust in my heart."

"You advised me to sin. You contradicted Church law."

"Now you're a Catholic?" She jabbed a fork toward me. "You ought to have enough common sense to know you can only go to hell once. Just one mortal sin is enough to get you there."

"So I might as well commit two, huh? Or a hundred?"

I spun around, marched two steps away, stopped and looked back. "I didn't commit a sin. I hadn't even thought about sex."

She smiled. "Clifford, our Lord knows what's in your mind."

"I've got to clean up," I said.

Hustling to the stairs I heard, "You can't wash away your sins."

That woman! I couldn't argue with her.

Worse consequences followed. While I was in the shower, Eden arrived. Keeping their voices lower than I could hear, the women allowed me, barefoot, in pajamas, to stumble back downstairs, enter the kitchen, and by God there she was, eating and talking with my wonderful aunt.

Like an automaton, I said hi, thanks for coming over.

Eden asked, "So your mother's no worse?"

My nightclothes told her that I had gone directly to shower, not to tend Mom, but her tone—was it sarcastic? I shook my head no, but wondered, What the hell had Aunt Judy told her? I grabbed a plate, heaped on pasta from pots on the stove, and worried, What would this meeting lead to?

Both women watched me sit down between them—hell, the round table offered no alternative place. I said, "Pass the Parmesan, please."

"It's right there beside you, Clifford," Aunt Judy said.

I shook the container so hard, it created a blizzard, snowing cheese over the tepid red pile on my plate.

"We eat together after all," Eden said. Without sarcasm?

I made a smile. "Yeah, your invitation beat one from me to eat here so this food was ready for us."

"What was wrong with your mother? What happened?"

I said, "Didn't you ask the good nun?"

Aunt Judy frowned and stood. "I'll leave you two alone and go check on Ruth. Want bread? There's some in the oven."

"Yes, please," Eden said.

"Thank you, Sister," I said, and gave her a mocking smile that prodded her more quickly from the room.

Eden and I buttered our garlic bread, wound spaghetti around our forks, and ate. After a few minutes, I remembered wine and poured us each a glass of rosé.

"This meal's better than you'd get at my house," Eden said. "Your aunt's a great cook."

"Hah! She can barely boil water."

"You made this?"

I nodded. "I bought the sauce, but precooked and froze the meatballs so that all she had to do was thaw them out in the microwave, dump them into the sauce, heat the mixture, and boil the pasta in water. For once she didn't overcook or burn anything. So we lucked out tonight. Oh, there's tossed salad."

I took the large, sealed bowl from the refrigerator, laid it with tongs on the table, then two small bowls and two kinds of dressing. We were soon gnawing like rabbits.

After a few minutes, with a raised forkful of lettuce, Eden asked, "What's the secret about your mother?"

"No secret. Mom's her usual self."

"What did your aunt think was wrong with her?"

I shrugged, shook my head, gulped wine, and changed the subject. "I liked that Mexican beer. Bring any with you?"

"I thought there was a crisis here, Cliff."

Clearly, there was anger now, along with wrinkled forehead and glittering eyes. "Look, I'm not trying to hide anything."

"Don't I deserve an explanation?"

"Christ!" I took a deep breath, then said quickly, "Aunt Judy just said something that shocked me."

"What?"

"It doesn't matter."

"Then say it."

"All right, goddam it. Aunt Judy said, and I quote, 'Use protection.' And she said it more than once."

"What? Use protection?"

She looked at me until I nodded, hoping that ended her interest in the subject. It didn't.

"That's all?"

I shrugged but thought, Shit! Here we go.

Eden insisted, "Meaning?"

I muttered, "Protection. You know, prophylactics."

Her mouth moved from stern, to amused, back to stern. "You told me your mother was dying."

"She is. She could die at any moment."

"You acted like there was something seriously wrong."

"Well, there was. The Catholic Church opposes the use of birth control devices."

Eden stared at me, waited, then said, "So what?"

"She's a member of the clergy, yet there she was, recommending birth control."

"And that upset you so much, you had to rush home."

"Well, no."

She laid the fork down in her salad bowl and clenched her right hand. The fist thumped down on the table by her plate. "I still don't understand."

Blood infused my cheeks as hadn't happened in years. Even my bald spot felt hot. I looked away and thought, Jesus! The shit was hitting the goddam fan.

She said, "Let me get this straight, Cliff. Your old auntie thought that I was seducing you."

I looked at her. "No, no, not at all."

"Then you thought it."

"No!" I shook my head. "No, I did not think that."

"What did you think?"

"This is so dumb," I said, and laughed.

She didn't laugh in response.

Only I could get myself into such a really stupid situation.

She said, "Will you explain, please?"

"I don't know if I can. I mean after what Aunt Judy said, I think I saw things from her point of view."

"By things you mean me."

"No, I mean you and me and the situation in general, and I guess I concluded that, well, sex was in the air."

Her lips tightened into one bloodless, straight line.

I said, "I mean you were in a robe, drinking beer, standing close, being friendly. It seemed obvious. I'm sorry. I know it's embarrassing, but there it is."

"It's not embarrassing," she said. "It's crazy. Could I have a conversation like this with anyone else?"

"That's just what I was thinking."

"So you sensed sexual tension between us and were repulsed."

"No. I want to get to know you. Okay?" She stared at me. "I'm attracted to you, Eden. Always have been, even out on the bike trail by Sammy when we met."

Another pregnant pause until she said, "You'd have stayed home with me if that were true."

I shook my head, not wanting to go on.

Her eyes narrowed and her left hand also became a fist.

"Don't get angry," I said.

"The idea of having sex with me turned you off."

"No, no, no." I reached across the table and patted a fist.

Her eyes glistened as if she might cry. Or explode.

I jumped around the table, squatted down beside her, gazed at a familiar little ear, and patted a fist.

She wouldn't look at me.

"Eden, I could hardly stop myself from grabbing you."

"Then why leave? Why?" Her voice was a whisper.

I said, "In a way I was afraid you wanted to have sex."

She turned toward me enough to expose one eye. "Afraid?"

"Not of sex per se."

"Who said it was going to happen?"

"No one. You're right. Maybe I was just afraid I would take advantage of the situation and you. As usual, I was confused. I wanted sex, but knew it wasn't right."

"Because of your Catholic beliefs?" With her face turned toward me, this arrived on a puff of garlic-scented breath.

"I didn't want to abuse you for my selfish pleasure. Okay?"

My right arm dropped off the chair, I touched a shoulder, she leaned toward me, and maybe we both made the move.

For sure, I kissed her.

And she kissed back. My feelings intensified, blocking out all else. Our tongues touched, then explored each other's mouth. We grappled, twisting so our chests came together. Then we were full length against each other, lying down. I was stroking her back, and we were lost in our kissing.

"Whoops! I'm sorry!"

Our lips parted, and I looked up with one eye through a haze of Eden's hair at Aunt Judy, who was looking down at us from the living room archway. Eden and I were lying on the floor between the stove and the automatic dishwasher.

Aunt Judy said, "I'm sorry. I heard the chair go over and thought—" Then she turned around and left.

Eden and I stood. I righted her chair, waited until she sat, slid her to the table, then sat across from her. We took a bite, looked at each other, giggled, and soon were laughing so hard, the table shook. We tried to muffle our sound from Aunt Judy, but that only made it louder.

For me, the rest of our evening was a romantic blur of pleasant sense impressions: my feet like puppies under the table snuffling at Eden's feet and ankles and shins. The clodhoppers I put on my bare feet and the winter coat I put on over my pajamas would normally have chafed my skin, but their hard touch was comforting. Eden's palm in my hand while we walked around the neighborhood ran such heat through me, the crisp night air on my cheeks seemed warm.

After Eden went home, I went to bed and imagined our

evening together, the wonderful onset of tender affection, our hour outside walking and talking. The actual details of what she said did not reengage me because I'd been concentrating on her closeness, not her words. Her voice had been enough then, and now it slowly lulled me toward sleep.

Ready to drop off entirely, I heard a dog bark. Insistently and excitedly. In the distance. But there'd been no dogs in my experiences with Eden so the barking seemed odd.

My awareness sharpened, and I listened with purpose. The dog was the mutt next door. Many times when I was in the yard, she'd put her front paws on the sill at the back-room window and bark through the panes at me.

Was someone out there now?

I jumped out of bed, ran through the computer room to its outside door, and looked down through its window. The angle was too steep to see anything along the wall or the steps going down the side of our house. However, a street light out front was throwing illumination between the houses.

I ran to the computer, leaned over the printer to the window behind, and with my head against a pane on the right, looked down left into our backyard. Long shadows moved in the light from the street lamp. Someone or something was down there.

What the fuck?!

The shadows jerked and swept around so I couldn't tell how many things or people there were. Was it a wind-blown bag? No, there was no wind. It was something alive. A person or people.

I remembered my house at the farm, the explosion, the fire, and I shook as if I were freezing, struck by fear of what damage could occur, and who could be harmed.

The fear became desperation. I ran to my bedroom closet and searched the shelf beneath and between stacks of shoe boxes full of receipts and canceled checks.

I found the shotgun flat against the wall and pulled it loose, raking everything that lay between it and me off the shelf. Boxes fell, their contents erupting.

I ignored the mess, pumped the mechanism back toward the trigger and fingered the chamber, but I'd known the gun was empty. Shells? There was a box in the linen closet on the ground floor.

I ran noisily downstairs, turned into the hallway, quietly opened the closet door, stood on tiptoes, reached carefully over toiletries stored on the highest shelf, touched the box back in the right corner, and lifted it out.

The box rattled softly, its contents rolling. It wasn't full, but there were some shells. Going farther down the hall into the bathroom, I opened the box, took them out, dropped the box, and stopped at the medicine cabinet's small night-light. In its glow I slipped one shell into the chamber, closed the pump handle, and pushed the other three shells into the loading tube beneath the barrel.

I held the gun up close to the light and made sure the safety lever on top of the grip pointed at the white dot marking on; a red dot marked off. Dad's old .12 gauge Mossberg! I felt strong and powerful, almost invincible with it.

I hurried down the hall, crept across the living room to the front door, stepped into the clodhoppers by the hall tree, put on a coat, unlocked the front door, opened it fully, and studied front yard and street as far left and right as I could see through the storm door. No movement out there.

I opened the storm door quickly, knowing it would squeak, closed it so it wouldn't slam, dropped down off the little porch to the right behind some bushes, and pushed past them as quietly as possible to the corner. I bellied up against the house beyond the last bush, and looked toward the backyard.

Lights were on now in the house next door, including in the

room where the dog had been. Somebody was running away around Mom's garage. Feet were thudding and kicking gravel.

I held the shotgun in both hands in front of me and chased him, but with my laces untied, I made poor time. When I reached the alley, nobody was in sight. I held my breath and listened, but heard no more footsteps.

I circled the garage and found both of its doors locked and the windows undisturbed.

The dog began barking again, louder. She was outside, and I saw her break through the hedge between properties. Her barking changed to snarls, rushing up to me.

I told her, "Lady, it's me! It's me, girl. It's all right."

When she could smell me, her tail wagged and she nosed my legs while I patted her head. She was an old Irish setter.

Somebody whistled shrilly at the neighbor's house, and she turned and ran back. I followed her to the waist-high pyrocantha bushes, and called toward the house, "That you, Ernie?"

The porch light came on in back. "Yeah! What's out there, Cliff, a raccoon?"

"A prowler, but I guess you didn't see him."

"A prowler! Want me to call the police?"

"Yes. Thanks. Ask 'em to come here. Meantime I'll look around and check the house."

I didn't have to go far before I smelled it: gasoline! The aroma was concentrated in the close space between Mom's house and Ernie's. I'd rushed through it obliviously, running to the garage. Now the odor gagged me, and the street light revealed something else I'd missed: an irregular dark line as high as ten feet along Mom's white wood siding, the top edge of where the flammable liquid had been thrown.

Chapter Twenty-One

City firemen hosed down the house, rinsing off the gasoline. It had been splashed on three walls. There were no signs of explosives being planted, but the bastards might have been chased off before getting to that. Officer Nelloms of the Bethel PD, summoned by Ernie Hathaway's 911 call, found no gas containers, and no neighbors who'd seen anyone suspicious nearby.

Dawn was oozing blood-like in the eastern sky when Eden prepared to leave, promising to check out the Crofts as soon as she met Shepherd.

I told her, "It's getting worse. Things are spinning out of control."

Through the living room window I watched Eden and Nelloms drive away, and Aunt Judy hike off to church on the sidewalk.

My relative's forceful strides were remarkable, masking the presence of artificial bones and old age. Modern science and Aunt Judy's extraordinary attitude had miraculously restored her physical abilities. Yet, with indifference, someone would have killed her last night—my helpless mother as well—to get me.

The twins? I'd bet on it!

I went in and checked on Mom, came back, kicked my boots off, lay down on the couch, closed my eyes, and conked out.

Being able to sleep so easily after such an experience may

seem odd, but I think events were taking a toll. Ever since my father's death, I'm never far from depression, having learned that a tragedy can happen naturally at any time. Having learned that our normal assumption of safety is necessary for daily functioning, but certainly not protection from catastrophes that can and do periodically happen. This new attack on me had resulted in energy-draining shifts among dismay, fear, anger, and sadness. That, plus a night without sleep, overcame me and permitted escape.

When I slowly, reluctantly woke up, rolling my head sideways, I glimpsed the clock on the wall: 10:00 a.m. I'd been asleep for over three hours.

I hurried outside, found the gasoline smell was hardly noticeable now, and went back inside to discuss the situation with an older, wiser head, Aunt Judy's.

She wasn't in the kitchen, the living room, Mom's room, her bedroom. I ran upstairs but she wasn't there. She wasn't in the goddam house, and I hadn't seen her outside either.

Could she have returned and left again?

Her missal was not on the coffee table, kitchen table, nor anywhere else. Her shawl was not on the hall tree, not in her bedroom. In the kitchen were no breakfast dishes dirty or recently washed in the rack. In Mom's room, the IV bag was empty.

Ergo, Aunt Judy had not been home since leaving for mass.

But she would never separate herself from Mom for hours without making arrangements with me. Definitely, something was wrong.

This idea knocked me back against a dresser. What should be done? I looked down at Mom. She was probably wet and dirty, and couldn't be left long in that shape because of the danger of infection, but I couldn't clean and change her now. First, I had to find out what had happened to Aunt Judy.

I looked up the church in the phone book, called the rectory, identified myself, questioned Father Gustav Gable, and he answered that Sister had not been to mass. In fact he had wondered if there was a problem with my mother. He'd been aware of my mother's condition for some time, you know. Hell, did he think I'd forgotten he'd given her the last rites six months ago?

I told him it was nothing like that, and he assured me mass had been attended by only Rose Emerald and Jasper Kuntz, two people I'd known since my childhood.

I thanked the priest, hung up, and leafed through the telephone directory for the mass attendees' numbers.

Mr. Kuntz didn't answer, and I remembered that he was nearly deaf and probably had a hard time hearing the phone.

Rose Emerald answered, insisted on pleasantries, then said no, she had not seen Sister. She had waited at the church door for her as usual, and when mass started, she had even gone out to the sidewalk and looked down the street for her.

I thanked her and raced outside, across the front lawn and up the street. Two alternatives were left. Aunt Judy was physically incapacitated or she'd been snatched—what else could keep her from coming back to Mom? Realistically, I doubted if Aunt Judy's health had been the problem, but that had to be verified.

Three and a half blocks from Mom's house, beyond where Aunt Judy would have turned off our street onto the church's street, I began knocking on doors. I raced up one side, tried two houses up the next block within sight of the church, then went door to door down the other side.

I told the five women I rousted that there was an emergency, that my aunt, a nun in a dark habit, was missing, and I asked if they had seen her or anything unusual like an ambulance or someone picking her up in any vehicle, which would be odd too because just before leaving home she'd turned down a ride with the police.

No one had seen a nun, and three of them knew Sister Merced. No one had seen an ambulance, and the only sirens heard had been much earlier when a fire truck and police car had passed, both of which one person had seen.

I ran back home, called the sheriff's office, identified myself, and asked for Detective Grimes.

She of course wasn't in, nor was Shepherd. I explained the emergency and its connection to the two officers. The dispatcher promised to contact them, and said the department had received no emergency calls at the time I'd mentioned.

"If it's not a medical emergency, then it's a kidnapping!" I said. "My aunt has been abducted."

"A deputy will be there shortly, sir. Remain calm."

Calm? With three hours' absence, Aunt Judy could be anyplace, in any kind of condition.

I called the Bethel Police Department and asked for Officer Nelloms, but he was off duty. I explained his involvement with me last night and my new problem. This office, the dispatcher said, monitored emergency calls, but there had been no radio communications for an ambulance that morning in the city. There had been no reports of anything amiss between 6:00 and 7:00 a.m.

"Then my aunt was kidnapped," I said, "and I think there has to be publicity to find anyone who might have seen something. Most people up at 6:45 are at work by now. Or maybe in school. Maybe a kid delivering the morning paper saw something."

My metabolism raced, a nervous condition controllable only with action. I wished I could go out physically and look for Aunt Judy myself, but no. Couldn't do that.

So what could I do? I called the county hospital, was put

through to the Emergency Room, and asked if a nun had received treatment that morning. Or any woman in her 80s. My aunt was missing and I was trying to find her. She might have collapsed on Bethel's south side about 6:45. When the receptionist hesitated, I pleaded with her just to confirm or deny the existence of anyone there resembling whom I'd described, and she said no such person had been admitted.

That was all I could think of to do for Aunt Judy. But other things had to be done. Something had to be done about the villains in this affair. And Mom, what about her?

I called Ed and left a message about the situation on his machine—he was probably outside in his studio, away from his phone. I called Home Care Inc. and requested help with my mother to include cleaning her, changing her clothes and linen, and handling the IV. The person on the phone looked through records, found a file on Mom, and asked if Doctor Zachary was still Mrs. Saunders's primary care physician. That confirmed, she asked if I wanted to go back on the schedule of two years ago. I told her perhaps, but I needed someone now, today, because my mother was comatose and her caregiver was gone. She promised by early afternoon, maybe by 2:00, to have help there, along with a nurse who would ascertain the state of the patient and set up procedures.

"Great! Thanks!"

What next? Okay, I could also prepare to confront the bastards who'd grabbed Aunt Judy, and I knew who they were.

But not where they were. I found listings in the phone book for George and M. K., first name and initials unrelated to my Crofts. No help there.

I thought of another way to get their addresses, hurried outside, into the garage, into Mom's car, which hadn't been driven in three weeks, and was relieved to find the battery strong. The motor cranked over a few times, sputtered, and started. I revved the engine, let it idle, checked the gas gauge—full—ran the motor a bit longer, shut it off, unlocked the door to the alley, raised it a few inches to be sure it wasn't binding, pushed it back down to the floor, left it unlocked and returned to the house.

There were no messages on the answering machine so no one had called. Okay, all set. Now to Mom.

In her room I rolled the portable table over by the bed, filled the plastic basin with water in the bathroom, grabbed a bar of antiseptic soap, wash rag and towel, took them all back and laid them on top of the table.

"Hi Mom. Time to clean you up."

I pulled down the blue wool cover and white sheet, carefully began to disrobe her, and was again shocked, lifting, turning her over, that she was as light as a goddam leaf, skin over bones, 90 pounds at most. She had her entire adult life weighed 140 pounds until her body began compressing into a tiny ball.

On her back near the shoulder and on her left hip were blue splotches streaked with yellow. Extra-tender spots. To avoid open bed sores, I would have to ask the nurse's aide to change Mom's position hourly.

The front-door knocker pounded, filling the living room with its metallic rat-a-tat-tat.

I covered Mom with the sheet and hurried there. It was Officer Nelloms. I let him in, shook his hand and thanked him for coming. Hell, I realized, he was a freckle-faced kid like Jones.

"I thought you were off duty," I said.

"They called me and I was still in uniform so when I heard about your aunt, well—"

"She didn't make it to church—I checked. She should've been back here by 7:30 at the latest. The church is just five blocks away. You saw her leave when you and Grimes left."

"Could she be lost?"

"No." I explained Aunt Judy's habits and my attempts to find her. "She was in good health so I doubt if she had mental or physical problems. I'm afraid somebody grabbed her—as weird as that sounds."

"Did you inform the sheriff's office?"

I nodded. "Nobody from there has come yet."

"Maybe your aunt went uptown or to someone's house."

"She'd never leave my mother for more than an hour. See for yourself."

I took him back to Mom's room and pointed out that the IV bag was empty and Mom was dirty. "Aunt Judy would never allow things in here to get so bad. This is her sister, and my aunt's a registered nurse."

"I'll call in and get people looking for her."

"Judith Merced is her name. She's eighty-three years old and has two artificial hips."

"Okay."

When he left, I concentrated on washing and drying Mom, a job intricate enough to demand close attention. The job was nearly finished when Nelloms returned.

I said, "Look, I have to keep on with Mom."

"Go ahead. Here's what's happening. Four patrolmen will hunt for your aunt, two in the neighborhood around St. Francis. We'll also put out a media request for assistance locating her so there's a good chance she'll turn up."

"I appreciate it."

"Call in if you hear anything, okay? I'll get back to you if anything develops with us."

As he left, I worried about what those developments might be, but continuing Mom's clean-up allowed me to avoid thinking about the possibilities.

I heard the front door open, then voices out in the living room. It was Eden. She and Nelloms spoke for a minute. Then the front door closed and Eden called out to me.

I yelled for her to come on back, and she arrived saying, "I'm so sorry about your aunt."

"Can you believe it?" I raised up from the large plastic trash bag, and one look at Eden brought the first tears of this crisis. I wiped them away with a forearm.

She came over and squeezed my left elbow.

"Careful. Dirty," I said, holding my gloved hands up, away from her. "It's incredible. They took Aunt Judy, who never did anything but good in her life. It never occurred to me they'd go after her. I mean I knew she could have been hurt if they'd bombed this house or set it on fire, but I never—"

"They may call you and offer a deal."

"Like pay a ransom to get her back?"

She nodded.

I shook my head. "I've got nothing to give them for her."

"Cliff, you don't know that for sure."

"Right now I've got to finish Mom before she chills."

"Okay."

She stood at the foot of the bed, explaining to me what was being done, police bulletins and so forth, while I applied Keri lotion, spreading it over Mom's body with my bare hands. On her feet and hands I used baby oil.

"Her feet and hands get rough and hard," I told Eden. "Sometimes we use Vitamin E lotion. I'm almost done."

I slowly worked the gown back onto Mom, rolled her onto her left side, pulled out the towel and the piece of plastic beneath her, covered her up with the sheet and the blanket, then replaced the empty IV bag with a full bag, hung it on the stand, connected it to the tube, and made sure its flow was open.

"Mom's only nourishment. That shunt in Mom has to be changed or cleaned or something. Maybe the rate of the dripping needs to be changed. Can't do any of that myself, but a nurse is coming soon. Let's go on out to the living room."

Eden led me from the bedroom, saying, "We'll get your aunt back."

"Did I tell you she has two artificial hips and walks as fast as I do?"

"We'll find her, Cliff. You got to have hope."

I rejected Eden's ransom idea, and tried another: that the kidnappers wanted Aunt Judy for information. But what could she know that they wanted? Whatever their reasons, wouldn't they dispose of Aunt Judy the way I threw out dirty diapers? They couldn't care less about her life. They'd shown that last night.

Eden probably thought the same thing, but she was playing her official and her nurturing-friend roles. She hadn't mentioned checking anywhere for Aunt Judy's body, but surely the police were doing that. I didn't ask, but I said, "I can't stand the thought of Aunt Judy suffering."

Eden hugged me until I asked, "Are you going to question the Crofts about her disappearance?"

"We'll check them out thoroughly. Believe me."

"The twins?"

"Them first."

"What'd they say about the gasoline dumped on the house?"

"They alibied each other. Said they'd been home all night."

"You mean they live together?"

"Yes."

"Okay, that means their alibi is worthless. When did you see them?"

"About 8:15."

"That's a long time after the gas was put on the house. It gives them plenty of time to kidnap Aunt Judy and get back to wherever you saw them."

"We may catch them both still home, and this time we'll search their cars too. We're already questioning their neighbors to see if the twins went out late last night. I'll pick up Shepherd and we'll go right there."

"Where's he?"

"At the station. I wanted to see you alone."

"I'm glad you did."

"We'll straighten this out, Cliff. Don't worry."

She kissed me. I thanked her, walked her to the door but not out to her cruiser. I had to hurry to do what had to be done.

I wrote a note telling the Home Aid people to go in if I wasn't home, taped the note to the storm door in front, took the loaded shotgun from the back closet, ran outside to my car, took the binoculars out of the trunk, ran around the garage, opened the door on the alley, threw all the stuff in Mom's trunk, started the car, and raced away.

Eden had never seen this car so it improved chances of her not spotting me.

I had to reach the sheriff's department before Eden and Shepherd left so I could follow them to the twins' home. Then, the first chance I got, if this mess with Aunt Judy didn't clear up, I would know where to find those pampered rich boys. Because they lived together, I might be able to interview, and forcibly extract the truth about their sneaky, vicious activities. With a little luck, from both of them at the same time.

CHAPTER TWENTY-TWO

Ed showed up and endured the brunt of my agitated attention for an hour, until Mom's new help came. I spent an hour with them, signing papers, watching the nurse examine Mom and instruct the aide. Then I went back to Ed—he was in the kitchen, eating of course—and started my frantic act again, complaining, speculating, cursing.

He interrupted me in mid-harangue. "Hey, you have to settle down or you won't be any good to anybody. Am I right?"

"Yeah, but—"

"While you were in with your mom, I called Georgie, Myra and Chuck. They can meet us at the barn, okay?"

"Exercise? Now?"

"It'll distract you and improve your mood."

"I can't leave here."

"What can you do here you can't do out there? We'll leave numbers for a pager and a cell phone that'll be at the barn with us so if somebody calls here, the lady with your mother can pass the numbers on. And you can inform the cops where you'll be."

"I don't want to be around other people."

"Bullshit, the more company the better for you."

"I don't know if the electricity's been reconnected to the barn yet."

"We'll find out."

So that's what we did. Ed arranged for us to meet his friends and went home for his exercise clothes. I dressed, explained to the nurse's aide Monica where I'd be, gave her the numbers on a sheet of paper, called the police and gave them the information, then drove out to the farm by myself.

The electricity was reconnected, and Ed was right. His friends were not only sympathetic, but Georgie and Myra were also formidable in leading aerobic exercise to music, taking us through routines that required concentration and relieved my worries. After more than an hour of that, we shifted into the improvised dancing I usually did, and they had done with me before, and that also occupied my mind.

Amplified percussion—Ed had brought four CDs, insisting drums were primitive and perfect for this occasion—isolated us from noises such as a police car would make, driving up, but we monitored the pager and cell phone, both of which remained dormant. A Buddy Rich song ended, silence hit us like a cold draft of air, Eden yelled my name, and we saw her, standing in the doorway.

The "Paradiddles and Hot Licks" CD banged into another frenetic number and chased me off the dance floor to her.

With the last flare of evening sun behind her, I spoke in an obviously inadequate volume, then bellowed my question just as Ed turned off the player. "DID YOU FIND AUNT JUDY?!"

"We think so," Eden said.

Beside her, I studied those beautiful eyes. They were wide, and she shook her head sadly. "I'm sorry."

I staggered backwards, bumped into the weight bench, sat, slumped forward, braced my elbows on my knees and propped my head up in my hands. There was nothing to say. There were no tears. There was only a numbing reality I could not comprehend.

After some time I looked up, and the four exercisers were on the edge of the dance floor, watching. Eden stood beside me, squeezing the back of my neck.

"You okay?" she asked softly.

"Where is she?"

"In the river south of Bethel."

"Will you take me?"

"No need for you to go there. Let them bring her in."

"I want to see her and the place where it happened. Okay?"

When she nodded, I said to all of them, "Excuse me," turned my back, and stripped off my sopping tee shirt and shorts—the hell with modesty. Eden walked over to the others and they talked. Nude except for socks, I toweled off, slipped on undershorts, tee shirt, long nylon jogging pants, sweater with a hood, wind breaker, jogging shoes, and wristwatch: 6:14 it said. We had been exercising for two hours.

I asked Ed to turn off the lights and secure both doors with the new locks I'd left open, hanging on the latches.

"I'll go with you," he said.

"Thanks, but it wouldn't help. You all can keep exercising."

"Whatever you need."

I nodded, thinking that in circumstances such as these, we all were helpless.

I left with Eden, climbed into her cruiser, which was parked behind my car, and she backed up past the black remains of my home and the other two cars. When there was room, she went forward, turned, and started down the lane, saying, "I haven't been there, but I think this will be hard to take."

Tires threw gravel so it hammered the undercarriage.

I asked, "What've you heard?"

"The body was found by canoeists."

"Is it Aunt Judy for sure?"

"The description fit. An elderly white woman."

"Where?"

"Near Spring Valley Preserve. By a public boat ramp."

I imagined the spot. "Christ, that's a long way from Mom's house. A long way from a morning walk to church."

"You know the place?"

"Been there many times to jog. The bike trail's nearby."

Eden turned south on Pekin Road.

I said, "I hope she didn't suffer much."

We rode into town silently with dusk and speed distorting the outside so familiar sights pressed in around us like threats. I was sapped, unable to appreciate things like the beautiful day just ending, with temperatures reaching the mid-60s and a soft breeze sweeping the barn clear of smoky smells and chill. Hell, the pleasantry cloaked death and horror.

Near town center I told Eden to turn off Route 86 onto 24 at their upcoming junction. "It's a straight eight miles from there."

She hit the siren, bolted through the main intersection, shut off the siren, and sped on faster than speed limits allowed. The emergency lights across the roof flared off walls and windows in the business district, and I realized those lights had been flashing across the hood ever since we left the farm.

I sank into a stupor that I emerged from only when Eden read a road sign out loud, "Spring Valley State Preserve, 1 Mile."

"That's it," I said.

We turned east on a county road, crossed a bridge over the river, and pulled into the small, paved lot on our right, passing a state highway patrol car at the entrance. We parked behind two other Shawnee County Sheriff's Department cruisers and a white van. I couldn't see any people.

"They must be over there," Eden said, pointing to lights glimmering through the underbrush ahead, but some distance away. "You sure you want to do this?"

"I don't want to, BUT—"

To our right the concrete ramp was a huge pale tongue, coated brown with silt, lapping the water. A rusty, green Chevrolet was parked in a lined space opposite the ramp to our left. An aluminum canoe lay on racks upside down across its roof, a single white rope at bow and at stern tied to the bumpers.

The air was thick with river and rot, an aroma that stimulated memories of previous visits. I'd leave my car here and jog on the road a hundred yards east to the bike trail. South, the trail went through swampy spots alive with critters, including in hot weather rare Massasauga rattlesnakes. Farther south were huge corn and wheat fields but no tree cover, making the bike trail very uninviting under a summer sun.

Floods had left ragged bunches of debris in the brush and on sycamore limbs as high as eight feet above our heads. Over the years, immediately after floods, I'd seen washing machines, dryers, stoves, even houses disgorged by the river. All the undergrowth was permanently bent by the current toward the south.

The lights were off in the other vehicles. Eden left our headlights on, but even so we had a hard time finding the narrow trail. Once noticed, it led us through dense flora along the bank four feet above the water.

Eden's flashlight lit the path, but behind her I stumbled over roots, broken limbs, plastic bags, Styrofoam containers, hunks of tar roofing shingles. Twigs and whippy limbs lashed us.

After several minutes of that, Eden stopped.

Coming up beside her, rubbing the backs of my hands, which stung from the whipping, I said, "Bad place for deer ticks."

She didn't answer, looking down at something that made me forget about Lyme disease or anything else.

Four men were down at the water's edge in a small pebble-strewn alcove up against the bank, all in knee-high black rubber boots, surrounding something that was long and fat and bluish white. I could tell that it once had been something alive, but human? Couldn't be, not the way the flesh spread out in totally flaccid, relaxed submission. That had to be animal. Butchered hogs looked like that, with bellies flapped out away from the backbone and ribs, like spilled milk spreading out over a dark tablecloth. That had to be what it was, a swine that had died somewhere upstream and washed up here.

Eden's flashlight or a noise we made must have clued the men that we were present. They looked up at us. One man was Shepherd. The other man not in uniform was older. He carried a black satchel and was bent over the body. The faces of the two men in uniform were hidden by their hats.

"Stay there," the older man said. "No room down here."

Then the uniformed men shuffled sideways, letting us see a human head, partially covered with short white hair, but its facial features were blurred among swellings and indentations of nose, ears, eyes, and mouth, which gaped, catching light oddly.

"It's not her," I said. "That's not Aunt Judy."

Elation filled me. Relief. I stepped over the bank, and though Eden clutched my left arm, she couldn't stop my momentum so I plunged down to the river's edge.

"Stop him!" shouted the older man.

Both uniformed men caught me so I didn't fall on the body. Behind me, Eden said something, but my attention was on the corpse, seeking proof that it was not Aunt Judy.

It was a woman all right. Up close I could see her sex, dark blood lines in her legs and breasts, large discolorations of the skin beneath the stringy, thin hair pasted on the scalp, a mole beside the nose—like the mole beside Aunt Judy's nose.

I stared at the hip by my shoes. Something there? Yes, a mark I squatted to see more clearly. It was a ridge of once-broken skin. A long incision, healed.

"Know her?" asked the man across the body from me.

I looked at him, then at the woman's face, and all of her features became familiar and separate, the brown eyes, the nose, the lips, the moles. The mouth had fooled me the most. Lack of teeth had distorted it, collapsing lips and cheeks as I'd never seen before. Decades of close association, and I hadn't realized she had false teeth.

That secret was out now, I thought, and so were others. I'd never seen much of her hair before, and now there it was, crudely cropped short and balding. Plus she was nude, sprawled out for all to see. Much heavier, flabbier than I'd thought.

My eyes labored, moving once more from her head to her feet.

"Recognize her?" the man asked.

I looked at him and heard myself moan, "Aunt Judy."

I stood, looked up into the limbs tangled against the sky, made fists, tightened all of my muscles and screamed, "FUU-UUUUUUUUUUCK!", wringing out the word until every molecule of air in my lungs was expelled and the cry echoed back.

What happened in the next half hour was largely lost to me, but a few things lodged in my mind.

"Get him out of here," somebody said. Hands pulled and pushed at me, but the muddy bank was chest high and sheer. Twice I slipped and fell hands-first against it.

I told them, "Let go," and when they released me, walked out into the river and waded knee-deep upstream. Somebody held an arm and helped me stay upright. At the boat ramp Eden grabbed my hands, pulled me up and out, then led me to her cruiser.

I came out of my daze when Eden parked in front of Mom's house. The living room light was on. I looked at my watch: 7:29.

"Can you take me to my car?" I asked.

"Tomorrow. I'll take you out there for it then."

"I'd rather now. So it's handy in case I need it. I have the time. The Home Care person will be with Mom until 8:00. But

191

if you don't want to—"

"No, it's all right."

She took me to the farm and dropped me off. The place was deserted. The night light on the barn had come on automatically, so that was still working. The rubble of the house was a black heap that absorbed all light falling in that direction, as if it were a huge, deep pit. I could see the barn door was latched and locked. I would trust that Ed had also locked the other door.

I climbed into my car, sat down, then realized it had been left unlocked. Damn! I felt on the floor for the shotgun I had transferred into this car from Mom's trunk. Not there. Oh shit!

It wasn't on the passenger seat. I turned on the dome light, twisted around and looked at the backseat. Not there. I knelt on my seat, bent over its back rest, and felt around on the floor behind it. Nothing.

I turned around, sat, and looked out through the windshield at the darkness. Goddam! Somebody had stolen the gun.

My car door opened and Eden said, "The shotgun's in my trunk."

"You took it?"

"Yes, I unloaded it too. I should have taken it with me this morning."

"You might've said something!"

She smiled. "You'll hear about it all right. Later."

"You're something else." She'd stifled her comments and was still stifling them—for my sake. I touched the back of her calf, patted a taut tendon, and kissed the air in her direction.

She bent, kissed my lips, raised up and said, "Ready now? I'll follow you back into town."

CHAPTER TWENTY-THREE

The nurse's aide left Mom clean, and she had even changed the bed linen. Some people were so good, they inspired me. Others did such evil, they lured me into hating.

I drank two beers, pacing through the house, stopped in Aunt Judy's room, pulled a large black leather suitcase from her closet, and heaved it up onto her bed. The damn thing felt eighty pounds empty. Her name was engraved on a metal plate attached to the handle. I unsnapped the locks and laid the lid back.

Six outfits of varying degrees of darkness hung on hangers in the closet. I looked through her bureau. She'd used only two drawers. A few other possessions lay on top, and a few more were in the bathroom and living room. That was it. A vow of poverty had meant something to Aunt Judy.

I stared at the gaping jaws of the suitcase, then at the habits hanging like old memories in the closet. Somebody would have to dress Aunt Judy in this stuff. Me? That would be fun.

I'd pack her possessions another day. The hell with it now.

I walked to the kitchen wondering what kind of people would destroy Aunt Judy. Sons of bitches!

I was half done with a third beer by the time I was upstairs, lowering a shoe box from its attic storage space above my bedroom. The box yielded a German Luger and a carton of 7.65 mm bullets. I stuffed the magazine with eight rounds. Took the pistol from its cracked leather holster, inserted the magazine in the gun's handle with the chamber closed and empty, wrapped the still-oily weapon in a handkerchief, and put the gun in a pocket of my heavy coat downstairs.

Between the front door and the hall tree holding the coat, I swore that, by God, I would end this crap myself. My mind traveled through town on the northeastern route Eden and Shepherd had taken from the station to the twins' new half-million-dollar home, and I watched myself push the button, ring a gong, and bring the pretty boys to the door. I imagined shoving the Luger into the mouth of one twin, kicking the other in the groin, forcing both to strip completely as they had stripped Aunt Judy.

I imagined making the bastards lie on the floor, demanding a confession, jabbing their heads with the muzzle of the gun. The desire to hurt them made me ache. Right now would be a good time. Mom was set for the night. It was dark and I could go there, do it and get back unseen in less than an hour.

With closed eyes and tightened muscles, I literally shook. "Not healthy thinking," I warned myself. "Not healthy."

Through the window in the door I stared at the empty street, finished the beer, walked into the kitchen for another, got it, sat down at the table and tried to think of all the things that had to be done. An image of the twins returned, however, and with them came the anger again.

The knocker on the front door rapped. I stomped to the door and jerked it open as if to rip it off the hinges.

Eden stepped in, hugged me, and asked how I was.

"In the twilight zone." I patted her shoulders, and smelled something sweet in her hair.

She pulled away and saw the bottle in my hand. "Have you eaten anything?"

"No."

"Come on."

I meekly followed her into the kitchen.

She pointed at the three empty beer bottles on the table, shook her head, but said nothing. I threw them into the garbage.

She asked, "What's to eat around here?"

I opened the refrigerator, took out three Tupperware containers, and set them on the counter. "Aunt Judy cleaned our dishes and put the leftovers away when we walked outside last night."

Eden opened the containers. "There's enough for both of us. Mind if I join you?"

"I'll be mad if you don't."

I sat down at the table, swilled a little more beer, and noticed her watching me. "What?"

"You are out of it. Pans? Plates? Et cetera."

"Oh, yeah." I got up and gathered and helped.

Ten minutes later we were eating.

Eden said, "Just like last night."

"Not quite." I stared across the table at her. "Why'd they take Aunt Judy and why kill her? Monica said no one called here while I was at the barn so they didn't try to contact me."

Eden shook her head and said the coroner's autopsy would soon establish the cause of death, probably tomorrow. No clues about the killer had surfaced at the river access area, but it would be searched again in the daylight. The body had probably entered the river near the boat ramp. The canoeists had found it snagged on submerged tree roots. "The body didn't drift far. That water's shallow and the current's slow."

"What about the Crofts?"

She sighed. "They alibi each other again, and other sources can't corroborate or contradict what they say."

"That's suspicious in itself."

"Not at the hours when the crimes occurred."

"What about their cars?"

"The twins let us search them. Nothing there either."

"That's why they let you."

"We haven't the first direct link between them and any of the events in question."

"They're clever."

"Or innocent." She frowned at me over a forkful of pasta. "We'll figure this out, Cliff. Don't you have other things to worry about?"

"Whether the house will blow up?"

"Funeral arrangements."

"Oh, yeah, that'll have to be done. I suppose the convent will want to bury Aunt Judy up there in Akron, and they'll want the funeral mass there. But she had friends here too. I'll have to see what Father Gable thinks."

As we finished the meal, Ed called, listened to my account of what had happened, then wanted to come over and keep me company. "Thanks, but Eden's here. I'm okay."

"I'll call tomorrow then. Ten o'clock at the latest."

Eden was at the sink, filling it with water.

I nudged her away from the sink with a hip and a shoulder. "Sit down and have some wine or a beer. Unwind a little."

She shoved back, and we threw soft elbows at each other, then hugged.

"I'm sorry, Cliff. I should've been more cautious with your aunt. Should have known the dangers."

"How could you know? Nobody guessed what would happen. Now sit down. I need to keep active so I'll do this by myself."

"I'll dry."

"Forget it. They'll dry in the air just fine."

She sat at the table, poured herself a glass of wine, and said to my back while I worked, "Can I ask you something? Why was the shotgun in the car?"

"For protection," I said, looking at the dark garage through my reflection in the window over the sink. Mom's car was back in there, still hidden from Eden.

"This morning you promised to put the gun away."

I continued washing and rinsing the plates. "Yeah, but having it nearby made me feel secure."

"It's too dangerous, Cliff. You got any other guns?"

Contemplating an answer, I put the plates in the drying rack, scooped up the silverware, and looked around at her.

"Huh?" she asked.

"There's one in the attic. A Smith and Wesson revolver, .32 caliber. My dad had guns when he farmed."

"I should confiscate it too."

I shrugged. "Obviously, I can go get a gun if I want one."

"You're not playing games, are you, Cliff?"

"I'm too tired for games." I laid the silverware on the rack, put the dirty pans in the water, and looked around. She'd finished her wine and was watching me. I said, "Don't let the shotgun upset you."

"I didn't mention the weirdness going on in the barn either. What were you people doing?"

I turned back to the sink. "Just exercising. Ed thought I needed a workout and some company. They're more his friends than mine. All four of them belong to a group that puts on rituals every equinox, solstice, or comet passing by."

"New age nuts."

"Their rituals are fun. I've been to a couple. There's dancing and chanting and roasting hot dogs and marshmallows at bonfires. Anyway, the dancing we did was good exercise."

"You call that dancing?"

"Whatever. It took my mind off things and released tension."

While I drained and rinsed the sink, Eden expressed surprise that I'd been at the barn at all. Anybody else would have stayed home and waited for contact from the kidnappers or police.

"You found me when you needed me. Everyone knew where I'd be." I sat on a chair. "I'd have gone nuts just sitting in here."

We stared at each other.

I dropped a hand over the one of hers on the table. "You don't have to baby-sit me, but thanks for coming."

"You smell like the river. Go take a shower and let's see how you feel. Then I'll leave."

"Damn, I forgot to clean up." I looked myself over: shoes still wet, pant-legs dried stiff. "Okay, make yourself at home and I'll be right back."

I went upstairs, shaved, brushed my teeth, showered, toweled off, combed my hair, put on pajamas and robe, and went back down.

The lights were off in the living room. I turned on the lamp by the stairs.

The heavy drapes were closed over the front window, and Eden lay on the floor, on a sheet with another sheet covering her.

"Sleeping?" I asked softly.

"Waiting for you. I got sheets from the hall closet. Okay?"

"Yeah, fine."

"I could use a massage, and you looked like you knew what you were doing with your mother."

"You want me to rub your back?"

"Please."

Call me naïve. Until I knelt, I didn't realize she had nothing on. Her trousers and blouse were draped on the rocking chair arms. Her knee-length hose, white bra and light blue panties lay on the seat. Her black flats lay on the floor.

I started at her neck, then did her shoulders, kneading the flesh, working my way down her upper arms, and down her back, keeping my fingers on top of the sheet.

"Ah," she moaned several times before I reached her waist,

digging my fingertips and thumbs in so I felt the tissues under her skin moving against the roundness of ribs.

I hesitated at her hips. "Relax. Your muscles are tight."

"Lotion would help. Got any left?"

"Like I used on Mom?"

"Yeah."

I went into Mom's room and picked up the plastic bottle. Mom was on her right side. I set down the bottle, rolled her left so she was more on her back, tucked her in, then took the lotion into the living room and knelt beside Eden.

"I'll have to—" I started to say that I'd have to take off the sheet, but obviously she knew that.

I pulled the sheet down to her hips, stared at the broad expanse of dimpled and smooth skin, then squeezed a thick line of the lotion across her shoulder blades.

"Aaaaah." Muscles twitched, tightening and relaxing.

"Sorry. I'll warm it in my hands from now on."

I fanned my hands and with them spread the goo over her shoulders and back. I worked my hands flat down her spine, pushing in so my thumbs felt the ups and downs of vertebrae. Then I put my thumbs on her shoulders, my fingers around under her armpits, and worked my hands down her sides, lingering along the soft swells of her breasts, proceeding on down to her hip bones. I went over her back again, rubbing in the lotion, making little circles. Then I pulled off the sheet completely and dropped it on the floor.

Her body resembled a statue, a nature goddess: a tawny, freckled landscape of soft undulations and long curves. My breath caught so I gasped, breathing again.

I filled my palms with lotion and covered the cheeks of her ass, rubbing my fingers down along the sides, fingertips just around and beneath the hipbones in front. I dragged my thumbs down the crack of her butt, and her heat touched them.

Applying lotion as needed, both hands kneaded the left leg, rubbing the lotion into the hamstring, the back of her knee, the calf, probing muscles and tendons with my fingertips. I took each foot in both hands, slid my fingers in between the toes, then milked each toe up and down between thumb and fingers. I cupped the arches and squeezed the heels between fingers and thumbs, caressed every callus and fold of skin. Then took more time on the soles, using my thumbs to press into the depressions between the balls of her feet.

I followed her right leg up, coating it with lotion, caressing until I reached the holy vee. My fingers slipped down into the snuggery between her thighs, inched up along contours I couldn't see, touched pubic hair, vagina, anus.

I kissed her neck and grunted, "You are so beautiful."

She rolled around onto her back and kissed me, thrust her tongue into my mouth, sucked mine into hers, and pulled herself up against me with her arms around my neck.

She lay flat again, untied the belt of my robe and pulled the robe off. She unbuttoned my pajama top, pulled it away, touched the hardness jutting out in my pajama bottoms, then reached for the snaps.

I grabbed her hands and said, "Let me look at you."

What loveliness. She raised her right leg, bending the knee, dragging the foot flat across the sheet until the heel stopped against her hip. She lowered the leg, sliding the heel across the sheet again until the toes pointed straight up and both knees rolled slightly away from each other, all movements as gracefully done as ballet.

Dark brown growth sprang from the belly button and trailed downward, thickening and broadening into a hummock at the juncture of her legs. The valleys alongside her stomach gathered up into the broad plateau of her chest, which in turn rose up into twin mounds that bulged toward her sides, the dark areolas slightly off-center in the oblong circles.

I bent and licked, sucked the left, then the right, and semi-hard pebbles formed in my mouth. My right hand traced the path of hair, combed through the thick patch, and my middle finger slid over the ridge and down inside the hot, slick ravine.

Eden groaned, "Ooooh!" as if I'd touched her heart.

I rubbed there with the fingertip.

Her body arched up at the hips, and within seconds she quivered, tugged at my arms and shoulders. "Come to me, Cliff."

"Soon!" I took her right hand, directed it down, and rubbed her clitoris with her own middle finger beneath mine. "Keep ready and I'll be right back."

I released her hand, covered her with the discarded sheet, stood and ran up the stairs, climbing two and three steps at a time, going to my dresser's bottom drawer, feeling in the darkness for the little box I'd left there three years ago. It was far back in a corner. I extracted the contents, ripped the end packet off at the perforations, dropped everything else, and ran back downstairs, unsnapping my pajama bottoms, kicking them off, taking the condom out and frantically rolling it on, bumping from side to side against the stairwell walls.

Eden threw off the sheet and reached for me. The lamplight reflected off thousands of fine hairs on her arms and chest and abdomen. I knelt beside her and ran my hands over the glazed fields, the hollows and hillocks.

"God, such beauty," I said, eyes feeding on her the way a glutton feeds on food.

She said, "Know what? Watching you dance turned me on."

"We'll dance together sometime. Just you and me."

"Now. Just you and me right now." She took my rubber-coated dick in a hand, my testicles in the other, and pulled me to her.

We sang, using words beyond their dictionary definitions, going back to prehistoric origins when feelings and needs first strained music from the human mouth. We loved each other on the floor. Upstairs I knelt on my mattress, anointed the front of her body with lotion, and we loved again.

When we slept, I dreamed of drums, booming, rattling, thumping. Babbling and dribbling and thrumming like rhythms of the heart or the wind.

CHAPTER TWENTY-FOUR

Eden and I woke up to loud knocking on the front door.

I said, "The nurse's aide. It must be 8:00 o'clock."

Eden said, "Damn! I wanted to be out of here by 7:00."

She jumped from bed, hustled downstairs to get her clothes from the living room, went into the bathroom to dress.

Quickly dressed myself, I let in the nurse's aide, Monica again, and she went about her duties in Mom's room.

When Eden emerged from the bathroom, I hugged her and whispered, "Nice waking up beside you this morning."

"Yeah, it was," she said, twisting loose, "but I have to get moving."

"You moved good last night."

She smiled, and rushed out the front door to work.

I smiled all through breakfast, remembering our night together. The memories stirred me as I hadn't been stirred in a long time, and the stirrings felt a lot like love.

This mood let me take care of some sad business without much pain, making phone calls: one to Ed, two to Father Gable at the church, one to Osvald's Funeral Home, two to Aunt Judy's convent, three to the coroner's office where I hung up twice after being left on hold for too long.

The third time the coroner himself answered, and his familiar voice brought me the image of the older man in civilian clothes with Aunt Judy at the river. The autopsy was incomplete, he said, but it'd probably be done by the afternoon. I asked when I could get the body. He was unsure. Maybe tomorrow. When should I call him? Don't call. The Sheriff's Department would inform me when I could claim the body.

"That's not very helpful." I felt too good to be very angry, but said, "I'm trying to make funeral arrangements."

"Best I can do. Sorry." He hung up.

Weren't coroners elected? I fantasized about campaigning to throw the bum out of office.

Then called Ed and described, to his answering machine, the arrangements I'd been making and the damn bureaucrat. "Frustrating, huh?" I concluded with a laugh.

I called Osvald's again, let them know of the problem, and was assured they would take care of transporting the deceased as soon as possible.

All of this phoning took time, and I didn't rush the calls, still flushed remembering the night before. Monica sat on the couch reading a book during most of them, I sat on the rocking chair, and between calls we chatted about life. Then the front door rapper pounded.

Sheriff Orndorf was on the porch, and behind him on the sidewalk were Shepherd, Eden, Burt and the other detective. Eden darted her eyes over me and away.

"Good morning, Sheriff." I crowded out onto the porch with him and breathed deeply. The sun was in a cloudless sky, and the temperature was already near sixty. "God, it feels good out here. Is the autopsy done? The body released?"

"No word on that," Sheriff Orndorf said. "We're here to search these premises."

Hitting me over the head with a club couldn't have stunned me more. I stared at him until my rose-colored lenses dissolved and my position became clear. I was at the bottom of a very familiar, very smelly hole.

"I thought we were long past this."

"No," said Orndorf.

"These two detectives already went through the place."

"Only the house, and they saw what you showed them. That wasn't a search. This investigation has to be thorough."

"You know, I was impressed as hell with how your detectives uncovered the facts. They have been thorough, and they told me their suspicions had shifted away from me."

"Then they spoke prematurely. My review of their data shows we'd be jumping the gun on you not to do this."

"Jesus Christ!"

"I think my investigators may have lost their objectivity, and that affected their judgments."

"What?!"

"In other words I know about you and Lieutenant Grimes."

"You know what?"

"That she stayed with you last night."

"Goddam!" I said, and looked at Eden.

She wouldn't raise her head, but I could see that a cheek just above the jaw line and an ear lobe were red.

Orndorf said, "I myself saw her car parked in front of your house at 6:30 this morning. She admitted she was here."

"Admitted? She saw I was traumatized and offered help. She had already confiscated my shotgun, which she'd found me carrying, loaded, on the front seat of my car yesterday."

Orndorf half turned around. "What's this about a shotgun?"

Eden spoke in a low voice, "He said he had it for protection. It'll be in my report."

I said, "Lieutenant Grimes thought I was suffering and responded like a fellow human being. Understand? As a fellow human being, she helped me get through the night. Heated up some leftovers, made me eat and calmed me down. Stayed at my house to be sure I was okay. Compassion, that's what she had. You used to have it too, Sheriff. What happened?"

Orndorf said, "Law enforcement officers can not get into personal relationships with suspects."

"How about with victims? That's what I am. Officers help victims all the time. That's their job. Let me tell you something. From under this big pile of shit that's been dumped on me, you look like the one who's not objective."

He raised a hand palm up, warning me to stop.

I ignored it. "Your relationship with Simon Croft is interfering with YOUR objectivity."

"Because of that friendship," he said, "I have stayed out of this investigation until now."

"Has your department searched the homes of the Crofts? Their vehicles and all their properties? Have you brought them in and questioned them the way you questioned me? I bet not."

"Simon could not have burned down your house. I was with him at the time. And he couldn't have killed his father because he was in a county commission meeting at that time."

"Even if that's true, he could have directed people like his sons to do the crimes."

"In contrast, Mr. Saunders, you cannot be ruled out of involvement, and it is quite possible you yourself did the latest felonies to lead us off track."

"Killed my own aunt? You've been harassing me from the start."

Orndorf stared, daring me to go further. I tried once more. "Look, use your brain. The Crofts are the ones who'll benefit from Sammy's death. Not me."

"That's yet to be established." Orndorf smiled, his first facial expression of any kind, and it wasn't pretty.

"It's common sense."

"Is it?"

The son of a bitch. He looked worn and tired, an old warrior gone to pot. And what else? Become insulated, unfeeling, arrogant in the application of his power?

Eden and Shepherd crossed their arms on their chests, said nothing, and wouldn't look at me.

I said, "You want to search my house now, after all I've been through. It's hard to believe. This is such an imposition."

Orndorf said, "I understand why you feel that way."

"You understand nothing. And to think of how I praised you over the years. God damn you! No, you cannot search this house."

"Yes we can. Here!" He held out a paper. "A search warrant."

"Shove it!" I turned around and went back inside, saying, "You are a pathetic excuse for a human being."

He followed, jabbed my back with the paper, then dropped it on a chair. "Consider yourself served."

"Fuck you!" But even as I cursed him, Burt and his buddy marched past and went back the hallway. On the couch, Monica sat watching this performance with wide eyes.

Those strangers were going to ransack Mom's room. Hell, her whole house. I started away across the living room.

Orndorf said, "Don't go back there."

I kept going.

At Mom's doorway, he caught up with me and grabbed my right shoulder.

I said, "I'm going to watch what they're doing."

"No you're not."

"I have a right to watch."

"Wrong." He pulled me back past him, then pushed me on into the living room. Still on the couch, Monica stared intently. Eden and Shepherd stood in the front doorway, looking inside.

Orndorf prodded me on across the room. When we reached the front door, he said, "Frank, keep him outside, but don't let him wander off. We'll be finished soon, Mr. Saunders. Then you can come in. Until then, I want you out of the way. Lieutenant, come in here and help with the search."

Halfway through the doorway, I remembered the pistol, stopped and turned around. "I need a coat. I'm sweaty and don't want to get chilled."

I took the coat off the hall tree, put it on as I went out, and felt the pistol in the pocket swing heavily against my hip. Dumb bastards didn't get that, I thought.

Shepherd didn't restrain me so I wandered around to the outside stairs by Ernie Hathaway's house and began climbing.

Shepherd hurried up behind me. "Don't even think about going in that door."

"I'm just getting into the sun."

Halfway up the steps I spread the coat out, sat on it, leaned back with my arms on a step at shoulder level, and stretched my legs out so a step pressed into my calves when my heels braced against the next step down. Like the day before, this weather was also ironically beautiful, even more so with the higher temperature. Shepherd was below, leaning on the rail, and he glanced intermittently up at me then away at the yards.

The pistol lay snug against my hip. If the cops wouldn't do their job, I would have to. The twins were waiting. Cushioned by the coat, I closed my eyes while anger churned inside.

I'd file a lawsuit later. No, that was hopeless. Orndorf had wrangled a search warrant from a judge without evidence. Friendly connections must have prevailed. So much for rule by law. The powerful and connected could obviously circumvent it.

God, I'd felt so good just five minutes earlier. Unbelievable! I had to stabilize myself. Gaining perspective on this turn of events might work. It had worked before.

"I have my health," I said out loud. "They say having your health is everything. If you don't have your health, you know, then nothing else matters."

Mom's house was so close to Ernie's, the walls amplified my words the way shower stalls amplified singing.

"I have money in the bank and I do pretty much what I want. I create stories that amuse people, and so I'm doing something worthwhile by doing what I like to do. I've been very lucky—"

Shepherd's voice was below my feet. "Hey, you okay?"

"I had everything a child could want. Good parents, a loving home, a good family. Dad died when I was young, but he left me with everything I could ask for. I was taught good values. What do I have to complain about?"

"Mr. Saunders. Hey."

"I've been very lucky with the many wonderful people I've known, neighbors and friends and relatives. They have supported me and loved me and taught me things. I had a good education with many wonderful teachers. I had a loving wife and daughter who put up with me for a long time and gave me a good home. I live in a wonderful place, and I have enough brains to recognize most worthwhile things and understand their significance. Life has been good to me. I've got nothing to feel bad about."

This time, cajoling myself didn't work. I remained angry while the cops went through house and garage. Thoughts focusing on the way I'd respected the sheriff silenced me. What had corrupted the bastard? Disappointment in him fed my anger.

I gave up keys for both cars and everything else they asked for. There was no other choice. But I refused to sign off on the list of items they took away: cars, gas cans, a few pieces of clothing. To get rid of the cops, I agreed to walk with Orndorf through the house while he tried to get me to say that nothing had been damaged and nothing had been taken except what was on the list. I told him to get the hell out.

As he and his troops finally left, however, so did Monica,

without a word taking her coat and brown paper lunch bag, and everything else she'd brought, including her respect for me.

Chapter Twenty-Five

By that evening, the negatives had so accumulated, I was convinced only two jobs remained in my life, and the German Luger, stuck beneath my belt, pressed into my crotch uncomfortably and confirmed this assessment. First Sheriff Orndorf, then the twins.

Was there anything better I could do? Well, I could go to Ed's, drink beer and cry on his shoulder about my troubles. Bullshit with him. Yeah sure. Fuck that. I'd lost Ed as soon as he'd dropped me off at the car rental place.

Renting a car, that was one in a long list of goddam expenses I faced. Thanks, Sheriff. You're a mighty fine nice guy.

I fingered the pistol grip—he was the one who'd caused all of my newest losses.

I went into the phone booth and got Orndorf on the line. He told me that our conversation was being recorded, and I said I welcomed it. Everyone should hear what I was going to tell him so recording it was good. It should be broadcast on the radio.

I snarled at him, "You are the son of a bitch who scared off the nurse's aide so she'd never come back. You are the one who told her that I was a murder suspect and made her afraid."

Oh, no, not him. It was somebody else, but he would find out who it was, probably Tweedledum Burt or Tweedledee, and he would let me know exactly what had been said, and if their conduct warranted reprimand, they would receive it.

I said, "Think that'll bring Mom back home, you son of a

bitch? Did you get that on tape or should I repeat it? You're the one who set up that stupid search and couldn't control what your people did or said. YOU are responsible. Nobody else."

"Something happened to your mother?" he asked.

"Yeah, you nearly killed her!" I screamed.

I called him every insulting name I could think of. Ranted a while and ended up, "You incompetent, bureaucratic bastard."

He said, "Calm down. Tell me about it."

I told him, though I'm not sure in what exact words, that I couldn't get another nurse's aide to come to my home despite calling every place I could think of. Without a nurse's aide, I'd had to hire an ambulance to transport Mom to the nursing facility of Home Care, Inc., and as she was being carried inside, she'd suffered heart irregularities that the doctor said could have ended her life. "She suffered, in other words, because of YOU!"

He apologized—but automatically, with no feelings.

"Sure," I said, and hung up.

Back inside my rental car, I sat and relived what had happened. Who knew what Mom understood? First, she experienced the furor about Aunt Judy's kidnapping and murder. Then her caregiver changed. Then strange men saying God knew what, making a mess, searched her room and nearby rooms. Then strangers hauled her out of the house into an ambulance and into a strange new place. No wonder she had developed heart trouble.

Bureaucratic ineptitude and indifference had caused Mom's suffering, the same things had killed Dad, and now they were getting me too. However, I would go kicking and screaming. I would leave signs of my protest against oppression by the state. I'd find the devils behind this mess, and I'd stop them myself!

I would bully my way inside the twins' home and hurt them until they told me everything they knew about Sammy and my farmhouse and Aunt Judy. I'd get the truth from them, and if they weren't guilty, I'd make them give me addresses for their sister and parents. Then I'd visit them and repeat the procedure. Yes, tonight the truth would come out, and the Croft people would be hurt. Not just the Saunders people.

I'd been victimized enough. I was justified to be angry.

"Saunders! Saunders, get out!" Knuckles tapped the window on my left, and when I looked there, a flashlight blinded me.

The voice was Tweedledum Burt's. A surge of new anger made me grab the pistol and lay my index finger alongside the trigger under my belt. All I had to do was pull it free.

"Leave the car, please!" He opened the door.

The outside air struck me, and I felt sudden relief. Thank God I hadn't hurt anyone yet. Thank God I was stopped.

I released the pistol, got out, spread my arms high and wide, faced him and said, "Take the gun from under my belt."

"Damn!" He took it, spun me around, leaned me against the car, and frisked me. After that, I compliantly stumbled into his unmarked car, and he took me downtown.

Eden stood waiting at the curb. She and Burt talked. Then she opened the back door, grabbed an arm, and led me inside the old courthouse.

"Sheriff wants to see you," she said, raising the pistol and magazine up in front of me in her other hand. "Where'd you get this thing? It's not the .32 you told me about."

"Doesn't matter."

"Snap out of it, Cliff. Talk to me."

"That goddam sheriff."

"Don't blame him."

"Searching the house and treating me like scum? The bastard! He caused Mom to have heart problems and be put in a home."

"Cliff, I'm sorry about your mother, but she was already very ill, and when Burkhoffer's lawyer contacted the office last night, to report that you're in the will, well—"

"What?" I was in Sammy's will?

Befuddlement. Was Eden defending the sheriff with the comment? I was in the will? What the hell? It didn't compute.

This was not a breakdown, I thought. You've seen breakdowns, and this was not one. A breakdown was when you panicked and surrendered to despair, hatred, anger or fear.

Well, wasn't that what you did? You had wanted and you had planned to hurt someone.

Eden took me into the sheriff's personal office and put me in a chair in front of his desk, herself in a matching chair. One wall held shelves of large legal-looking tomes. Another wall held two windows facing the new County Administration Building. A third wall held framed pictures and papers.

Orndorf rocked back in a swivel chair, braced his elbows on the chair's arms, and put his hands together as if he were going to pray. "You really raked me over the coals when you telephoned, Mr. Saunders. I haven't heard language like that since I was in the military, and even in boot camp I was never called so many names so fast. Some were real inventive, reflecting your writing profession, I suppose. *Neolithic ninny* was pretty good."

He stared at me, and smiled. Then he shrugged. "Okay, I deserved it. We could have searched the house so less strain was put on your mother. When I think of my own mother—Well, I'm sorry, very sorry. There's nothing I can say to relieve the pain your mother suffered, but I want you to know that when things settle down, I will talk to that nursing home and see if we can't get your mother back home. And I will try to be more sensitive in the future. Which was one of your suggestions when you called. Along with dropping dead and having my head examined."

"I didn't make any threats."

"Except to fight my reelection."

"I will do that too."

"Okay, that's one thing I wanted to tell you. Another is your call alerted us because it seemed, well, so frantic. The Lieutenant had already received a call from a friend of yours—"

Eden said, "Ed Hilliard."

"Who said that you were acting peculiar."

Eden said, "He said you ordered him to leave you alone right after he'd driven you to the rent-a-car place. He got worried that you planned to do something drastic."

Orndorf said, "Then Detective Shepherd said that you were talking out loud to yourself while we searched the house. See? Putting all that together made apprehending you a priority. Looks like it was a good thing we had you under surveillance." He held up the German Luger that Eden had laid on his desk. "Nasty little weapon. Why'd you have it?"

I said nothing, unsure of myself. Maybe I would have gone through with my plan, maybe not.

"Were you thinking about using this on someone? Or yourself? You don't seem suicidal. I hope not, but it's hard to tell."

Eden said, "Burt said he surrendered it voluntarily and made no threat. The magazine was full but the chamber was empty."

Orndorf said, "Isn't it called a clip? Anyway, carrying a concealed weapon is a serious charge. Okay, we're gonna keep this," Orndorf said, laying the pistol back down, "but I won't file charges. I'll assume you had it for protection like you had the shotgun. You've got reason to worry about your safety."

He studied me with a proverbial furrowed brow, then said, "Meanwhile, get some counseling. For grief and for anger. You've been through a lot and it would help. Here are the names of two good people I've used myself one time or another."

He stood, stretched forward over his desk, and handed me a card. It had his name and phone number printed on the front.

Written on the back in blue ink were two names, a male and a female, and phone numbers. I put the card in a jacket pocket.

"What do you think?" he asked.

"I've got plenty to be upset about."

"Yes, but how you handle your emotions is the thing. You don't want to blow up."

I said, "You act concerned, yet for no good reason you searched Mom's house the day after her sister died."

Eden said, "I told you we learned you were in Burkhoffer's will."

"So what?" I looked from her to Orndorf, who slouched back down in his chair. Both stared at me as if my stupidity were legendary. Well, they were right about that. My mind was always slow with complexities, and I was far from normal now, too overloaded to understand much of anything. Kindly, they spelled it out for the dullard.

To confirm a ride home from the Columbus airport, Burkhoffer's lawyer Benjamin Brook had telephoned a nephew, who presumably lived somewhere in the county, and learned by chance about Burkhoffer's unsolved homicide. The lawyer then phoned the department to ask if the Burkhoffer will had been recovered.

Eden said, "Obviously, the lawyer thinks the will is important for our investigation, and when he mentioned your name, that got the sheriff thinking about you as a suspect. Get it?"

"You mean I'm an heir?"

Eden said, "We don't know."

Orndorf said the call had come in at 4:00 a.m. this morning, and the dispatcher had not known enough about the Burkhoffer case, nor been authorized, to supply the lawyer with more information. For similar reasons, the dispatcher had not inquired for more information about the will. That he'd thought the news important enough to relay it to the sheriff's home answering machine was even surprising.

The rest of the lawyer's message was that he would be available to discuss the will upon his return should that interest the department. When? Tomorrow maybe. At the moment of the telephone conversation, he'd been in Rio de Janeiro, transferring planes, in a hurry to catch an arduous flight home. Exhaustion might put off such business until the day after next.

I tried to fathom the mystery but failed. "Sammy said nothing to me about his will."

Orndorf said, "Well, with luck we'll learn about its contents soon, and that may shed all the light we need to clear up this case."

I shook my head. "If you were that optimistic, then why search Mom's house?"

Orndorf sighed, then said, "Here's the way that went down. I heard the dispatcher's message when I woke up at 5:15. I had planned to review the Burkhoffer case file at home over breakfast so it was conveniently on hand. After reading through the reports, I deliberately drove by your residence on the way in here, and saw the Lieutenant's car there. Considering everything, including the possibility you knew you were in the will, I concluded that we had missed a real opportunity not searching your house thoroughly before. Okay?"

I frowned, trying to follow the logic.

He said, "Here was my thinking. You claim to have been sleeping on the couch in the house when your aunt was abducted and killed, but we can't confirm that. You claim somebody threw gasoline on your house, but your neighbor saw only you in your backyard. Your farmhouse blew up and burned down, but you were outside camping, sleeping on the ground in freezing temperatures. That especially seems too strange to be a coincidence. Nobody I know would choose to sleep outside on a night like that."

I said, "But why would you think I'd kill Aunt Judy?"

Eden said, "She was religious, right? And therefore honest?"

I nodded. "Okay."

Eden said, "What if she knew things that would implicate you in Burkhoffer's death, or the crimes at your farmhouse, or the gas thrown on your mother's house? She would feel obliged to tell us, especially if we questioned her directly. If you were aware that she was about to implicate you, then you'd silence her to protect yourself. Make sense?"

"Brother!" I shook my head, surprised there might have been good reasons to search the house.

Eden said, "The sheriff wasn't picking on you."

Orndorf said, "We have to rule out all possibilities. Detectives Grimes and Shepherd argued against the search, but I over-ruled them. So like you said, the search was all my responsibility."

I said, "It was a waste of time and very destructive."

Orndorf said, "It had some bad effects, but if the search confirms or eliminates you as a suspect, we're a step ahead."

"How could it do that? It feels slow and redundant to me."

He smiled. "Well, we'll just have to do our job as best we can. Okay? And you have to do yours too. Do not do anything more to get into trouble. Be patient. We all have to keep plugging along, and maybe soon with the lawyer we'll find out all we need to know. What do you say?"

I shrugged, holding onto my anger like an old friend, unwilling to change my opinion of him. I couldn't think clearly enough to judge anything.

Orndorf said, "Okay. That's all I've got for now. Lieutenant, please see that Mr. Saunders stays out of trouble."

Eden took me outside, walked me around courthouse square, and prodded me to explain myself. I opened up, basically telling her that I had felt helpless, hopeless, agitated, frustrated, taken advantage of, victimized, overwhelmed by everything. I had missed my daily work-out, which generally calmed me down, and losing my aunt, then nearly losing my mother had simply propelled me into something like despair. I gushed it all out in almost two full laps around the block.

Eden finally said, "Friends can help you over the hump when things get hard to handle, Cliff. Talk to me or Ed or some other friend when it happens. Give us a chance to help. Now then, are you hungry?"

"No, but I haven't eaten since breakfast."

"You like pizza? Let's take one home. They tell me this place is pretty good."

We were standing in front of Antonio's Pizzeria across the street from the old courthouse, looking in through the plate glass window.

Going inside added new stimuli. We were purchasing one of my all-time favorite but for decades neglected foods, Antonio's large pizzas. I remembered the spongy, thick circles of food, and the pleasure during my teen years of eating dozens. Tony Turino was long gone, but two kids with hair in cornrows, presumably hired by Tony's son Mike, a high school classmate of mine, efficiently served us the boxed-up meal.

Eden drove me south on 86, took side streets to Mom's house, parked in my space off the alley by the garage, and said, "This'll be less conspicuous than out front."

"I need my rental car," I said.

"Not tonight."

"What if it gets towed?"

"Then you'll have to pay."

Okay, I thought, why not?

Inside the house, I went through the motions, eating without awareness, the house throbbing with too many memories of its own. We devoured the pizza and a bottle of wine, but I hardly noticed.

When Eden reached across the table and held my hand, I said, "The sheriff dislikes our personal relationship."

She smiled. "He's not sure anything went on between us. Not after what you said this morning. You made him feel guilty for his assumptions. And I believe he did say to be sure you were all right tonight."

"Your job could be jeopardized."

"I don't think so. Now if you're full, let's clean up."

Obediently, I rose from the table and washed the dishes and silverware. Then Eden dragged me upstairs where I stopped and looked around as if I'd never been in my bedroom before.

"Take it off," she said after a minute, and pulled off my jacket. "All off. Time for a shower."

I looked around at her then. Her clothes were on the floor, circling her feet. I followed her example, stripping, but folded my clothes and laid them neatly on a chair.

Showering together in such a narrow stall, we bumped each other with every movement. Steam billowed, and under the hot flow we lathered. At her suggestion we washed each other, then rinsed. We ended up face to face, body against body. She kissed me and we hugged. Like windshield wipers, my hands swept over her slick back and butt, wiping off moisture. When she fondled me, I stood there and watched.

Eden applied the bar of soap, then moved her hands so fast, they made a blur, mounding foam around my genitals.

I said, "I think I'm clean down there."

"That's not all. You're as limp as a rubber band."

"My mind won't focus."

"We'll see about that."

After we dried off, she pulled down the bedcovers, laid me down on the sheet and used the lotion on me as I'd used it on her yesterday. She worked on me until I was erect. Then she found the condoms in the drawer, put one on, and slipped me inside her hot, liquidy self the way a cork might slide into an oily bottle.

"Concentrate," she said when I started to wilt. "Think about what we're doing."

Like a robot, I caressed her hips and her back and her arms and her breasts and sucked on her tongue while she bucked above me. Gradually, the sensations took my attention, building until there was nothing but us pounding against each other, grinding away, panting and sweating, climbing a long, dark hill until we fell off a cliff that seemed to take an hour to reach.

She collapsed onto her side next to me and within minutes slept, her breathing like moth wings against my left ear. I pulled a sheet over us, closed my eyes, and thought, If I was in Sammy's will, what did that mean? What did that explain?

CHAPTER TWENTY-SIX

Sammy's inclusion of me in the will had importance or the lawyer wouldn't have mentioned my name, but in what way? An insane thought blossomed: he'd left me all of his land. I snorted in derision because something like that could happen only in romantic novels, not real life, but the idea persisted.

Chores and commitments helped me suppress the speculation. Wednesday's schedule called for fasting so I sipped water for hours and struggled with funeral arrangements—Aunt Judy's body had been released by the coroner to Osvald's. The coroner's findings? There were bruises on her shoulders and arms, but cause of death was drowning. Someone had held her head underwater, probably at the boat landing where I'd come out of the river.

I talked to the parish priest, talked to Aunt Judy's convent again, contacted organist and florists, and wrote an obituary notice which I e-mailed to the town and the Dayton newspaper. My worst job was informing the Saunders family, i.e. my daughter and her mother, of the murder, Mom's condition, and the loss of their old home.

Contacting Laura by e-mail was easy to do but hard to endure because it promoted such an extra feeling of loss. I wondered where she'd be, reading her Hotmail message—Spain? I wasn't sure where she lived because we hadn't communicated in many months. She'd be upset by my news but unable to get back home for proper grieving. Feebly, my writing tried to offer comfort, but I felt helpless and missed my daughter so the effort distressed me.

Then I was forced to talk to my ex-wife. It had to be done. She and Aunt Judy had once been very close. Luckily, her New York City number produced only a computerized voice. In grateful relief, I left Angela a message much more gracious than I could have delivered in conversation with her.

Mid-afternoon I broke free in a long run that purged the body as well as the feelings. The exertion left me in a decent mood, driving to the will's reading. A crimson sunset promised a nice day *mañana,* and experts predicted clear skies for a week with unseasonably hot temperatures. A voice on my car radio told me so—this thought reminding me of Eden's help hours before, returning the rental and retrieving my cars.

Jesus, I moaned, parking. I'd been so busy all day, I hadn't joined Eden at her condo for lunch—and for the other pleasures she'd hinted at when inviting me.

I entered the county commission's private meeting room on the second floor of the old courthouse, and there were Sheriff Orndorf, Detectives Grimes and Shepherd facing the Croft family across a long, polished, four-foot-wide table.

Sight of the Crofts tightened my muscles so I stopped in the doorway.

"Mr. Saunders?" an older man asked, struggling to rise from a chair at the table's head.

I hurried over to save him the trouble and shook his hand. In his 70s at least, he was short, slim, elegantly dressed, with curly white hair and a dapper mustache. He stared up into my eyes and squeezed my hand. "I'm Benjamin Brook. We met once before, in court when you were answering a trespassing charge."

"Oh yes." I remembered him now, seated in the court by Burkhoffer. "You weren't so friendly then."

He smiled. "Probably not."

"Yet I end up in your client's will?" When he nodded, I said, "In what capacity?"

"Have a seat and we'll get to that."

"Saunders!"

Across the table Orndorf pointed to his left at an empty chair that Shepherd was pulling out.

I went around behind the lawyer, behind the police, sat, scooted my chair in and looked up. All the Crofts were watching from the other side, prompting me to frown and glare back.

Orndorf said, "Okay, Counselor, we're ready."

"Thank you, Sheriff. I shall remain seated for this. An old man has only so much energy, and traveling has depleted mine. Believe me, Brazil is far, far away. The Burkhoffer will."

He lifted some papers head high, then lowered them. "It was completed sixteen days ago when two copies were signed by Samuel Burkhoffer in the presence of two witnesses, who also signed. To be precise, all three signed each page of each copy. It was a preliminary document in that Mr. Burkhoffer planned to replace it with an Irrevocable Living Trust. Because of his failing health, he wanted the will in place as an interim measure before my trip. I think he was prescient about his death although not in regards to its manner."

Brook glanced down at the papers and said, "This document begins with the usual declarations of being in sound mind and under no duress in its making. More legalese follows, all of this a prelude to the major stipulation. To that I go directly. It reads, 'I leave my entire estate—lands, buildings, chattel, bank accounts, stocks, all property of any pecuniary worth—to an as-yet unformed incorporated, non-profit organization, henceforth to be known as the Burkhoffer Old Town Land Trust, which will oversee the property's management in perpetuity under the conditions stated herein. Creation of the Burkhoffer Old Town Land Trust and its direction to fall under the auspices of this will's executor, Mr. Clifford James Saunders, of—' "

Me?

Brook read on, giving my address on Pekin Road, naming an alternative executor should I be unable to perform the role, but I was too surprised to grasp specifics.

"He inherits everything?" one of the Crofts asked minutes later, drawing my focus back to Brook.

"Mr. Saunders is the will's executor," the lawyer said. "The will asks him to set up and direct the land trust, whose conditions of existence and purpose are stated on the second and third pages of this document."

"But he gets everything?" the Croft voice repeated.

The lawyer said, "The land trust is bequeathed the estate, which is to become, and I quote, an 'historical nature preserve.' Here are photocopies of the will. Please share them."

He handed two copies to both sides of the table, one copy coming to rest between me and Shepherd. The Croft parents looked at a copy, and the Croft children huddled around another.

I scanned the first page, the second's five paragraphs, then the third's three paragraphs.

"That's some will," Shepherd said.

I looked at him. "It's wonderful. What an idea."

"Sam had great faith in you, Mr. Saunders," the lawyer said, perhaps overhearing my comments.

I looked at him. "It's fantastic."

"We aren't even mentioned," Mrs. Croft said in a tone that contained anger, disappointment, and sadness. Her husband looked equally disturbed, bent over with his eyes only inches above the will. The Croft children were mumbling among themselves.

The contents of the will elated me, but the Crofts infuriated me at the same time. They had ignored Sammy until his illness, one or more had murdered Sammy and Aunt Judy, yet they were complaining as if they deserved something. What goddam egotism! Justice was definitely being served.

The lawyer said, "Mrs. Croft, I have something that may answer any questions you have. If you would, Sheriff?"

Orndorf stood, rolled a five-foot-high, black metal stand from the wall over by Brook, and sat back down. The stand held a large television on top, a VCR on a shelf below, and a black cord that arced from in back to an electric outlet.

Brook said, "Sam Burkhoffer made a videotape to inform me of his wishes for the will, and it contains his reasons to exclude the Croft family. I'm sorry if the will comes as a shock, but I believe Sam's reasoning is clear. Let me warn you, however, he minces no words. This might be painful. Understand?"

Brook looked at Simon. "Should I play the tape for you?"

Mrs. Croft nudged her husband.

Simon sat upright and refocused on Brook. "Go ahead."

Brook extended a black remote control in front of himself, pointed it up over his left shoulder, and the monitor flickered into a snowy pattern that dissolved into Sammy, seated, wearing a blue sweater that gaped open on a dark shirt beneath.

The familiar cadence, intonation, word choice, pronunciation and grammar startled me. Sammy's mode of expression! It was like a voice speaking from the other side.

It said, "I think I got her set up all right now. I been testing how close I gotta be so I can talk natural. I don't want to shout. Ben, I'm gonna try this here instead of talking it out in person or writing 'cause it's easy to take my time and cut out and put more in 'til I get what I want. Type up what you think I mean, and we'll look her over and make changes."

Brook paused the picture and said, "That is precisely what we did. I printed a draft of the will after receiving the tape, and we altered it twice to achieve its completed form."

On the monitor Sammy shimmered, blurred by an unsteady pausing mechanism, glowing as if his aura or his soul were appearing. What struck me most was how cords of skin stood out from his throat, hanging down from his chin. How his face was sallow, and his eyes lay deep in hollows. How liver spots on his skin were visible, even beneath his thinning goatee and hair. I had never noticed this frailty before, maybe because Sammy had always been heavily clothed on the bike trail.

Brook aimed his remote again, the picture resumed animation, and Sammy said, "You told me we can replace this will with a living trust when you get back. Anyways, you pretty well know that I want to save my farm. That's the main thrust for the will. You called it a preserve set up as a not-for-profit corporation, a land trust, so that's what I'll go with right now.

"I want it run private. I don't want no government getting ahold of the land. That'd ruin it for sure. So would making it into some kind of public park. The public be darned. People stomping around in here any time they want would ruin it. I stopped letting hunters on my land years ago. Dang people knocked down fences and left gates open and shot anything that moved. But, heck, that's not what I wanta talk about."

He coughed hard, the picture jumped, and he was wearing a long-sleeved, gray undershirt.

"Here's some ideas to put in the will. Make it so the trust can set up programs to educate people. This here farm is where all kinds of things happened with the settlers and Indians and people ought to be aware of it. There's the history of the land itself, and animals and the river. There's plenty that people can learn about here.

"Cliff Saunders knows all about it. He's been a teacher, and he can explain it better than me. He's studied on all these things, and I've heard him talking about them so strong, he wore me out. Ben, put him in as executor. I'll talk to him one of these days before we do the living trust, and make sure he understands what all I'm thinking of. I don't believe he'll have any objection to these plans. Heard him often enough say how important the place is and what oughta be done. Heck, Ben, you heard him yourself go on about it in court some years ago.

"Now you told me setting everything up is gonna cost money. Well, give him use of my stocks and savings, which ought to add up to about eighty thousand. That'll get this thing started. To get him more money, put down that he can raise it by holding events and so on, taking in donations to support the trust and keep up the buildings and fences and equipment.

"Be sure to make it so he won't put up buildings or pave the place over into parking lots. Cliff wouldn't do that, but we got to set it up so the people that take over after him don't. One more thing. I don't want none of the land sold. Don't leave it so little parcels can be sold off to raise money.

"If need be, I suppose Cliff could lease some of the land on short terms for farming purposes, like I do, but I think we ought to put a limit on that too.

"What buildings are here can be used for storage, and meeting rooms and show places. Like over by Freeman College where that man willed his land to the county for a park. In his house they hung all the paintings he did like an art museum. My buildings can be redecorated, but not to set up a business here, like a restaurant or something. I don't think that'd be necessary. But there's lots of things like that I want to talk over with Cliff and get his ideas.

"What I think he'll do and what I'd like to see is to let it go back to nature. I mean bringing it back like it used to be before the settlers came.

"Now that reminds me. Cliff talked about Indian dwellings. We ought to make it so things like that could be put up. Buildings of the kind that the Indians had.

"Another thing, along with the old hen house I got full of Indian stuff, there's antiques in the basement and attic from early settlers. Some old farming equipment in the barn. All that could be put on display too."

When the picture jumped into static again, my muscles were so tense, I almost jumped up and shouted. The reality envisioned by Sammy was such a wonderful idea, tears welled in my eyes. The monitor captured Sammy again, this time with a light blue blanket around his shoulders over what looked like a green and white checkered pajama top.

He said, "Just thought of something else. Cliff commented on different groups, Conservancy something, and Audubon and what not. We got to make it so the land trust can work with these nature groups. Not for them to take it over, you understand, but to work with him if he wants to do that."

The picture fluttered and jumped to Sammy in a yellow, red and brown turtleneck sweater. He wiped his brow with the back of a hand and looked at the camera.

"Cliff got me to thinking today." Sammy shook his head and smiled. "He still don't know who I am. Never has asked for my last name, but that don't mean he's not interested. Got me to talking about my childhood and called me Sammy like my Mama did. Can you beat that? Asked about my wife and child too.

"So I thought to say something about my son Simon and his family so you'll know that I ain't cracking up. Cliff said he was sorry that me and my son had drifted apart. My gosh, until I got sick, I hadn't even talked to Simon in thirty years. So when he and his family came to see me, it smelled fishy, if you know what I mean. I don't trust them.

"If I find out they're different than I think, I'll change things later. But right now, I want everything to go to the trust. The Crofts don't need it, but to get started the land trust does. I wonder if we should put these reasons in the will. If you think so, then do it.

"What does my son or his family need from me? I can't think of anything. There's nothing here they love or respect. Simon made that clear years ago by gettin' rid of my family name. I want the Burkhoffer name to continue right along with the land.

"What people do shows where their hearts are. Cliff told me about him, and I read about him in the newspapers. Saw him on television a coupla times too, talking about new building projects. Far as I can see, he cares about land according to what cash value it has. How he can make money building on it or digging something out of it.

"Him and his kind get ahold of this place, and it'd be gone in five years. Cliff told me that and I believe he's right. Several times Cliff got excited about how all the farm land is gettin' ate up. Well, any darn fool can see it's true, but not my son. No sir. Not him."

"That's all of it," Brook said, flicking off the picture and rewinding. The whirring tape was clearly audible in the silence.

"He tricked him!" one of the twins said. I still couldn't tell Richard from Jason.

Brook said, "Excuse me, sir?"

"This man—" The twin pointed at me. "Tricked my grandfather. He was sick and senile, and he—" The twin pointed at me again. "He told him lies about us. Took advantage of him."

Brook said, "There is no indication of that. I think Mr. Saunders is as surprised by the will as anyone."

I said, "Sammy was far from senile."

"Let's see that will," the other twin said. "The one you read from. The good copy with the signatures. Let's see it."

"Yeah," said his brother. "The official one."

Mrs. Croft said, "May we see your original, Mr. Brook?"

Brook glanced at the sheriff.

Sheriff Orndorf said, "We don't have the original, Diane. Mr. Brook's copy was stolen from his files. Samuel Burkhoffer's original of the will may have been stolen as well."

Simon asked, "You mean there is no original to probate?"

Brook said, "At the moment all we have is this photocopy I made of the original and kept in a file cabinet at home."

Damn! I thought, then said, "Isn't the photocopy good enough? We've got your testimony and the witnesses' that it's a copy of the original. We've got the videotape too."

Brook said, "Of course, it can be offered to the court for consideration. And proof could be offered that it reflects the final intentions of the decedent."

Simon looked at me and said, "It'd never fly. The court would accept only the original with the actual signatures."

The awful truth was clear to me before Brook responded, "Correct. A photocopy could almost surely be broken if challenged. If an original copy is not recovered, Sam will have virtually died intestate, or so would rule the court."

Mrs. Croft said, "Wouldn't my husband inherit then?"

Brook said, "Mr. Croft IS Sam Burkhoffer's only child."

"All right!" said one twin.

"Okay!" said his brother.

Both grinned and glanced at their sister, then stared at me triumphantly. The transfer of Sammy's estate was not a question of legitimacy to them. It was more like a goddam game. Their sister smiled, the mother smiled and patted her husband's right arm, but Simon just stared blankly at me.

My stomach turned over and the bile climbed back into my throat. I said, "But the originals were stolen."

Brook said, "That probably would not sway the court. The videotape and the will's completion occurred many days before Sam Burkhoffer died. The court's logic would be that a person can change his mind in just a few moments."

I said, "But there's no indication that happened. There's all kinds of proof the will is what Sammy wanted."

Brook shook his head. "You can so argue in court, but probably without effect should the will be challenged."

The twins laughed aloud. Mother and daughter whispered to each other. Simon continued staring at me.

I felt drained, disappointed, angry, but also resigned—I should not have let my hopes get so high. This would be nothing less than another loss architectured by the law.

Simon Croft said something that silenced the other Crofts. Louder, he repeated it. "Why did you present that as the original? You knew a copy wouldn't be acceptable in court."

"That was my idea," Sheriff Orndorf said. "I was hoping to get a reaction from your father's killer."

Simon said, "What?"

Orndorf said, "Only the killer knew the wills were missing so I wanted to see who questioned the signatures. Your boys and Diane implicated themselves."

Diane protested, "It was a natural thing to ask about."

"Mr. Brook," Orndorf asked the lawyer, "do family members generally ask to check the signatures on a will?"

"Not in my experience," Brook said. "Of course, wills are usually not controversial, and family members often have a copy of the will or know its contents already."

"It was natural to ask about it," the vocal twin said.

"Yeah, it was," said his brother.

"Simon," said Orndorf, "do you know where each one of your family was on the nights in question? Which of them had access to your father or Mr. Saunders's houses or his aunt? You know the times involved. I'm not going to pussyfoot with you any longer. It grieves me to say it, but somebody in this room, perhaps more than one, is responsible. You have a duty to help me out."

Orndorf looked along the other side of the table. All five Crofts seemed about to explode in denials and protests.

Instead, Simon declared, "I'll sign a waiver."

Brook sat up even straighter than before. "Really?"

"Yes, I'll sign a waiver."

"What?" asked one of the twins.

Brook said, "A waiver would mean your father accepted this will as valid and would not challenge it. He would be giving up any claim he has to the estate."

Simon said, "The will states what Father wanted."

"Dad, think about it!" the vocal twin said.

He and his brother, their sister and Mrs. Croft began speaking at once. They stood and clustered around Simon.

Simon shuddered under the onslaught, then stood and pushed past them to the head of the table. There, he leaned down and talked privately to Brook.

When Simon straightened back up, he said loudly, "It's settled. I won't fight Father's last wishes."

"Are you nuts, Dad?" the vocal twin asked.

Mrs. Croft said, "Darling, you're overwrought. Let's take our time and think it over."

Simon said, "You all go home. It's my decision."

Brook said, "We can get a waiver form at my office."

"Tomorrow," Diane Croft said. "Bring one by the house tomorrow, Mr. Brook. You can get Simon's signature then if that's what he really wants to do."

The family surrounded Simon again, all talking, bombarding him with their opposition, trying to drag him away from the lawyer and the waiver.

Tears covered Simon's cheeks. He dropped down onto a chair and slumped forward, resting his head on his forearms as if his family's words were crushing his chest against the table.

What an act. He'd never sign a waiver. Yes, I was cynical, and why not? Obviously, Simon's sudden desire to go along with Sammy's wishes was nothing more than a ploy to lead the sheriff away from making further allegations and inquiries about his family. And it had worked. The sheriff's quizzing of Simon about his family's activities was done. My cynicism went even further.

Would the police bring the family in for questioning now? With warrants would police immediately search their homes? I doubted that too. The cops had probably planned to observe what happened at this meeting before moving in those directions. Plus they would still accord the sheriff's influential friends enough courtesy to get a lawyer and prepare for a police ordeal. Maybe tomorrow they'd get a warrant and search. Not tonight.

It was all very screwed up! Not to my liking, but there wasn't a thing I could do about it.

Seeing that Brook was left momentarily alone, I went around the table and asked him if I might copy the videotape to have a memento of Sammy. Having often wished for a video or audio recording of my father to help remember him by, I was not going to ignore this videotape if it was available.

Brook said, "Certainly. This one is a copy. Take it."

CHAPTER TWENTY-SEVEN

Thrown into something like despair, I sought comfort that night by sleeping on the ground west of Sammy's barn at Old Town. I woke up in the same emotional state. Dropped my sleeping bag off at a Laundromat for cleaning. Ate breakfast with Ed at Mom's house. Stopped at Osvald's funeral home to check developments there. Confirmed food choices with the caterers. And started exercise-dancing with friends in my barn.

Into our fourth song, there was Eden, waving.

I turned off the music, and she replaced it with "Simon Croft is dead."

The news echoed back off the rafters and stunned me.

I said, "Jesus Christ! His family murdered *him* too!?"

It was 11:00 a.m. so we'd been whirling around for only fifteen minutes. We made a circle with Eden, and I introduced Lt. Grimes to Myra Suchac and Georgie Carlin.

"You're missing the other male this time," Eden said.

I said, "Chuck Shirley's working today."

Ed asked, "What happened to Croft?"

"Sorry, but this is an active investigation."

I said, "They all know what's gone on since Sammy died. I told them about the will and yesterday's meeting."

Eden opened up, surprising me. "His wife found him in his car. The garage doors were closed, his windows were open, the ignition was on, but the car was out of gas. The wife's car was idling, but had only a little gas left after being filled yesterday so the cars had probably been running for hours."

"He committed suicide?" Ed asked.

Eden shrugged. "There was an empty bottle of his wife's prescription sleeping pills on the car floor. Ten were in the bottle when she went to bed, and she said only one pill was enough to put her out. On the seat beside him was a fifth of vodka, nearly empty."

Myra shook her head. "Get drunk, take ten strong sleeping pills and pass out forever. A painless way to go."

Eden said, "Now I need to talk to Mr. Saunders in private so excuse us. Outside?"

"Okay." To the others I said, "I'll be right back."

A few feet away from the barn, I touched Eden's arm, but she said softly, "Frank's in the cruiser."

It was parked by the sweat lodge with Shepherd on the front seat, looking down at something in his hands. The car was running, the windows were up, so the air-conditioning was probably on. What a change in the weather! What a change in other things too.

When Simon Croft had been sitting like that on his car's front seat, with the exhausts filling his lungs, I'd been sleeping outside Sammy's place in fresh air—fresh except for the sleeping bag's stench from my burned house.

I said, "Croft's death is too damn convenient for his wife and kids, considering their reaction when they found out the will was a copy and when he said he'd sign a waiver."

Eden looked up toward me, but the sun drove her eyes back down and she said, "Let's get in the shade."

"East side of the barn." I pointed, and as we strolled that way, I said, "Couldn't Croft's death be a murder?"

"No outer signs of trauma. Asphyxiation is the probable cause of death. We're waiting for autopsy results, but I think there's little chance it'll show anything but carbon monoxide poisoning with sleeping pills and vodka. Maybe something else will turn up, but—" She shrugged.

"Yeah, that'd be too much to hope for."

"Frank and I went over it a dozen times. This was a perfect way to kill him. He was already drinking. They could put the pills in his vodka, and when he passed out, put him in the car, turn the motors on, and if nobody sees them, they're home free. They'd never be caught unless one of them confessed."

Did this honesty signal a change of attitude? After last night's revelations, maybe her department finally regarded me and my friends as supporters, potential helpers in the case.

I asked, "You think the whole family's involved?"

"Could be. Diane's a bit flaky, though. She's taken sedatives for years and would be a loose link. Then again, it could just be a suicide. Diane said she saw the kids drive off before she went to bed. And Croft seemed despondent last night."

"Yeah, very down. But it could have been an act."

"Possibly. But it could also be a real reaction."

"I suppose learning that your kids are probably killers would make anyone despair. How can you sort out the truth?"

"Let me and Frank worry about that. You think about this. When're we gonna hook up again? You ran off on me yesterday afternoon, and then you weren't home last night when I stopped by. Who were you out with, Myra or Georgie?"

"Both," I said. "We were dancing nude in the moonlight."

"All night long?" Eden leaned back against the barn's old wood siding, and ran an index finger across my bare abs.

We were in shade, on the rough, once-fenced-in ground of a loafing pen. Winter-beaten thistles and hogweed surrounded us.

Her touch switched my interest away from Croft. "Let's meet tonight, okay? After Aunt Judy's viewing? Seven-thirty or eight o'clock?"

She pulled out the front of my running shorts, raked

fingertips down through my pubic hair and grabbed my penis, which immediately began to harden.

I grinned like a chimpanzee. "Brazen hussy."

"You complaining?"

I remembered Shepherd, looked with alarm toward the cruiser, but only the backseat was visible. Eden must have known the corner of the barn was hiding us.

She squeezed my rapidly expanding flesh, and I leaned forward, bracketed her head with my hands on the wall, lowered my head, craned my neck, and kissed her.

I said, "Careful. My sweat can stain your pretty suit."

Her hand moved farther down, cupping and gently kneading my testicles. "My clothes come off easy."

I said, "Want to see how quick I can get you naked?"

She laughed. "Not right now."

"Look how we're acting. A dead man's at the hospital being cut open, and we want to have sex."

"That's how it works. Death's an aphrodisiac."

"A natural mechanism to insure survival of the species."

"Sometimes we just need a good lay in the hay. Farm boys like you oughta know that."

A car door slammed, and she withdrew her hands so quickly, the elastic top of the shorts snapped back and stung me.

Shepherd yelled, "Hey! Come on! Let's go eat!"

I pointed to my blue shorts, tenting noticeably in front.

Eden smiled, stepping away from the wall far enough to see Shepherd.

"In a minute," she yelled, but my Henry Mancini CD resumed blasting just then so she pantomimed her words, raising a fist with its index finger extended.

I walked up behind her and said in an ear, "Don't tell him I have a hard-on. It's bigger than that finger anyway."

Laughing, she reached behind with her other hand for my

erection—I was still out of Shepherd's line of sight.

"No more of that." I backed off out of her reach. "Did you say Croft had already been drinking before he went home?"

She said Croft had left the courthouse with the sheriff, gone straight to Harry's Bar and Grill, and chugged three double shots of vodka. Within thirty minutes the sheriff talked Croft into leaving, drove him home in Croft's Cadillac, parked it in the garage and went inside the house with Croft. The wife and kids immediately started in on Croft about the waiver, but Croft locked himself in his den and told everyone to leave him alone. The sheriff exited by the front door and was picked up by Shepherd and Eden, who were waiting behind the kids' three cars out front. At the station the two detectives and Orndorf finally were able to plan how to follow up the meeting about the will. They decided the obvious, to bring the Crofts in for questioning, to get warrants and search all their homes and belongings. Too slow to my thinking, but at least logical.

Eden concluded, "Of course, we got no warrants yet with the call about Croft coming in at 7:15."

"Does the sheriff think Croft's death was a suicide?"

"I don't know. He went to a meeting in Cincinnati this morning, but he's on his way back now."

"I don't suppose Benjamin Brook showed up last night at Harry's Bar with a waiver that Croft signed before going home."

"Afraid not. Now I have to go."

"So I'll see you this evening at Mom's house?"

"Have the lotion ready." She reached for my shorts.

I thrust my hips back away from her.

"Chicken." She hurried away toward the cruiser.

I followed, hiding the bulge in my shorts from Shepherd by staying behind her.

As Eden climbed into the cruiser to drive away, I was distracted by sexual desire, the sun's heat, and the thought that

Croft's death assured Sammy's and Aunt Judy's killers, who seemed to be escaping prosecution, of inheriting the land Sammy had tried to save. His grandchildren were Sammy's closest living relatives now. Very goddam frustrating.

Only one thing seemed certain. More dancing. Three hours of it might stop my obsession with bad events, with people victimizing me and those I loved. And Myra had said something about teaching me some "real dances."

Eden, in place behind the wheel, backed the cruiser away between the three other vehicles and the charred pile that used to be my house, drove forward, and turned up the lane in front of me. I half-heartedly waved, the car completed the turn, flared sun off the rear window so I blinked, and an idea came to me as if the bright flash had occurred in my mind.

I yelled at the car, but it continued driving away. I yelled louder, but the car gained speed. I ran after it, screaming and waving my hands, afraid they'd never see me. Time was of the essence. We had to contact the sheriff before he saw the Crofts.

Eden stopped halfway out the lane, at the crest of the hill, then backed up. She was still reversing when I opened the back door on Shepherd's side. She jammed on the brakes so suddenly, the tires skidded on the gravel.

I threw myself inside, and both turned around on their seats to look back at me.

"I just thought of a way to catch the killers tonight."

CHAPTER TWENTY-EIGHT

About 2:00 a.m. the next morning, when Eden dropped me off at Osvald's parking lot, I wordlessly let her scoot off. Maybe the quicker she got to the station, the sooner she'd finish work and meet me at Mom's house. Besides, there wasn't much to say.

I unlocked and opened my car door, laid my good clothes neatly on the passenger seat, straightened up, and propped my forearms on top of the door. Eden's taillights had already vanished, leaving this neighborhood as dark and as silent as Benjamin Brook's had been.

What a goddam day! First the tedious exchange of clichés attending to Aunt Judy's coffin inside Osvald's, topped off by the last-minute hectic arrival and placation of Angela, who'd driven non-stop from New York. Escaping her, I'd sat six hours on hard ground at Brook's house only to see my plan fizzle bigtime.

Oh, the detectives did capture someone: a curfew violator, who occupied their attention at the station now, a damn kid cutting across Brook's yard, going home from a friend's house.

Jesus! I had had to talk my ass off convincing the sheriff not only to try the plan despite Eden's and Shepherd's objections, but also to let me join the stakeout.

The idea was simple: tell the Croft family that Simon had signed a waiver in Harry's Bar after the meeting, show it to them, and make it clear that Brook was taking it home for safekeeping that evening, until tomorrow. Then we'd wait for the killers to visit Brook's home to destroy Simon's waiver, and capture them.

It could have worked. Ed had cooperated, forging Simon's signature on a waiver. Brook had cooperated, and the sheriff had fed Diane Croft the disinformation in what Eden herself called a convincingly natural way. Enacting the plan had gone well.

Damn right it could have worked. The killers had a history of going to their victims' homes: Sammy's, mine, and Mom's.

Of course we'd rushed implementing my plan, and it had many variables that could have tipped off our subterfuge to the Crofts. Maybe it was so obvious a scam or risk, they'd just not fallen for it. Hell, maybe the Crofts weren't even the killers.

Really, my goddam plan had been pitiable, inconveniencing all the detectives, the innocent kid, and the Brooks too!

I shook my head, and my stomach growled loudly. The ham sandwich I'd wolfed down about 3:30 hadn't been much sustenance.

Antonio's Pizzeria! It was on my way home, and although I'd been too preoccupied to enjoy the pizza Eden had treated me to the other day, a vague memory of it stimulated saliva.

I drove straight there, found it still open, and thought of running over to ask Eden what she liked on her pizza pies. The new County Administration Building was just cater-cornered across the street. No, going there would tell the others that she and I would be together.

I went inside and ordered two large pizzas with extra tomato sauce, sausage and mushrooms—what I liked and what she'd eaten without complaint before. When the pizzas were boxed for me at the counter, I brought over from the cooler two six-packs of the Mexican beer she'd had at her condo.

"Having a party at the jail?" the kid asked, taking my credit card.

"Not hardly." What an odd comment, I thought, signing the receipt and leaving. Seconds later, looking back inside, I saw my reflection in the window and understood. I was still wearing the blue jacket with DEPUTY in yellow letters on the back.

I drove through the business district, stopped for a red traffic light, opened the top pizza box, threw its lid up against the passenger door, picked a small outer piece from Antonio's crisscross cutting pattern, and put it in my mouth. Distinct tastes closed my eyes and made me chew and swallow slowly. No traffic appeared behind in the rearview mirror so I sat through two cycles of lights, disposing of three more bite-size pieces.

An idea hit me. Something might be amiss. Weren't we giving up on my plan too soon? I'd better contact Eden.

I spotted a pay phone on a pole at a filling station that was closed for the night, gunned the engine, made a right turn on red, an immediate left, drove to the phone, lowered my window, put in a quarter, and punched in Eden's cell phone number.

She answered on the third ring. Other voices chatted in the background, but after I asked, "How's it going?" I heard a door close, cutting off the voices.

"I'm busy, Cliff. We're waiting for the boy's father."

"Anyone watching Brook's house now? Is the stakeout officially over?"

"Nobody will be on the property if that's what you mean. But the patrol around the house will continue every half hour."

"That's no good. You can't see anything from out on the street. The car patrol was intended to make the killer think it was the only surveillance. What if somebody sneaks in there now?"

"How likely is that after all of us came out of hiding? We all were out on the driveway in open view."

"Yeah, but that also showed anybody watching that the cops weren't there anymore. I'm going back."

"That is not necessary."

"The Brooks assume we're watching and keeping them safe."

"They are safe, Cliff. I told him the stakeout was over."

"But what if the Crofts show up? They could still believe in our signed-waiver story."

"We did what you wanted. We gave it a try. Now forget it."

"Okay. You're right, but I'll be there until whenever. Dawn probably. I'm not asking you to come. This is for my own peace of mind. It's just something I have to do. Don't worry. I'll stay out of sight and won't disturb anyone. You go get some sleep."

"Cliff, listen to me. Go home!"

"No, I've got to do it. Goodbye."

"Don't—"

I hung up, pulled out of the station, turned northeast toward Brook's house, and smiled, realizing that I'd forced Eden to meet me there, and she would be pissed. Well, hell, maybe I could appease her with the food. We could picnic in the dark. Anyway, there was no other choice. I really did have to be sure Brook was safe. Anybody showing up was very improbable— that was true—but I didn't want to take the slightest chance of creating more innocent victims.

I drove around the city block that Brook's property occupied. Over a half hour ago, maybe fifty minutes, we had walked away from it via the driveway, but I didn't want to be so obvious returning. I circled the perimeter again, edged toward the curb near the southeastern corner and studied the brush by the sidewalk. Turning the corner, heading west, I saw, just as the kid we'd caught had said, a path—so well worn it showed up easily at night from twenty feet.

I parked, shut off my lights, and looked around to be sure I wasn't attracting attention. Across the street was a dirty white panel truck with rusty sides, a swept-back antenna on top, and a sign ACME INTERIORS beneath dark windows on the door.

Also dark were the few cars parked farther off on both sides of the street in back and in front of me, and the houses. There was no movement, no one walking around.

I looked north where Brook's large Victorian house lurked behind trees. Eden shouldn't be long in arriving. She'd probably drive around the block and look for my car.

I twisted a cap off a beer, drank half the bottle, picked out a large piece of pizza, and ate it. Then downed the rest of the bottle and put it back in the pack. A loaded stomach made me sluggish, and I yawned.

The pizzas radiated heat, and they had a wonderful smell. I'd eat another piece and wait for Eden.

Better not. That would put me at risk of falling asleep. Damn! I wanted to stay here and relax.

Well, this was a private stakeout so it could be done in comfort. I stuffed a beer into each jacket pocket, one in a rear pants pocket, closed the lid on the top box, grabbed the full pizza box beneath it, left the car and went to the path.

The path narrowed leaving the sidewalk, curving down among thick honeysuckle-type bushes so I had to hold the pizza box in both hands in front of me and push through. The noise of branches scraping on cardboard and my clothes alarmed me enough to slow into a pace at which I could move soundlessly.

At the path's lowest point, it met the creek, which turned south beneath the street, a trickle of water disappearing into a large pipe. The path curved away in the opposite direction, up a rise toward the house.

Topping this little climb brought me to mown grass where I stopped and oriented myself. The pine-tree field was on my left; little flower-beds and clumps of waist-high bushes were ahead; then the house.

I went from pine to pine, worked my way to the lilacs, sat down, and leaned back against two of the larger ones on the house side, thinking that was enough camouflage. No need to go behind the lilacs where Eden and I had been before. That seemed unnecessarily cautious.

I took the beer from my back pocket, pocketed the cap, set the bottle down carefully, screwing it around in the grass to a level seat, opened the box, took out a large piece from the pizza's center, and ate it. Then ate another slowly.

The pizza was as delicious as anything I'd ever eaten. This was the way to conduct a stakeout, I thought, reaching for another piece.

The two dark gaps in the pizza stopped me. I didn't want to offer a half-empty box to Eden. Besides, I should check the house. Just a small portion of it was visible from here.

Armed with the box in my left hand, the beer in my right, I ambled from pine tree to pine tree to a point off the southwestern corner of the house where I could see the whole front. The porch light lit an empty western wall, and the yard and the brick driveway were empty out to the street.

I reversed direction back through the pines as close to the southern wall as their coverage allowed, went back to the lilacs, began to set down the pizza, then decided not to, afraid it might attract animals or not be handy should I run into Eden elsewhere. I kept it out in front of me, swallowed some beer, went farther back in the yard to the trees along the creek, and stayed in front of them inside their darkness, strolling around the eastern and northern sides of the house.

Reaching the northwestern corner, I looked toward my earlier southern position and was unhappy. The other three sides were the dangerous areas, yet I'd been too far away to see raised or broken windows. Why not be sure and walk next to those walls on my way back to the lilacs? The Brooks were asleep, and there'd be no noise. I might as well do the job right.

The detached garage was only thirty feet away, and from it to the house was only twenty more feet. Other places along the tree line by the creek were much farther from the house and would expose me for a longer time.

Staying in shadow, I walked over to the garage, checked its closed double doors by poking my head out around the closest front corner into the light, then went around behind the garage directly to the house, and started east, glancing at the five ground-floor windows, passing them so close to the wall, my right elbow brushed it occasionally. I turned at the east wall, stepped into the dark rear entranceway, saw the door was closed, hoped it was locked but didn't try the handle, stepped back out, wondered what kind of ivy was twined on the metal trellis, sipped beer, and proceeded on.

The largest part of the lawn was on these two sides. East was basically a large open field back to the trees along the creek. The south lawn was equally large, and so perfectly flat with the six-foot high pine trees so evenly spaced, it reminded me of a chessboard with pawns in position.

I rounded the southeastern corner of the house on a line of slate squares. They paralleled the wall on this side just out beyond three shoulder-high, wide and deep rhododendrons. One bush was near each corner, one was in the middle, and each obscured the bottom third of a window.

I walked silently on the grass between the slate squares, went beside the first bush, between it and the wall, checked the window, moved back out to the slate, and proceeded on. Reached another window, checked it, then crept on.

The middle section ahead looked different. It was the darkest part of the house, and the blackness seemed to sway slightly as if a breeze were disturbing the bush.

Weird. Why would the wind whirl only there? I approached it, stepped toward the wall alongside the bush to check the window, and turned my face up, trying to catch the breeze on my cheeks.

My left foot came down on something uneven, something rounded and too hard to give with my weight, something that moved so I lost my balance and lurched sideways. Beer sloshed out onto my hand, and the box in the other teetered so the pizza inside it shifted. Had I stepped on a small animal? An out-of-place ball?

Part of the shadow broke loose from the bush and rose up beside me. It brushed my legs, then the box, raising it so the lid flopped open and the pizza tipped toward me. Had I kicked loose a limb that had been held down somehow, allowing it to spring up into its natural position?

Something lighter appeared level with my eyes inside the shadow. The paleness had an eerie quality, a pasty, wet-like insubstantiality. It resembled a grotesque human face, an ancient Greek theater mask, the sudden apparition of a nightmarish, dormant evil.

I screamed and something slammed against my chest. I fell, going down so fast I was helpless to catch or to cushion myself. Then something smashed against my head.

Chapter Twenty-Nine

"With that head injury, you shouldn't be drinking," Eden said. "There could be a concussion."

"Doctors examined my head last night and found nothing."

"Listen to her," Ed insisted.

"Where'd your sense of humor go?"

Myra, Georgie and Chuck clucked similar disapprovals.

"Hold it, everyone. Aunt Judy's with the nuns up north, Mom's in a nursing home, I put up with my ex-wife all afternoon, along with her mother and father, who never did like me, and we just finished cleaning up this house. In other words, I'm too damn tired to care. So have a drink and relax."

"We don't drink," Georgie said, including Chuck in her "we." She proclaimed further, "Alcohol is poison."

"We think your body's a temple," Chuck said, devoutly.

"My body's a temple? For what, gas?"

"We have to leave," Georgie said, standing, bringing Chuck to his feet like her shadow.

"Smooth talker," Eden said, accusing me of something.

Myra said, "Cliff's just trying to be funny."

I whined, comically I thought, "I'm stressed out."

Georgie waved a palm at Eden, Myra and Ed, all seated at the kitchen table. "We really do have to go. Goodbye."

I took Chuck's right hand in mine. "I appreciate the way you've helped me."

"We didn't do nothin'," Chuck said.

"You two helped clean up this place. Exercised with me. Came to the funeral and the reception. Supported me, in other words." I noticed Georgie fidgeting, caught in place between us and the kitchen table and the wall.

Chuck muttered, "Well—"

I stepped up against him, hugged him, patted his back with both hands, then stepped apart.

At once Georgie tried to rush between us and away.

I caught her in mid-stride. "Thank YOU very much too."

I embraced her sideways, bent, tried to kiss her, and when she turned her face away, grazed a cheek. A very cold cheek.

"Okay. Go in peace." I released her, telling myself to leave them alone, but then I dropped my arms across their shoulders and walked between them to the front door, our legs and hips bumping awkwardly all the way.

As the two hurried outside, I said, "Let's dancercize at the barn again soon."

They moved along to the street with halfhearted waves.

I closed the door, turned around, and my three other friends were standing there, watching.

Ed said, "I couldn't say it with them here, but you're drunk."

I said, "Did I insult them somehow?"

Myra said, "They just don't understand you."

Eden said, "Who does?"

I asked, "Were they really offended?"

Ed shrugged. "They're reformed alcoholics."

I shook my head. "Sorry, I knew that and forgot. I'm just feeling too good."

Ed smiled. "Like I said, you're drunk. You're no hugger."

"The hell I'm not."

"You curse social hugging every time you see it."

"Shit. Listen, I want to thank each of you personally for standing by me through all this. You first, Ed."

I hugged him and playfully kissed a hairy cheek.

He lifted me off my feet, and strong as a goddam gorilla, squeezed so hard I gasped, "Uncle! Uncle!"

"He's high as a kite," Ed pronounced, releasing me.

I said, "Thanks, Myra," and hugged her. "For being here for the caterers and everything. Really. You did a lot. The most."

She hugged back and kissed me on the lips. "You're welcome. I'm glad to help."

Tasting the paraffin from Myra's gloss, I hugged Eden and kissed her. "Thank you too."

"Sarcasm for me? I did nothing and you know it."

"Not true. You put the silverware away when you got here, and you saved me last night. Plus, you haven't shot me yet. What more can I ask from a woman who carries a gun?"

I stepped away and looked at them. "Now sit. Sit!"

I fetched Ed another Mexican beer, poured Myra and Eden more white wine, uncapped another beer for myself, and sat on the rocker facing them. The women had chosen the couch, and Ed was in an easy chair. The women crossed their legs, and Ed grinned at me as if he were watching an idiot child. I gave him the finger.

"Are you on medication?" Eden asked.

"Forget it." I deliberately put down a big slug of beer.

"He's feeling no pain," Ed said. "It's been a while, but I've seen him like this before."

"He's just relieved," Myra said. "That's nice."

"Yes it is," I said. "Here's to you but not these killjoys."

She raised her wine glass and we sipped together.

Eden said, "If he's feeling no pain, then he's cross-medicating. Mixing alcohol and drugs can be dangerous."

I said, "I feel good, very good. Is that so abnormal?"

Ed said, "For you it is."

"Bullshit, but I know what you mean. I've been through sadness, anger, lusting after a woman whose name I refuse to divulge, and that whole gamut of feelings was predictable, I mean given my nature. But now you can't understand why I'm happy."

"Beer and dope," Ed said.

Myra said, "Give the poor guy a break."

I laughed. "That's exactly what my mother would have said. You're a good person, Myra."

"Ignorance is bliss," Ed said. "That's why he's happy."

"Words of wisdom. Words to live by. But the truth is I'm happy because my plan worked over at the Brooks' house."

Eden said, "Worked? Your assailant got away."

"The killer showed up. That's my point. After all our reservations about that plan, it worked. I was feeling low until then. Unsure and out of touch with reality. But the goddam plan was a good idea after all. I wasn't just whistling *Dixie* the way everybody thought. So there's joy in Mudville tonight."

"You look like hell."

"Thanks, Ed, very vague and trite."

"Your head looks like a football. Clear enough?"

Eden laughed and Myra smiled.

"Now he tries a simile. Okay, I shall plumb its depths. You must mean my head is empty and full of air."

"That's true too, but I meant those stitches look like seams on a football."

"Oh, that's an exaggeration," Myra said.

Eden said, "You should have kept the bandage on."

"And look like a skunk?" I imagined the white gauze and tape against my dark hair, but didn't explain, saying instead, "Anyway, it'll heal faster in the open air."

Eden said, "It'll get infected easier too."

I patted the stitches with my fingertips, stimulating prickles of pain, stood up, turned around, leaned forward, and fell over my chair because it was farther from the wall than I'd thought. It was close enough, though, to put my hands on the wall and catch myself. I tilted my head up and down in the mirror.

"Goddam, that is beautiful." The sutures and the blackish residue they'd collected made a jagged seam on my bald spot from directly above my nose to the back.

"You sick?" Ed was beside me in the mirror.

"I'm looking at the stitches."

Eden appeared on my left. "Sit down before you fall down."

Ed said, "Go to the bathroom if you're gonna throw up."

"Goddammit, I'm okay!" I pushed up off the wall, turned around, and sat. "Mom used to rock me in this thing. It's older than this house. Her parents made it."

Eden and Ed glanced pointedly at each other, then sat.

I said, "Okay, look. I ought to be frustrated or sad but I'm not. I said that a minute ago, didn't I? Anyway, you know what gets me the most? The goddam killers are going to get away, and if they're the Crofts—and who else could they be?—the bastards will even inherit Sammy's farm at Old Town."

Eden said, "Something will turn up. They'll be caught."

"Hah! People get away with murder all the time, and in this case the law seems helpless. Wait a minute. Stop the morbidity. I'm too happy tonight. I will not let the shit get me down. Whoever showed up at Brook's house got me feeling too good."

Myra asked, "Couldn't you see the person?"

"I couldn't even see if it was a him or a her, a white or a black."

I flashed back to the Brooks' house and told them it was hallucinatory, how the person who must have been the killer had knocked me down and how I'd awakened to voices, blinding lights, dark forms running into and out of sight above me.

Eden said, "You were out of your mind long before that, walking around with a pizza in one hand and a beer in the other. That made you worse than defenseless."

I said meekly, "You're right for once."

Ed said, "Why would you be so careless?"

"I thought it was safe. Hell, even experts like Lieutenant Eden Grimes thought the killer'd never show up."

Eden said, "I thought Cliff was dead when we found him. So did Frank and Leroy."

"Leroy? I never heard the other detective's name before."

"Leroy Driessen," she said, and described how my chest had been covered with tomato paste that looked like blood. Their only clue concerning the assailant's identity was the panel truck I'd reported being parked on the street. It hadn't been there after the incident, none of the neighbors knew anything about it, but of course I had failed to get its license plate number.

My imagination still had me back on the ground at Brook's house. "Lucky my head just scraped that metal stake. A square hit would've killed me. Even so, I was so out of it, it took a while to realize the pain in my back came from lying on a beer bottle."

Eden said, "Whoever it was probably would've tried to get in through the back door if Cliff hadn't shown up. Heavy storm windows made breaking in through them almost impossible."

Myra said, "Then Cliff prevented a crime. A crime where people might've been hurt."

I said, "Mom, there was a crime, and I did get hurt."

Ed said, "Football-head is an all-American hero."

They prodded me to talk, probably to help me remain lucid. No prodding was necessary, but lucidity was beyond reach. I skimmed over events since Sammy's death, heard myself rambling, looked around and said, "The world's spinning."

Eden said, "I told you."

She or somebody else, maybe all three helped me upstairs and put me to bed. Tears covered my cheeks by then. "Even if the killers are convicted, they'll still inherit Sammy's property. It's the goddam pits. Where's justice when you need it?"

Somebody said, "The game's not over until the final out."

Fighting nausea, I woke up alone in the dark in my suit, shucked off the duds, then rushed to the throne where I knelt in homage, spilling my guts out in confession to the gods, wrenchingly over and over until nothing remained inside me but hot and fetid air.

Sometime during my collapse into sleep after that, I heard Aunt Judy's voice, lulling me into calm: "Keep on doing your best and everything will be all right."

CHAPTER THIRTY

The next night, from the same bed, freshly made with clean linen, I said to the darkness, "It's been a day of miracles."

"Uh huh," Eden purred in a post-coital daze.

Miracle referred not only to Eden's innovative sexual enthusiasms, but also several other happy surprises.

I pulled a sheet up over our nakedness, rolled over against Eden, draped my left arm over her stomach, lay my nose in the hollow between her neck and shoulder, closed my eyes, and the day's miracles paraded through my mind.

Ed had first used the term miracle this morning, entering Mom's house without invitation, climbing to the second floor, and batting my ass with a rolled-up newspaper. He grabbed an arm, dragged me around half off the bed, and said, "There's a miracle on the front page. Look at this."

"Get the hell out of here!"

He swatted me again. "I'm not kidding."

"Who cares?!"

I got up, pulled on some clothes, went downstairs, made coffee, faced the window over the sink, and refused to look at, listen or talk to him. When the coffee finished perking, I slopped some into a container and had a swallow that came back up and almost out my nose. I took three aspirin tablets from a bottle on the counter, washed them down with more of the vile liquid, then sprawled on a chair at the table.

Ed asked if I'd heard him.

"I don't give a goddam what's in that paper."

"My, my, and you felt so good yesterday."

"I'm dying."

"Yeah, but look at this before you go."

He threw a Bethel paper down in front of me, pounded an index finger on a front-page article, then went to the counter, poured himself a mugful, which I hoped would choke him, and became a noisy pig foraging among the piles of leftovers.

The paper caught my attention. It had today's date, and the article started, "BREAK-IN FOILED."

Despite my hangover, I laughed as the story unfolded, four brief paragraphs describing a hero who'd personally thwarted a break-in at the house of local attorney Benjamin Brook. Ten to fifteen sentences, but who could count?

Ed plopped down a plate to my left and sat. It was overloaded with two huge chunks of pastry.

"Jesus Christ! Any pie left?"

"The pecan pie's gone, but there's still some lemon meringue." He nodded toward the paper. "What about that?"

"The story's crazy. I shouldn't even be in it, let alone its focus."

"The sheriff gave you all the credit."

"Weird! The cops chased off the bad guy and executed the plan. Not me."

"The article omits my contribution to your plan too."

"Shit! Write a letter to the editor and describe what you did."

"Maybe I will. Any publicity's good for my business."

"Orndorf got this printed so the Crofts would know the waiver story was a hoax and wouldn't try to enter the Brook home again."

"Don't you think the cops were all over the Crofts yesterday? They had to know about the hoax before this."

"Yeah, right. And they wouldn't have gone back a second

time anyway, would they? I'm beyond figuring anything out. Except that both kinds of pie are all over your beard."

He brushed a hand across his mouth, shoveled in a mound of bakery, and swept his soup spoon like a squeegee over the plate, which was already empty. How the hell had he done that so fast?

The front door rapper pounded.

I said, "I'm not home."

"It could be important."

"I don't want to see anybody. Ignore it."

He shook his head. "I'll go, you antisocial jerk."

Ed's feet made heavy drumbeats, thumping off into the distance. The front door opened, there were voices, female and Ed's, and then the thudding returned to the kitchen.

Ed said from the archway, "You better come."

"Who is it, a neighbor?"

"Get up and see."

He stomped across the room, grabbed me under an arm, jerked me up, dragged me all the way to the front door, and went outside pulling me along. "Here he is. Mr. Clifford Saunders."

"You clown, get out of the way."

I edged past him, careful not to trip on the sill or his feet. He draped an arm across my shoulders, squeezed against me, and was smiling inanely when I looked up.

My visitor was a middle-aged blond woman hiding under heavy make-up. Beside her a younger woman was aiming a video camera at us. The blue van at the curb had a dish antenna on top and CHANNEL 8, WHIP TELEVISION on the side.

The blonde spoke into a microphone, "Here is the man the Shawnee County Sheriff praised, Clifford Saunders. Mr. Saunders, how do you feel about being a hero?"

I shook my head, looked at Ed, then back to the woman and

her right hand holding the microphone near my chin. My instinct was to sneer and run back inside, but maybe a word on TV could do some good, assuming what I said was not edited out.

Before I could say anything, Ed dipped his head down to the mike. "He's modest and shy."

"Too bad you're not," I said. "Look, the sheriff and his detectives are the ones. They saved me."

The woman brought the mike back to herself, asked, "Didn't you devise the plan that lured the criminals to that house?" then pointed it at me again.

"Well, I proposed the idea, but Sheriff Orndorf and his deputies deserve all the credit. The sheriff must feel sorry for me. I'm just a survivor. Look at this."

I lowered my head so the sutures were in the picture, held the position a second, and raised back up.

The woman asked, "Is that the injury you got saving Mr. and Mrs. Brook?"

Ed butted in, "Don't encourage him. He's beggin' for sympathy."

I said, "Ed thinks those sutures look funny and calls me football-head because of them. Ed of course is very odd. He's a sculptor and an artist and he's listed in the yellow pages under Ed's Arts and Crafts."

"You must be good friends," the woman said.

Ed cracked, "I wouldn't admit that on television."

I said, "Actually, I've been lucky. Did the sheriff tell you that somebody blew up my house in the country? Then when I moved here, they tried to burn this place down. Then they hit me over the head. This was the third attack on me. These bad guys are stupid, incompetent idiots. They've killed two people eighty years of age. Old people. Victims of greed. And the low-life cretins that did it are still free."

The woman pulled back the mike and smiled, inappropriately it seemed because she said, "That's awful." Then she re-extended the mike toward me.

I said, "We all need to help the sheriff capture them before they hurt somebody else. I say that in case anybody knows something. This can be like a public service announcement."

The woman said, "Let's stop here for a minute."

She turned to her companion and asked about lighting and sound. The younger woman began rewinding the tape in her camera. The older one glanced at notes on a sheet of paper.

Mom's phone rang so I went inside and basically ended the interview. I said nothing more than farewell to the TV people.

Ed and I were surprised when Channel 8's noon news program ran their tape uncut, adding introductory and concluding comments by the blonde and the sheriff. An announcer said the "story" was part of the station's ongoing series called "Local Heroes."

Ed said, "We look like a comedy team."

"The two stooges."

"You look worse than me."

Ed had at least been clean. I'd been unshaven, uncombed, in a white dress shirt with a dark stain on the chest. Well, fuck, I didn't care how I looked on the damn television.

I had cleaned up by noon, though, for Benjamin Brook. When the television people were present, he'd been the one on the telephone. He'd asked to see me, and arrived with his wife soon after the broadcast. He introduced her as Bea, short for Beatrice, met Ed, and then both Brooks thanked me for what I'd done at their home.

I apologized for putting them in danger.

They sat on the couch, drank coffee, from a new pot since I'd tossed out the old, and Ben, as he insisted we call him, asked me to let him file the photocopy of Sammy's will for probate. Ben said we might get the Crofts on the stand and provide in public court records clear indications of their greed if not their guilt.

The prospect of fighting the Crofts in court over the will—with the free help of an expert like Brook—elated me. I said, "Maybe we'll even win."

"Very unlikely, but winning the court case isn't the point. We'll do this because it's the right thing to do."

Beatrice invited me to their home for dinner. She'd call, she said, and set up a time.

"We can plan our strategy then," Ben said.

"I look forward to it."

Two hours later, another minor miracle: I started my long jog crawling, held down by lethargy and dissipated brain power, but my pace quickened as I went along and I ended up stronger than I'd been starting out.

The aspirins had kicked in, of course, easing my pains, but the praise of the sheriff and the media and the Brooks had energized me too.

After that surprisingly good run, another miracle came when I returned to Mom's house and deviated from my entrenched habit of never answering a telephone's ringing.

A computer said, "Will you accept a collect call from—"

"Laura."

"Yes," I said.

"Hi, Dad." I had not heard that familiar voice in over two years. God, the girl had really been angry at me.

"Hi, Baby," I said.

Laura was so relieved I'd picked up the phone. Her phone card had run out, and a machine in Andorra had seized her ATM card so she'd run out of cash and everything had just gone wrong. Then she'd called me collect over and over but I wouldn't answer. Well, that was all right. She knew how I was about telephones. But it was so frustrating because she wanted me to know how sorry she was about Aunt Judy and Granny and the house.

She ran on for a while, listened to me describing events, then expressed sorrow over our fight. It was her fault, she said. She'd had to get some distance and some time between us and grow up a little. Now she was able to accept the divorce. Of course, her mom had helped her understand too.

"Angela's staying with her parents the next few days," I said, "in case you want to talk to her."

"We already talked. I may return to the States later in the year. Then you and I can talk things over in person. I miss home an awful lot."

"Little girl, home is gone forever."

"Home is more than that house, Daddy. I miss the town and the people too. The atmosphere. I miss it all so much."

Uh huh, I thought, then why have you been in Europe the last two years? I only said, "Come back now if that's how you feel. I'll pay for your ticket. Round-trip if that's what you want."

"Thanks, but I can't right now. There are complications."

"What's his name?"

She laughed. "Gerard Bateau. We've been together for five months now. Andorra's a side trip on the way from our apartment in Barcelona to Jerry's parents' home in La Rochelle, France."

"He might be the one, huh?"

"Yeah, maybe. Anyway, I'm fine right now. I just don't want him helping me with money. I love him and you too, and I'll work my problems out all by myself. So don't worry about me. Goodbye, Dad. Check your e-mail. I'll keep in touch from now on."

Lying in bed alongside Eden, nearly asleep, I smiled at these memories. There was one more good thing to contemplate.

Eden had surprised me even before her astonishing acrobatic performance in bed. This other miracle had come in the early evening, after a brief argument caused by my complaints about Laura's living with Gerard.

"What's the problem?" Eden asked. "Her sex life is her business. She's an adult. Besides, you're doing basically the same thing with me."

"Well, we're older, and we have something special going."

"Maybe she does too. Being old-fashioned is one thing, Cliff. Being hypocritical's another."

I dropped the subject before disaster struck, and the miracle followed. It arrived during a candle-lit dinner at a restaurant nestled in an orchard on a hillside above a pond in the countryside north of Red Springs. Between salads and the main entree Eden said, "We have a new suspect." The department had located the panel truck I'd seen near Brook's house, and identified its owner. Our case was far from dead. This suspect could lead us to who knew what?

The possibilities were so obvious I didn't name them. I inhaled the faint smell of Eden instead, breathed on her shoulder, raised my hand off her belly, laid my forearm along her smooth thigh, and fell asleep wondering what else was going to happen. There had to be more good things ahead.

CHAPTER THIRTY-ONE

In the next three days Eden and I saw each other only once. Given the hectic pace she set, developing evidence, and the many jobs I had to do, twice-daily phone calls were all we could manage. They informed me of her progress, the new facts, but did not keep me from worrying about her success in solving the case.

My tasks were more depressing than hers. I visited Mom at the nursing home and tried to ascertain that she was being well cared for. Though it was clean, I smelled urine and heard a patient yelling mindlessly in another room. The home's director appeared, said the sheriff had talked to her, and whatever he told her, she was now sure that Home Care, Inc. would again be able to supply day care help at Mom's home, perhaps within a week, if I preferred to keep her there. Relieved, I told her I so preferred and looked forward to the change.

I went back to Mom's residence. Most of Aunt Judy's possessions had been taken by the convent's nuns who'd come to town to accompany her body back north where they conducted a private funeral service and burial. I disposed of the meager things that remained, and this little job led me to cleaning house completely—packing up the clothing Mom would never use, organizing her papers, disposing of all her unneeded things.

After several telephone contacts with the insurance company, an adjuster checked my home's inventory of contents, visited the rubble, and recommended a reasonable settlement. I'd receive the check for my losses within six weeks minus the $250 deductible. The demolition people arrived after him, and three truckloads of debris and five hours' work reduced the site to a raw scar.

During the demolition, scrounging among the ashes, I found the Indian tool, the shaped rock from Old Town. Never thought I'd see that again. Scrubbed with a stiff brush in the creek, it shed a coating of soot, but remained so darkened, I put it on top of the barn's audio player to remind myself to take it away later for washing with soap.

Even with a sewed-up scalp, I stuck to my usual work-out schedule, but its focus changed. Since Christmas, I had used exercise to build up my strength after my last writing project and to prepare for the next. E-mailing Laura had given me the tactile experience of typing on the keyboard. That and the magical appearance of words on the monitor pleased me in a way no other activity could. I felt strong now and wanted to do something worthwhile—more accurately, I needed to do something that made me feel worthwhile. It was time to start a new project.

I thought up a few plots, characters and settings, noted these down. I surfed the web, read news reports, funny stories, information on scientific breakthroughs, anything that caught my eye, and jotted down more notes.

I'd learned over the years that the right subject would excite me. I tried to look at the world with the expectation that every particular thing could provide material if I were sharp and in tune with it.

But the police case and Sammy's will distracted me. I consoled myself, thinking their resolution might be near. Eden's intermittent communications certainly provided me with a positive flow of discoveries concerning the case, but was conclusive evidence accumulating? I constantly mulled over the facts she gave me with this question in mind.

A Franklin County deputy sheriff, responding to her query for information, had reported moonlighting for a private security firm and riding in a panel truck such as Eden had described. Inside it he had seen ACME INTERIORS on a magnetic sign.

Eden apprehended the vehicle's owner, Morgan Edward Rauch, but the man refused to cooperate. On principle, he said, he would not answer questions. He knew his rights, invoked the fifth amendment, and told Eden to charge him or let him go.

Eden held Rauch on suspicion of assault to commit bodily harm while she and her colleagues compiled information about him. A licensed private investigator, he'd served six years as a patrolman with the Columbus Police Department, which he left with a clean but undistinguished record. Prior to that, he'd put in three years with Explosive Ordnance Disposal units in the US Army. As an EOD expert, he was therefore familiar with the use of dynamite, which the arson investigator thought had been used on my home. A search of Rauch's home in Plain City, a Columbus suburb, uncovered no evidence connecting him to the case.

Shown Polaroids of his rusty white panel truck, I confirmed that it looked like the one near Brook's house. In the truck were the ACME INTERIORS sign and two five-gallon metal gasoline containers that could have been used to carry gas to Mom's or my house. The truck also held carpentry tools and a large collection of skeleton keys. A forensics sweep of the truck, however, found nothing specific to connect it to the case, no proof that Aunt Judy had been in the truck as Eden had hoped.

At the same time, the department had been pressuring the Crofts. The day after the Brooks' house incident, the same day we'd buried Aunt Judy, Sheriff Orndorf had met with each Croft alone to convey the salient facts. One, the autopsy of Simon could not rule out homicide. The drug found in his system might very well have been put into the vodka he'd drunk by a family member who then arranged the asphyxiation. Two, the assault on me at Benjamin Brook's home also suggested someone in the Croft family. No one else had been told the bogus, signed-waiver story. That, along with the two homicides in the case, showed that the murder of Simon by a family member was a real possibility.

Considering this logic, Sheriff Orndorf asked those Crofts not involved in the crimes to cooperate. Social responsibilities were more important than family loyalty. All of them denied knowing anything about my assailant at the Brooks' house, and claimed innocence in the murders. After that, detectives grilled them about their movements.

When Rauch was identified, Eden showed the Crofts, again one at a time in private, his picture. The twins recognized him as a friend of Penny.

Shown a picture of Rauch, Penny denied knowing him, but told of the twins' statements, she admitted that he was her lover. She'd met him when the computer software company she worked for had used Rauch for investigative purposes. Why had she lied? To keep their relationship a secret because Morgan was fifteen years her senior. She had wanted to avoid hassles with her brothers, who could be snide, and her mother, who would be upset by such a boyfriend. That the twins knew about Rauch surprised Penny.

Eden thought that the brothers, learning of their sister's affiliation with Rauch, honestly tried to supply information, but the best they could do was place Rauch with Penny in two popular nightclubs at times unrelated to the crimes. The mother Diane said she'd known nothing before about Rauch, but he did not seem to be a good choice for Penny. What could they have in common?

Warrants gave the detectives access to all of the Crofts' possessions, but searches provided only one more relevant piece of information. The Crofts owned a gravel company south of Bethel in Warren County, and Simon had been active in its management. It was near where Aunt Judy's body had been found, and four sticks of dynamite were missing from its supposedly secure storehouse. Penny could have known where the dynamite was kept, and Rauch had keys that would open every lock at the pit site.

After hearing all this, I ran into Rauch in the hallway outside the County Prosecuting Attorney's office. I'd described under oath my experience at Ben Brook's house, in particular the panel truck, and confirmed its identification in the Polaroid pictures I'd seen before. Doing this took about thirty minutes. I left the office, and there was Rauch, sitting on a bench beside a well-dressed man, presumably his attorney.

While I waited for an elevator car, Rauch stared at me without expression. He wore blue slacks, black shoes, a blue, green and tan plaid, short-sleeve shirt, and looked several inches over six feet tall. With short black hair swept back without a part, a long, broad nose, somewhat protruding ears, a small, round face, and a short torso connecting a basketball player's long arms and legs, he resembled a spider.

When I described him to be sure that was who he was, Eden said, "Rauch should never have seen you. There was some kind of foul-up for that to happen."

"Yeah, well, I couldn't connect him to that distorted face I saw at Brook's house. Wish I could but I can't."

"I wish you could too," she said. "Circumstantial evidence ties him to you and the murders, but there's not enough of it."

"Wonderful!"

Eden shrugged. "There's even less on Penny. The prosecutor won't seek an indictment for either without more evidence, and I just learned something that clinches their guilt for me."

In phone calls to Hopper Security Systems, which had employed Rauch on special assignments for several years, Eden had learned that Hopper Systems had completed work two months ago for Samuel Burkhoffer. When Hopper executives connected Eden to the operative assigned that work, he said he'd gathered information about me and made an oral report to Sammy, detailing my jobs, habits, political activities, financial, family and legal status, those sorts of things.

I said, "Wow! I wonder how much he found out."

Eden said, "I may get a court order to look in their records for a written report. Seems odd to me there isn't one. Hopper could be withholding it. This is a murder case, and they're afraid of being sued."

"By me?"

"Who else? You're one of the victims."

Hopper's operative also told Eden that Morgan Rauch had met him, seemingly by accident at Hopper headquarters, and asked about the Burkhoffer assignment. This was four weeks after the job's completion. Rauch said he'd seen the operative in Bethel and wondered what was going on. The operative claimed he'd told Rauch only a vague and general outline of his work because every assignment was confidential. Claimed he'd mentioned to Rauch neither my nor Sammy's name.

Eden said, "That's a questionable statement too. The guy may have told Rauch everything since they were acquaintances and colleagues working for the same business."

"Doesn't that give you enough to charge Rauch?"

"Not according to the prosecutor."

"I knew it."

"Cliff, we're canvassing people who live near the crime scenes. Someone may have seen Rauch or Penny or their vehicles."

"You did that before and got nothing."

"We're exploring other leads too."

"They'll get off. Nothing's changed."

"Except that we know who the killers are."

"That makes the failure of justice even worse."

Her voice lowered into a seductive tone. "*Que sera sera.* Forget them for now. Let's go home. I got enough free time for a quickie."

I was in no mood for love. "Later? Tonight? Right now I have to get Mom's car titled and registered and licensed in my name."

Chapter Thirty-Two

The next morning, I went to the post office only because I had nothing better to do and was listless.

On the way I added up the evidence again, and concluded again that it was not enough for any jury to convict Rauch or Penny Croft. The killers would certainly get away with their crimes. Damn the injustice! Damn my helplessness.

I drove to the post office by habit, passing traffic and buildings and everything else without conscious attention, entertaining childish fantasies like those that had impelled me to take a pistol and go after the twins. A saint might not want revenge, but I imagined inflicting pain on the killers.

I tried to clear my head, but couldn't. I was as addled as I'd been yesterday evening, and remembering that fiasco made me feel guilty. I'd been able to give no more than desultory attention to Eden so our romp in the sack had succeeded for neither of us. She went home frustrated, and I phoned Ed. He let me rave for half an hour, told me to get some sleep and everything would look better in the morning, then hung up.

When that memory dissolved, where was I? Inside an airy room surrounded by glass walls. Aha, the post office. Refocused on the here and now, I turned in a request to have the mail forwarded from my farm address to Mom's address, and received the farm-addressed mail that had been on hold the past week. At a wooden table, I sorted through the pile and threw in a trash can all of the advertisements, coupons, and requests for charity.

That left two bills, one from the utility company, one from the phone company, and a 9-inch by 12-inch white envelope bearing no return address. A thick-nibbed black marker had printed my name and address on it in large capital letters. I tore open the flap and pulled out three sheets of paper.

It was Sammy's will.

Why had Ben Brook sent me this? And why to the farm address? I already had a photocopy of the will. The one from his meeting at the courthouse was back at Mom's place.

Turning the pages confirmed that it was the complete will, but nothing else—no cover letter, no note scribbled anywhere. I looked at the first page again, lifted it up toward the lights, brought it closer to my eyes.

"Damn!"

It looked like an original. Each page held what looked like original signatures, slightly thicker black ink than the print, which looked produced by a printer, not a photocopying machine.

I looked at the pages closely again, and came to the same conclusion. "I'll be goddammed!"

A woman in the lobby glanced at me, startled.

"Good news, I think." I waved the pages, smiled, hurried to the parking lot, and because the outside was considerably brighter than inside, studied the papers in the sunlight.

Definitely, an original!

I smelled something that reminded me of jasmine, noticed a pretty white flowering shrub in a large pot, noticed my car was in a Handicapped space, rushed over to it, jumped in, started the engine, then wondered where to go. Mom's house? To Eden? Ben? Ed?

Slow down, I told myself. Don't get your hopes up. Be sure of what you have before bothering people about it.

I sped back to Mom's house, retrieved the photocopy of the will, dug out Mom's magnifying glass from a dresser drawer in her bedroom, hurried into the kitchen, and at the table beneath two 100-watt ceiling bulbs compared both wills.

The photocopy's impressions were dark and clearly defined. The original's impressions looked lighter and not so even, maybe from a nearly empty ink-jet cartridge. On the original, the signatures were broad bands of darker ink than the print, and the cursive letters' ink ran unevenly along the edges, becoming lighter as they spread farther out in tiny splatters. On the photocopy, the signatures' letters seemed to be evenly dark without lighter edges, the same darkness as the print.

But I couldn't be sure. My magnifying glass wasn't powerful enough and I wasn't knowledgeable enough.

The paper? Again my knowledge was limited, but the original's paper seemed better quality, thicker with threads of fibers showing. The photocopy's paper was slick and shiny and probably less expensive than the original's paper.

The computer-generated print on each looked exactly the same in spacing and content, but the signatures? Comparing the same signature on original and photocopy showed differences in spacing between first, middle and last names, between the spaces between signatures and the lines for signatures below them, between sizes and shapes of letters, between lengths of the same signatures.

"Damn!" The photocopy did not match the original.

Wait a minute. There'd been two originals, and my photocopy was of Ben's original—to be exact it was a photocopy of a photocopy of Ben's original. This from my mail must be Sammy's original. So naturally there would be minor differences in the signatures. Nobody signed exactly the same every time. Sammy's original had not been photocopied. That explained the differences in signatures on the two copies before me.

Then explain this, I told myself. Why hadn't this original arrived in the mail before today? I sat back in the chair and tried to think it through.

Sammy died two weeks ago. If mailed before he died, why did this original get to me just now? Even not checking my mail for a week couldn't explain such slow delivery. Okay, the explanation was that it had been lost, laid aside, then recovered and sent to me only now. The envelope had stuck to the side of a mailbox or a mailman's bag and stayed there a few days unnoticed. It had slid under a package or something else and lay hidden. Then a few days later, wherever it was, somebody noticed and put it back into the mail being processed.

Sure. Those things could have happened. But they seemed unlikely. Suspiciously too convenient. Could there be something else? Some other reason?

Our recent "signed-waiver ploy" with the Crofts, the forged signature we'd used, suggested another reason. It was a fake.

This thought struck me with certainty. Ed! That crazy shit had forged the waiver. He had heard my belly-aching about the lack of justice, then done this. Hadn't he said last night on the phone that today would look better?

Was it possible? After I'd shown him my photocopy of the will, I'd stored it away in the telephone table's drawer. Hell, he could have easily taken my photocopy, made his own photocopy of it, and returned mine without my knowledge. He'd been in and out of this madhouse a dozen times while I'd been distracted.

Yes, the silly bastard could then have forged the signatures because he'd had copies to imitate, three copies, each signature being on each page of the will, Sammy's and the witnesses'. So that fit. But could he have gotten a blank copy of the will?

I called Ed, let the phone ring six times, then drove to his home, shoved past Brute and his wet tongue, and found Ed behind his house, behind his garage, extracting things from his kiln.

I bellowed my complaints at his back.

"I can't stop now," he said. "These have to fire a specific length of time at a specific temperature. Then they have to come out or they're ruined. Then I have to put in those urns over there. We can talk after that."

I ranted on, stopped for breath, and Ed twisted around enough to see me. He was wearing goggles, a shiny fireproof outfit, and big mittens. "Who cares where the will came from? Take that sucker and run. Shove it up the Crofts' asses."

"Did you do it or not?"

"How could I, you idiot?! You wanted justice, and now it's possible. Don't look a gift horse in the mouth."

He turned back to the kiln, whose open door emitted so much heat, it blasted my face although I was standing behind him.

I said, "I'm going to check with Ben Brook," and hustled back to the car, holding shoulder high the manila folder into which I'd put both copies of the will. Brute was leaping at it as if I were playing keep-away. The damn Clydesdale of a dog could knock the folder out of my hand and destroy the will.

"Down!" I snarled, got him to sit, and escaped.

Beatrice and Ben Brook were home, and learning of the will, Ben rushed me through the house to a room adjacent to his kitchen, a den-like space with book shelves, leather easy chairs, pipes on a rack, and large cans of tobacco that exuded a pleasant smell. Ben sat behind a desk, and compared the original and the photocopy as I'd done. Then he took two documents from another drawer, and compared them to the original.

"The print is the same," he said. "I printed these two wills yesterday at my office."

I asked, "Do you mean they were printed by the same

machine that printed Sammy's will?"

"Looks like it to me."

"But if this is Sammy's original, why did it take so long to reach me?"

All smiles, his wife touched my right arm. "I've heard of things being delivered months, years, even decades after they were mailed. Isn't this wonderful?"

"If it's true." I couldn't smile back.

"What are you thinking?" Ben asked, staring at me.

I started off about Ed and the waiver and his access to the photocopied will at my house.

"Stop right there, young man," Ben said. "What you are suggesting is fraud, and you are accusing your best friend of doing it. As well as me."

"No, I'm not saying for sure—"

"I would have to be involved according to what you're saying, and frankly that's offensive."

"Is the pen that was used for those signatures at your office downtown?"

"Yes it is, and before you ask, there has been no sign of unwanted intrusion in my office since I returned from Brazil."

I wanted to ask if he had told Ed what pen had been used to sign the will and where the pen was, but I didn't. I wanted to ask if he had told Ed about the computer containing a document file of Sammy's will, its folder and file names, or if he had printed up a blank copy of it and left it on his desk or somewhere else where Ed might have found it. These thoughts occurred to me, but so did thoughts about the history of Old Town, the injustice of the killers escaping punishment, the deaths of Sammy and Aunt Judy.

I said, "Can you prove that is the original will?"

"The proper question is, Can the Crofts prove it is not an original?" Ben paused and smiled. "The answer is no. Now, this will should be filed for probate immediately. I want to get it within the court's province and out of harm's reach. Today. At once. All right?"

"If you think that's what ought to be done."

His wife said, "We're on the Board of the County Historical Society, you know, so we think this development is splendid. We've liked the idea ever since Mr. Burkhoffer approached Ben about it. Mr. Saunders, Clifford, think of the good you'll be able to accomplish with this will."

She was very attractive, a slim, gray-haired woman in a flowery print dress and unfashionable jogging shoes. Her enthusiasm was infectious, and I began to reply.

But Ben was already up, tugging at my arm. "Come along then. I'll need you at my office."

I was only able to nod to Mrs. Brook in answer.

Ben pulled me outside, led me downtown—I followed his car in mine—and hurried me into an office that was more like a storage room, with two filing cabinets against a wall, a lamp, three chairs, three tables holding various things, and a desk.

He sat behind the desk, took papers from a drawer, a fountain pen from the middle top drawer, handed it to me, spun the papers around, and pointed at two lines on the bottom of each.

"Sign there. Those are the Application To Probate and the Application To Appoint the Executor. You sign both, and I will notarize your signatures and get the applications and the will over to the courthouse. It won't take long. I'll be old-fashioned and fill these out with the typewriter. Now where is it?"

"Behind you." I pointed to an electric machine on a small, wheeled table against the wall.

He rolled his chair close enough to grab the table's edge, then towed the table along, scooting his chair back to the desk.

"Cliff, as an officer of the court, I'm telling you to inform police authorities that you received this original. It is evidence in a homicide investigation. Please give me an hour, however. I want the will recorded and in the court's possession before the police get hold of it."

"I'll stay with you until you say it's time."

Not listening, looking through me, he said, "I'll call on a judge friend of mine to expedite matters. You need to have access to the Samuel Burkhoffer property to set up security. Executors must protect their estates. Does that meet with your approval?"

"I guess we ought to protect the farm."

"Good. Now go home and compose yourself. Mention to no one else your worries about this will's authenticity. Otherwise you might jeopardize your friend or me."

"The police think the killers stole the originals of the will and destroyed them."

He smiled. "No one knows if that is true except the killers, and they can't say anything. Consider this will, as I do, to be the original that Sam Burkhoffer possessed until he mailed it to you just prior to his death. Keep that in mind at all times whenever the subject of the will comes up."

"Okay."

"After I finish at the courthouse, I intend to draw up papers for the land trust and the incorporation that Sam wanted and the will calls for. All right?"

I went back to Mom's house, sat down on the rocker, and tried to ignore doubts and imagine possibilities. Obviously, the land would not be destroyed by urban sprawl. Experts of various kinds could advise me how to preserve and enhance the place, how to create valuable programs for the community. Ben and his wife and their historical society might know people I should talk to. Indians? Shawnees? Miamis? Was that possible? I would surely be able to recruit all kinds of wonderful people to help. Great, if the will was probated.

I closed my eyes, imagined Sammy's farm, its buildings and its fields, and dozed off. When I woke, the time was 12:30, well over an hour since I'd left Ben, and it was Eden's lunchtime.

I thought about calling her cell phone number, but wanted to tell her the news in person. She'd been going home for lunch this week. That's where she'd be.

Since her condo was less than a mile away, the day was so nice, and I felt so good, I'd jog over. No, I didn't want to get sweaty yet. I'd ride the bike. I locked the back door, took my old three-speed Schwinn from the garage, squeezed the tires, found them full of air, and started pedaling. It was an easy trip down the alley, along several side streets, heading south and west. Within a few minutes I turned into the north entrance of her condominium complex, passed the front unit and approached hers. If home, she'd park her car or cruiser on the west side, where the front of the unit was, but I'd have to go clear around the building to check there.

Instead, I biked off the driveway onto the grass, maneuvered past the tennis court, around the blue spruce screening her little patio from the driveway, cut behind the solid wood, six-foot high fence, which screened the patio from the large central commons area and the next unit over, bounced up onto the concrete slab, and stopped with squealing brakes.

I looked through the glass doors, and the outside light penetrated the room enough to let me see Eden and a man on the couch deep inside near the fireplace. They were naked, looking toward me from prone, side-by-side positions.

Perched on the bike seat, I leaned to the right near the glass, stared for a moment, and my large grin transformed into a gaping mouth. I pushed off with the right foot, backing up until both tires were on the grass, turned the handlebars, pushed forward, then stopped as the glass door clicked, slid open, and Eden's head craned outside.

She had wrapped the blue drape over her left shoulder down under her chin and right arm so only her right arm, shoulder, neck and face showed to me, her whole backside remaining bare to whoever that was with her—he was no one I knew.

We stared at each other. I started to apologize, but didn't because I wasn't sorry I'd seen them.

"What is it?" she asked.

"I'm surprised."

"Don't throw one of your tantrums."

I shook my head, thinking, I should have gone home with her at noon yesterday. No, that was stupid. What difference would that have made. I must've been staring at her accusingly.

She said, "Cliff, we never made any promises."

"You're right. Sorry I intruded. See you later."

She may have called out to me. I don't know because my bike clanked and creaked, crossing the grass, bumping over the curb onto the driveway. I concentrated hard, first on not losing control on the rough ground, then on finding my way back home.

Chapter Thirty-Three

I pedaled back to Mom's house, changed into my running clothes, called the sheriff's office, and left Lt. Grimes the message that the US Mail had this morning delivered to me Sam Burkhoffer's original copy of the will. Then I drove to the bike trail and did a long run too fast, exhausting myself so badly, I had to walk the last two miles back to my car.

The run helped me escape talking to Eden, but not thinking about her. What had Ben Brook advised—to get composed? How could I do that?

At Mom's house, a sheet of yellow, legal-pad-size paper stuck out head-high between back storm door and frame: a note from Eden, asking for the envelope the will had come in. I wadded up the paper, threw it at the trash can, went upstairs, showered, dressed, and flopped down on the bed.

Wasn't the envelope at the post office? I dug a hand into my pants pocket, found the two damn bills in there, smoothed them out, and lobbed them over in front of the stairs. Yes, the envelope was at the post office. I hadn't brought it home.

Why would she want it? The date stamped on it? I hadn't noticed that, and what could it matter anyway? Well, a postmark from before Sammy's death might matter. A postmark after might raise questions about the will.

Also, Eden and Shepherd might want to check the envelope for fingerprints and DNA. I'd read about saliva on envelope flaps being tested. Only Sammy's or the killers' prints or DNA on the envelope would benefit me. Other people's, Ed's and Ben's especially, would be trouble.

My watch showed a little after 4:00. The post office closed at 5:00. Eden or Shepherd could stop here any second. I wouldn't destroy the envelope, but why help the cops get it?

I rolled out of bed, picked up the two bills off the floor, put them in the bowl of bills-awaiting-payment downstairs, locked the back door, and drove away in Mom's car to cruise without destination. Route 24 took me south over the freeway and a few miles farther. I turned east on a county road, followed it to 86, and followed 86 north back to town, crossing over the freeway again. Reaching the business district, where 86 and 24 merged, I meandered northeast, noticed my nearness to Ben Brook's property, drove there and went to the front door.

Ben was still at his office. Beatrice took me inside, offered a snack, then connected me by phone with her husband.

Ben was working on documents for incorporating the non-profit land trust. He'd filed the will for probate, gained the co-operation of his judge friend, and as required by law, all of Samuel Burkhoffer's relatives, as potential heirs, had been informed that a hearing on the will would take place on Friday next week. He and Sheriff Orndorf had visited each Croft, hand-delivered written notice about the will and the hearing, and explained to each Croft that the will was Sammy's original, which had apparently not been stolen after all.

"Any hassle from them?" I asked.

"No, and hopefully there won't be any. Do you know the mechanics of probating a will?"

"Not much."

"If the will is challenged, it can take a long time. The court has dual responsibilities: to provide for the estate's inheritance according to the legator's wishes if those can be established. And to protect the rights of legitimate heirs."

"So a Croft challenge could mean months of delay."

"Years, but the Crofts seemed to be in shock. Of course we encountered them alone. Maybe in a group they will be different, but I think the family is in disarray at this point. They lost the head of their household, and then received proof that one of their own might have killed him. Our filing of an original will could be too much for them to deal with now."

"No challenge would be nice," I said.

"We'll have to wait and see what they do."

Ben's good news didn't pep me up, and neither did Beatrice, who started describing the County Historical Society's accomplishments. I excused myself, not able to chitchat, assuring her that sometime I did want to ask her which society experts might advise me about the Old Town Land Trust—should that ever become a going concern.

Avoiding the sheriff's office downtown, I wandered east through increasingly newer suburbs until my street ended. There a lane took me south to Route 53 where I pulled into a nursery.

Sitting with the windows down brought in a sweet odor that reminded me of funerals. I got out, walked around aisles of displays, went through a greenhouse, and bought two red and two white already-blossoming geraniums. I drove to Mom's garage, picked up a shovel, drove to the cemetery, and planted them on my father's grave near the tombstone.

I looked around and noticed most flowers on the other graves were also planted in that location. Why was planting flowers there better than anywhere else? Did a tombstone mark the actual head end of a grave? Damned if I knew.

The monument was ready for Mom. She'd had her own name engraved beside Dad's and a blank space left for her year of death. Mom had also selected and prepaid Osvald's for her casket.

I took a plastic gallon milk jug from the trunk, filled the jug at a faucet, watered the plants, started back to the car and stopped. My feet pointed down the length of Dad's grave toward the headstone, and I thought, Beneath my soles in the earth lay my roots.

Did the Croft children think something similar at their father's grave? Or was Simon in the mausoleum where they'd put Sammy's ashes?

I didn't stop at the mausoleum and check, steered around it instead, reached the road, and drove a mile west to a hilltop just north of the freeway. I left the car and walked downhill in the gutter. At the base of the hill, I crossed the street into a driveway that snaked around among four long, gray, two-story, warehouse-like buildings: apartments redone thirty years ago into Bethel's first condominiums.

At the farthest-in, southeastern edge of the property, against the twenty-foot raised earthen platform that elevated the freeway, I stopped before the party house. The fenced-in swimming pool beside it was empty, Memorial Day being more than a month off. The long, one-story addition on the rear, somebody had told me, contained a weight room and an exercise room that doubled as an area for dancing.

Dad's old house. The kitchen, the living room and my bedroom upstairs were vague memories from my sixth year. There'd been a large red barn to my right, its location buried by the freeway now. There'd been fields north, south, east and west of the house—all gone now. Despite aluminum siding and fancy new windows, the front of the house resembled what had been there before, but nothing else looked familiar.

I went back to my car and looked down at the scene. Cars and trucks whizzed past on the freeway. Freeway? Their speed was possible only because they stayed on a road that occupied the center of my Dad's family's homestead, which had once been 210 acres of rich farmland.

Fighting the sale of the place had killed my father. He'd bought Mom's house in town, moved us there, and later bought the smaller farm I'd bought from Mom on Pekin Road. His struggle in the courts had sapped him so badly, he died from frustration and sadness. Eminent domain was declared, and his heart gave out.

The day of his death, a neighbor drove Mom out to the Pekin Road farm because Dad hadn't come home for dinner. She found him lying by the tractor in a field he'd been plowing. I came home from playing in the neighborhood and found her rocking in that chair of hers, crying. She'd said, "I knew it'd come to this," pulled me onto her lap, and we rocked together for a long time, until she thought of my hunger and made supper for me.

One more look at my obliterated inheritance, and I drove to Ed's place. Years of Dad's complaining filled my head on the way. He'd developed the habit of repeating certain things aloud, but to no one except himself. The goddam government this. The goddam government that. Worse than communism. Those goddam thieves!

I asked Ed to go to a movie with me, but he was unable and asked me to join him at dinner with some friends. He mentioned four names that told me they were actually business contacts of his. I begged off, asked him to exercise with me at my barn tomorrow, and we agreed to meet there at 2:00.

"Should I bring the crew again?" he asked.

"If you want to."

I drove west toward Dayton, loafed along on back roads, eventually encountered that city's bypass, and took it southwest to a shopping mall. At the complex of ten screens and second-run movies, a large sign listed the next showing of my movie choice to be in an hour. I found a fast-food joint nearby, ate supper, and returned to the theater with time to spare.

Cast Away—I'd read reviews and was glad it hadn't left town yet. After it was over, driving back to Mom's house, I rated the performance a *tour de force* and wished for someone to discuss it with. The Tom Hanks character had struck a familiar chord, the way he developed after long isolation, coming home to people and a world as changed as he was. There had been the usual over-reliance on technical tricks in the beginning, when the plane wrecked and sank, but I could accept that and the overly obvious ending's positive message because of the script's humane values and believable characters.

Back at Mom's house another yellow paper awaited me in the back door. It urged me to call Eden, NOW, no matter the time. She'd even used the magic word please and underlined it.

My watch said 11:15. There was a good chance that by now the envelope had been thrown out with the other post office trash and was, hopefully, buried in the county dump.

Might as well get the call over with. I went to the phone and punched in her cell phone number.

When she answered, I said hi and told her I didn't have the envelope, must have left it at the post office, at the wooden table nearest the entrance or in the trash can beneath the table because that was where I'd thrown the junk mail. And no, I had not noticed the postmark.

"Why didn't you tell me this earlier, Cliff?"

"Calling you is awkward so I put it off."

"Want to come over? Or I could come over there."

"No thanks."

"We can talk this out, Cliff."

"I feel betrayed."

"We made no promises."

"Yeah, you said that before. Well, I thought we did. I thought we had something special and that implied commitment."

"I made no commitments to you."

"I know that now."

Silence, a pause, then I said, "I don't think we can work this out. Our values clash too much."

"You're gonna cut me out just like that?"

"I'm sorry, and I'll miss you a lot, but that kind of difference is too much for me."

Lying in bed, I felt as if another beloved person had died. She had never apologized—obviously because she didn't think she owed me an apology. Lust and loneliness had guided me— and her. I should have gotten to know her better, found out her thinking, and reached a clear understanding with her before trying sex.

Sex wasn't a recreational activity like going to a movie. A loving sex act implied commitment even if commitment wasn't discussed—otherwise having sex was using the sex partner selfishly. That was what I thought, and it was the truth, a truth out of touch with the times, but a truth nonetheless.

CHAPTER THIRTY-FOUR

The next morning, "The Lord giveth and the Lord taketh away" blinked on and off in my mind like a damn neon sign. I told myself that the saying offered no comfort.

No comfort? It very wisely suggested the need to accept realities, to trust that a plan beyond human understanding guided all things. Without that belief, I might be headed for nutsville. Insanity. All-consuming anger or despair.

But if I adopted that Biblical notion, wouldn't any comfort from it depend on self-deception?

My thoughts seemed so incompatibly at odds, and the saying itself was so insistent, I turned on the computer, went on-line, plugged "Lord Giveth and Taketh" into my search engine, and clicked on one of its findings, bringing up a home page that listed hundreds of thousands of innocents killed at God's behest according to The Old Testament. The page had a USC.edu address, suggesting that some anti-religious intellectual at the University of Southern California was urging his disbelief on everyone. Its messianic anti-theism drove me off-line.

I pulled up my word processing program, began typing, and more than two hours later scanned what I'd composed: free association, rambling nonsense, then more orderly descriptions, the best of which was about finding Sammy dead.

"I'll be goddammed," I said, realizing only then that I'd concentrated so much on that subject.

I saved the Sammy material and printed a hard copy. Read it

over more carefully and thought it had potential. This could be my next project. Think about it, I told myself.

A memoir about the murder case?

Why not?

I'd never done a memoir. I didn't know how the story ended.

Yes, but I never knew how my books ended at the start. When I thought I knew, they ended a different way.

Arguing with myself, I shut off the electronics, dressed for exercising, locked up, and set off for the Pekin Road farm.

Isolated inside the house all morning, I was surprised that the hot, dry weather had broken. There'd been showers, and after a week of 70- to 80-degree temperatures, the day felt very cold. It was in the low 50s, cloudy and windy. The car radio reported that thunderstorms were probable and tornadoes possible. Dropping temperatures might bring frost tonight. An arctic cold front was colliding with our muggy heat.

At the farm, wearing long pants, jacket and ball cap, I barely worked up a sweat in the chill, jogging the lane to the road and back, repeating the route enough times to complete four miles, double the normal length of my warm-up. On the barn floor, my feet left a trail of soggy prints. Jogging in the grass past the barn to achieve the measured distance had soaked my shoes. Damn! The wet socks might impede my dancing later on.

I began lifting weights, following my usual order, doing the usual number of repetitions, paying attention only to their demands, taking my time to avoid muscle strains.

I completed one whole cycle of nine exercises, took a break to recover my strength, recorded numbers in my log, and checked my wristwatch, which I'd laid on top of my jacket and hat. It was 1:35 already. Well, I didn't care. When Ed and whoever showed up at 2:00, I'd quit the weights and join them in dance.

A monsoon hit, rain pounding so hard, two huge callused

palms seemed to be drumming on both slanted sides of the roof. Thunder boomed and crackled, and lightning flashed just outside the barn doors, which were a foot open. The temperature plunged further, and my breath puffed, suddenly visible before me. I glanced out the doors again. Water was pouring along the ground as if the barn were an island in a stream.

"Good. We need this," I said, but shivered, and yearning for warmth, swung the long steel bar loaded with ninety pounds of weights up behind my head onto my shoulders for a second set of thirty squats. The up-and-down motion heated me at once, excluded thoughts about morality, weather or Eden, and made me feel whole, a component of the old barn's peacefulness inside the storm.

I was thinking twenty-two, counting, standing up out of a squat when something struck my left temple and knocked me sideways. My fingers uncurled, the bar rolled free, and weights struck my left hip, hurling me farther right.

I must have staggered several feet because, awakening, I lay on the dance floor looking up at the lights underneath the big cross beams supporting the hay lofts.

Two figures flew toward me, and not wholly conscious, I thought of huge bats. Their clothing flared out from around their bodies the way bat wings stretched between front and back legs. With only the shadowed side of their clothes showing and bats dwelling in the barn, I'd made that connection.

Light caught the figures, revealing blue plastic ponchos with hoods, the wet faces of Penny Croft and Morgan Rauch. They took off the rain gear and threw it aside.

"Stand!" Penny yelled.

Rauch grabbed my left ear and jerked so I screamed and struggled up. He released the ear, rapped the sore side of my head with his knuckles, and I almost went down again.

"Let me," Penny said. "I want the pleasure."

As the spidery Rauch stepped away, the woman's right hand shot out, ball-peening my chest. My shoulders hunched forward, she shouted something, a foot slammed into my left shin, and her left hand hit my right cheekbone.

I fell backwards, landing on my rear, then my shoulders, whipping my head back, whacking the floor.

When consciousness returned this time, I was already on my feet with the spider tugging on my ear again.

"Too easy. Too quick," the woman said, assuming a martial arts stance.

When the spider let go and stepped aside again, she circled me, balanced but taut, reacting to any movement of mine. I ducked my head beneath my forearms, but she landed short, painful jabs on my arms, shoulders, and sides.

The blows jackhammered uncountably fast, accumulating impacts that threatened to break whatever was hit. My arms went numb, and my hands dropped below my waist. To get blood circulating, I flexed, but she then pattered the exposed area around my eyes with rapid blows that stung and dazed me.

I gasped, and my open mouth drew her punches, precise, staccato strikes that sent me reeling back with her in pursuit. Two pebble-like masses swept down my throat, my tongue found jagged stumps, and I realized I was swallowing dental crowns.

She stood before me, her fists in position—they were blood-stained—and her dark eyes studied me.

I swayed, tried to speak, swallowed blood and choked, then managed, "Killing me won't stop the will."

"You weaseled your way into Grandfather's favor. You played Daddy for a fool, bothered him his whole life and at the end turned him into a cream puff. Then you came up with that so-called original will. You turned my whole family against me. Killing you is something I've wanted to do for a long time."

"Why Aunt Judy?"

"The nun? That old bitch said she forgave me. Said you forgave me. Said the Lord forgave me. Who did she think she was?"

"She did nothing to you."

"You did. Let's see if an incompetent cretin can teach you something."

Her fist came from nowhere and hit my nose THUMP! Pain slashed through my sinuses and traumatized my eyes so badly, I couldn't see. Clutching my face, I was defenseless.

This was how the world would end, I thought, with a whimper, but at least that would stop this pain.

"Had enough fun?" the spider asked the woman.

"Yeah."

"Put him down. I'll get the gas. This place'll go up like a torch."

Killing me wasn't enough. They were going to burn down the beautiful barn. I WAS a goddam wimp to give up.

I forced my eyes open. She stood between me and the weights. Rauch was gone. Behind me was the stall and the audio player.

The woman balanced her weight on her left leg, bent her right knee back to her chest, yelled something that sounded like "Die!" and kicked up at my head.

I moved just enough so her heel hit a shoulder. The force of the kick spun me around away from her backward against the stall. The wall of the enclosure buckled with my weight, the audio player jumped up in its box, and the Indian stone on top of it fell to the floor. I slid off the wall and bent over, dropping my hands to the stone as if I were collapsing again. With the rock in my left hand, I looked behind me and started straightening back up.

Penny had her fists positioned and was coming toward me

for the *coup de grace.*

I turned toward her, swinging my left arm and the stone around so centrifugal force increased the speed of my hand. Released at the last moment, the rock struck Penny's forehead.

She dropped at my feet without a sound.

I tripped over her, stepping on an arm, remembered the back door was locked, and ran to the front. I stuck my head out between the open doors and was blinded. Dark clouds were everywhere except for one clear blue spot that lined up perfectly between me and the sun. I blinked, looked down, refocused, looked up more guardedly, and saw Rauch thirty feet to the left with his back to me, bent over a squat, four-wheel, all-terrain vehicle.

I ran outside to the right, passed the big tree, crossed the backyard, passed the swing, and started down the mown trail. One leg hurt where it had been kicked, and I couldn't coordinate my upper body because pains had twisted my head and arms and chest into awkward positions. Breathing was hard with an unusable nose and a throat choked by blood and mucous.

I did my best. What else could I do? I ran on as hard and as fast as I could, hoping Rauch hadn't seen me.

Something rammed into my calves, knocked my legs out from under me, and dropped my butt down onto something smooth. I slid off, rolled onto my feet, heard the engine and saw Rauch leaving the little vehicle. I stumbled away, but he caught me. Smashed the back of my head, knocking me forward and down.

I landed in water, spit out a mouthful, and my hands slipped on mossy rocks. I was face down in the creek.

Behind me, Rauch said, "No more foolin' around! You're dyin' right here and now."

With my head raised above water, this pronouncement rang out like a fiat, voicing an inescapable evil.

Was there no stopping it? I looked for an answer around me.

Less than an arm's length away was the sycamore that leaned over the creek. The water was higher now than the last time I'd been here, when the bastard behind me had ruined my house. The tree's largest root was now fully submerged. I had probed beneath it many times before when it was partially out of the water, and almost always found an inhabitant. Let it be there now. Please God, let me have time.

My left hand touched the sandy bottom by the root, reached into the hollow that had washed out of the bank underneath it, and I felt hardness. Was that it? I flattened my palm over a dome-like carapace, and along its roundness was the line of bony eruptions. My fingers followed them down to the end nearest me.

I hesitated. I'd been taught that snapping turtles always went into their lair head first. I'd never known this "belief" to be wrong, but still there was fear.

I dropped my fingers farther down, touched the tough spike of a tail, and filled my palm with it.

Rauch stepped into the water, splashing, straddling me so his ankles touched my shins. He was ready to beat in my head.

I yelled, "Please wait!" and pulled the tail toward me.

The stubby legs churned, scrabbling to stay there. I turned over and sat up. It wasn't a dangerously fast move that would alarm or threaten Rauch. I was too weak for speed, and he probably expected me to roll over and plead for mercy.

My left arm twisted across my chest and dragged behind so that what strength remained could gather into my left arm and hand. The turtle came out of its lair, out of the water, fighting mad. Its webbed feet clawed the air, its beak opened, and it hissed. I swung it up backhanded and flung it headfirst at Rauch.

He was leaning forward over me, his knees bent down together, preventing a kick at his groin, but he straightened up, protecting his face, perhaps thinking a rock was coming toward him but too weakly to be dangerous. Maybe he was stunned, seeing up close a predator unchanged after eons of life.

Instead of swiping it aside, Rauch caught the turtle with a hand on each side of its shell, leaving his arms vulnerable. The snapping turtle would have undoubtedly attacked those targets, but this one was fairly big, over a dozen pounds of fury, and its surprising weight, velocity of descent, and perhaps Rauch's sudden fear and weakness brought it farther, up against his waist, and here the beak could do worse damage. It bit.

Rauch screamed and slowly sat straight down as if taking a seat he didn't want but couldn't refuse. He screamed again and continued screaming. His torso was clear of the creek, but his lap and his legs remained in the water as if he were hoping the water might entice the turtle to release its grip and swim off. Snappers I'd seen never let go. They snapped and stayed snapped until what they'd bitten broke free or their head was cut off. Even with a severed head, though, the beak would hold on, and the heart would beat on for hours.

The screaming chased me out of the creek. I clambered up the bank to the little vehicle, found its motor rumbling, climbed onto the seat and shifted into a gear. The ATV jerked forward into a briar patch, shoved through it, curved back onto the trail, and bounced away. I sprawled forward, slumped full upon the handlebars, pressing down so my weight held the movement in a basic direction toward the swing and the backyard.

The vehicle rammed into something that twisted the wheels so the handlebars turned abruptly, throwing me off to the ground.

There were voices and blurry people, and I tried to warn them about Penny and Rauch.

Someone wiped my eyes, and I recognized Ed.

"Danger! Police!" I said. "Nine-one-one."

"Take it easy, Cliff," Ed said, but he looked beyond me toward the creek.

Georgie appeared beside him with a cell phone. I heard her call and ask for police and an ambulance.

Rain pelted my face. Thunder rattled as if the sky were trying to speak.

Somebody touched my face.

"Don't move him," somebody said.

Myra was kneeling beside me and she put her face close. "I was gonna teach you some dances today."

"Save the turtle," I said. "Don't waste the turtle."

I tried to explain but passed out.

CHAPTER THIRTY-FIVE

The first clear sign of my recovery came after three heavily medicated days in the hospital when phantom-like visitors left me with vaguely remembered fragments of information.

On the fourth day, just moderately doped, I went home, officially pardoned from my fears of imminent death, but struggling to do the simplest things: disembarking from Ed's pickup, stumbling inside, descending fully onto my right side so the pains were only sporadic, and so I could see the three people present from Mom's couch. Surprisingly, one was Eden.

I heard Myra ask, as if she were scolding Eden, why Rauch and Penny Croft had not been under surveillance.

Eden said they'd been under so much suspicion already, no one expected another attack on me. Also, the depth of Penny's hatred for me had not been understood then.

The source of it was Simon. All three children had adopted his attitude toward me, but Penny was most affected, maybe because she was the most anxious of the children to win her father's approval. All three pursued Simon's avocation of karate, but she alone imitated him by attending a military academy.

Her hatred grew as Simon's bitter complaints about me intensified over the years. When I wasn't charged with arson in the burned-up bulldozer incident, Simon became furious, then openly gloated over my incarceration for contempt of court. Although I was out of his hair for five years after that, my connection to Sammy's death and then Sammy's property aroused

Simon's old animosity a hundred-fold because I was now directly intruding in Croft family affairs.

Simon's feelings incensed Penny, and my comments on television and her failures to harm me at the farm or at Mom's house so stimulated such hatred of me, she had to get revenge. Her father's suicide, which she blamed on me, along with the original will I received in the mail, forced her to seek me out even while she was under intense suspicion.

Ed said, "Cliff does have a way with women."

Dumbass, shut up, I thought. He didn't know I'd found Eden with another man. Never would know either. I snorted, "Huh!" and let him guess what I meant.

Eden said that the twins, Diane Croft and Rauch had given her this information, but input from Rauch was questionable. He blamed Penny for everything: she'd killed Sammy and Aunt Judy, and she'd burned up my house. She'd told Rauch about these acts, but he himself had participated in none of them.

I blurted, "Bullshit!" causing my head to turn and muscles to ache so much I vowed not to speak again.

Eden said, "Of course Penny can't defend herself. The doctors don't know if she'll ever wake up. If she does, they say she'll never be competent. There was severe brain damage."

I kept my words quietly under control, "Odd how things work out." Somebody had told me the Indian rock had cracked open Penny's skull like a walnut. I shook my head, and with that movement, my neck and shoulders throbbed so painfully I cringed.

"You feel bad about her?" Ed asked, rocking on Mom's old chair.

"Hell no," I said, remaining calm. "She'd have killed me."

"You did a job on both of them," he said.

"Pure luck." Explaining was beyond me, but I would have told them some Power had had me in its grasp. It gave me the

Indian tool and the turtle so I used them. I contributed a little willfulness and knowledge, but the outcome depended most on chance, or on some unknowable, universal plan.

At that point, lulled by the sounds of friendly voices, I fell asleep, and an hour later awakened alone in the house. On the coffee table lay the envelope the will had been mailed in, with a note from Eden: "The sheriff said to give you this. Get well." No signature. No complimentary close. No apology.

I filled the kitchen sink, soaked the envelope in it until it was mush, and threw it away in the garbage.

One whole week after returning home, I felt good enough for a turtle soup celebration with friends in Mom's living room.

Able to speak without pain if I didn't overextend my jaws or touch my tender cheekbones, wearing ugly temporary plastic dental crowns that spared me the pain of six bare snags, I said, "Before you dig in, let's honor the critter that saved me. He was home at the right time and available for service, so I humbly thank Mr. Snapping Turtle from the creek behind where my house used to be."

"The least you can do," Ed said. "He gave his life for you."

"He most certainly did. To Mr. Turtle!"

"Here! Here!" were the cries. Or something like that.

I hoisted a can of domestic lite beer in our town's first-ever toast to one of its most permanent residents. Raised glasses and mugs responded. People smiled, drank, then tried the soup.

The taste was entirely appropriate to its wild source, and so strong it drove all eight of us to the large shell, which I'd scraped out, cleaned, dried in the sun, and upended on the coffee table. The shell's inside was lined with Saran Wrap and heaped with crackers, clear little plastic sacks of oyster and square saltines. The first wave of takers depleted the supply, but the boxes lay near, and Myra replenished the pile.

I told the assembly that we should thank my Mom, who'd

returned home yesterday to her bedroom, for the soup's recipe, and thank Deputy Clayton Jones for the turtle's preparation. The sheriff praised Jones for the departmental training program Jones was setting up, and that put Jones on stage center.

He described his "apprehending of the alleged perpetrators" and the slicing of turtle from Rauch. Ernie Hathaway innocently asked what parts of the turtle we were eating. Jones then described in gory detail the butchering process, to the disgust of the Brooks but the delight of Georgie and Chuck, who said they were into natural foods and didn't know how to do turtle.

When Jones mentioned that he used to catch snappers on trot lines baited with chicken liver, as I had done as a child, the fact he was the first officer responding to the 911 call seemed serendipitous enough to confirm my divine plan idea. Or whatever you wanted to call it. No one else would have known how to handle the turtle or would have butchered and cleaned it.

Jones ended up his comments, "Rauch was sittin' in the crick, yellin'. The snapper had a right good grip on his leg."

That startled me. "I thought Mr. Turtle bit off the family jewels."

Ed laughed. "That would've been perfect."

Eden said, "Wishful thinking."

Jones grinned. "No, sir, that didn't happen, but even so, he won't walk straight for a while."

I said, "We're lucky Rauch didn't pull the turtle loose. He might've killed all of us before you got there. Or at least escaped."

Jones said, "He was afraid to pull it loose. He told me to be careful 'cause he thought the femoral artery might get broke. From what I heard at the hospital, he was right. That coulda happened easy."

★ ★ ★ ★ ★

A month after coming home, dangers from a concussion minimized, improved enough to do more than walk around the neighborhood, I convened our fivesome at the old barn, and Myra taught us some folk dances. They wore me out, circling around with relatively easy maneuvers to exotic foreign songs. I rested, but joined back in for about two hours' worth. On the way home I told Myra I really liked her kind of dancing.

"I thought you would," she said.

I surprised her when we danced again three days after her introductory session. I'd had the stall-walls dismantled, the audio player put up front, more lights on separate circuits hung under the mows, and four-square-foot oak parquetry installed around the original tongue-and-groove oak. Except for right inside the front doors, a 15-by-20-foot section holding weight-lifting equipment, the entire ground level was dance floor.

Myra taught us more dances, faster ones as I grew stronger, and performing them, just being on my feet for two or three hours, was challenging exercise and fun. Myra led us around, and I stumbled along at the rear, imitating her steps.

Why did I like this dancing so much? The idiosyncratic movements and sounds seemed mysterious, having risen from particular people in particular places at particular times. Bending and straightening up, grapevining, walking, skipping, kicking and spinning, coordinating our feet, arms, hands, and bodies to the music and each other, snaking around my old barn's rough, hand-hewn upright beams beneath the lights, conveyed beauty.

No, that was inaccurate. I was certainly not beautiful, tripping around so awkwardly. The others could be, especially Myra, whose practiced grace I liked to watch. The doing was the important thing, concentrating my energies, attempting to reach beauty, to physically join myself to the ethereal flow of what was best in life, and occasionally, momentarily being carried along by its force. Yes, that was it. Reaching for beauty was more important than creating it. Giving my energies over to this universal impulse celebrated life and gave me joy. One thing our dancing conveyed was the certainty that beauty existed.

A little over two months after the assault, I was at another kind of dance, sitting in Sammy's westernmost field, facing a soft breeze, leaning back on outstretched arms.

Forty feet away, fourteen Indians were taking a break. Most had wrapped a blanket, jacket, or heavy shirt around their shoulders. They were probably chilled, having danced continuously the last four hours, so evaporation of sweat and depletion of bodily fluids would be affecting them. They were also out of the sun down there on the bottoms this side of the high ridge above the distant curve of the river.

The men resembled denser than normal shadows, three-dimensional silhouettes. In the quiet since they'd stopped, the darkness shading them had been climbing the slope toward me.

The warmth of the day's last sun caressed my bare arms, legs, chest and head, inducing me to close my eyes, straighten out my legs, and stretch all my muscles.

Ah! Not one spritz of pain occurred anywhere. The bruising around my eyes, the swelled and split lips were healed, the cheekbones were knitted, and I breathed freely through the reconstructed nose. New crowns topped half of my single teeth in front. Only my two cracked ribs emitted an occasional pang when I twisted funny or strained, but there was no pain now.

Wasn't it time to jog and lift weights again? Yes. Tomorrow I'd try a few miles and a few curls, flies, squats and presses.

I opened my eyes, and Ted Cantrell was standing in front of me. What now? Another hassle?

"You look like a Buddha," he said.

"It sure is peaceful." I hoped it would stay that way. His presence punctured the daze I'd fallen into.

Ted was a surprise. Even wearing ornately decorated deerskin moccasins and loin cloth (with white jockey shorts underneath), he was brown haired, brown eyed, and although reddened now by the sun, as Caucasian looking as me, not what I'd expected for a Shawnee Indian. However, the Hopper Security System's final report, which was written, had sealed my confidence in him. The firm had never admitted giving Sammy a written report on me.

Ted turned to face west and crossed his arms on his chest.

I asked, "Do they want you to tell me to keep my hat off?"

He looked down at me. "That what those two got mad about?"

"They said to take off my hat because the dancing was sacred. I pointed out that half the dancers had hats on, and they said Indians could wear hats but non-Indians couldn't."

He chuckled. "They didn't explain. Just called you a name."

"I told them to quit playing games or leave. I hate elitist bullshit like that."

He laughed so loud a couple of the dancers looked our way. Then he said, "They're the two guys you invited."

"Yeah, I'm the damn dope who insisted they join you. I thought some locals ought to be here."

"Did BIA recommend them the way it did me?"

"No, a state Council for Native Americans identified them as Shawnee Indians."

He snorted. "More likely members of the Want-To-Be-An-Indian tribe. Lots of people like that."

"Aren't they Shawnees?"

"I don't know, but I think they're confusing this with a Powwow. Every Powwow has different rules, and some ask for hats off. You got to be careful about people claiming to be Indians."

"I should've stayed out of it. I don't know beans about Indians. See how much I need you to accept my offer?"

"The caretaker-manager job?"

"Until the positions have to be separated. Then we'll hire another person."

"It's a big move. I got to talk it over with the wife."

"The house would be rent free. A school bus comes right by here if you ever have kids."

"There's a lot of other things to consider."

"Right, like pay, benefits, responsibilities. Let's put them in writing and get the Board's feedback on them."

"The lawyer Brook and the sheriff?"

"Them and a guy from a nature preserve up the road. As manager, you'd be on the Board, and we figured on maybe another Indian you might help us choose. Then there are two other slots to fill."

"I could do the farming all right. And the maintenance. I don't know about the fund-raising and educational work."

"Well, a lot of us will be here to help, and I know you care about this place because of how quickly you came and got these men here to dance. Tomorrow, we'll talk it all through and see if we can work it out, okay? Christ, I need help. I got other things to do besides dealing with the Trust."

"Aren't you retired?"

"Retiring doesn't mean I'm dead. I have to tend to Mom and build myself a new house." And write a book, I thought but didn't say. The damn thing was only two short chapters along. "I'll also have to be at Rauch's trial, which starts next week. Hey, sit down. You have to be tired."

I lifted my butt and shifted left on my new blue plastic drop cloth.

He flopped down and said, "When the fire's going good, we'll start again."

"How long will you dance this time?"

" 'Til dawn."

"Really? Everybody looks exhausted now."

"We'll survive."

We'd find out about that. Dawn's first grayness was six hours away, and hell, all the men were much older than Ted's twenty-eight. Not one looked in good physical condition.

I lifted the backpack onto my lap, reached inside, and said, "How about a beer and something to eat?"

"You go ahead. Most of us won't take any food. That's the tradition as I know it. Your two guys brought ham and cheese sandwiches. That's okay, but some of us won't even take water."

I pulled out a can of lite beer, unsnapped its tab, set the can between my legs, and pulled out my plastic thermos. "You ought to try this turtle soup at least. It's great."

"Made from your turtle?"

"This is all that's left of him. Want me to save it 'til you finish dancing?"

"Now is okay. A little taste."

I unscrewed the cup from the thermos, gave the cup to him, swirled the thermos around to mix the contents, unscrewed the plug, and half filled his cup. "Want a spoon?"

"Don't need it." He sipped from the cup and within seconds said, "Very good. Thank you."

"Take more. You can have it all."

"The rest is yours."

He handed me the cup, took the thermos from my other hand and filled the cup, more or less forcing me to eat now.

Well, okay, I was hungry. I sipped a mouthful, chewed the tough little pieces of meat, and, swallowing, had a crazy thought. This felt like communion, which I hadn't taken in years.

I glanced over at Ted. He was staring straight ahead, but noticing my cup was lowered, he emptied the thermos into it.

I drank a second time. The soup seemed stronger than it had tasted at Mom's house weeks ago. Freezing the leftovers until this morning had enhanced its flavor.

When I finished the soup, closed the thermos and returned it to my pack, Ted said, "The turtle has a lot of meaning in Indian cultures. A famous Miami Indian chief who lived around here about 1800 was named for the turtle."

"Really?" I needed to explore native American mythology and history. Maybe he'd talk about them when he trusted me more.

A minute later Ted said, "Why don't you go back to the house and go to bed? No sense hanging around if you don't have to."

"Does it bother you that I'm here?"

"Not me, but your two friends are complaining about the white man looking over their shoulders."

"Keeping an eye on things is my responsibility. And those two guys are good reasons not to leave."

"Yeah, but this land's been raped for hundreds of years. What could they take or destroy?"

I shrugged.

He said, "Only some clover and weeds growing on it."

"You got any ideas what ought to be planted? I'm collecting ideas now. The naturalist on the Board wants to make it a prairie. It'll be restored as well as I can get it done. That's all I can promise. Far as I'm concerned, though, this is a magical place whatever shape it's in."

"Shawnees believe that everything has a spirit. Even rocks and dirt."

"Then lots of spirits have to be here."

Fifteen minutes later, Ted was back with the others. Below me, the flames were high, blowing aloft embers that winked out within a few soaring feet. Over to my right was the cedar post they had erected and danced around until now.

Once all fourteen men were settled down, sitting around the blaze, they lit and shared a two-foot long calumet. Each man held it out on extended arms in front of himself, exhaled a cloud of smoke, then passed the pipe left. All the while, someone chanted or recited something, maybe in Shawnee.

A few minutes later, the drum and flute began. Both musicians remained seated, playing on the west side of the fire, while the dancers rose and circled it, slowly and evenly spaced. One shook a gourd rattle. Several, usually at different times, sang monotonous, monosyllabic sounds, and others broke in occasionally with high-pitched yells.

The drums were steady as a heartbeat. In fact my heartbeat seemed to assume their rhythm. I centered myself on the cloth, set the open beer can aside on the dirt, lay back, put my hands beneath my head, stared up at the sky, and soon dozed.

After a while a chill made me shiver. I woke, sat up, put on my ball cap and tee shirt, and draped a jacket over my shoulders. Then I glanced down at the fire and the dancers.

So that was how they'd continue through the night. Five dancers were sitting while seven others danced. They were taking turns. Apparently, no one would dance the whole time.

I lay back down and closed my eyes, wishing Myra and Ed, Georgie and Chuck were here. Well, this wasn't a party so maybe their absence was good. They were with other friends at Serpent Mound tonight, doing their new age thing, which was against the law. The Park Service had denied permits to enter the area after hours so I wondered if they'd been chased off or arrested.

I would find out tomorrow when we met in the evening for dancing. Uh oh, I'd forgotten about that. Okay, no jogging or weight lifting tomorrow. Dancing would be enough exercise. I'd plug back into the old jogging and lifting routines on Saturday.

The thought of seeing Myra made me smile. She was good company, a friend, and maybe becoming more. The song for

Tzadik Katamar, an Israeli folk dance she'd called it, ran through my head and put me to sleep.

At 3:21, I sat up, rubbed my eyes, and checked my watch. Mist had oozed from the river, crossed the field in low spots and risen up in little spirals at its closest points. A three-quarters waxing moon poured down with an almost tangible glow. Thick air washed over me like warm cream.

The drum below me thumped, dum, dum, dum, dum, dum, but only one dancer was on his feet, Ted. He pranced in time with the beat, slowly did half turns, full turns, inexorably making his way clockwise around the flames. I envied Ted. Hadn't I been trying to do alone, free-dancing to cool down after lifting weights, what he was doing now? If so, without his cultural background, I had not known how nor understood my purpose.

One of the seated men stood, lay two more hunks of wood on the fire, and started dancing on the opposite side of the flames from Ted. Somebody began a low chant like a rising and falling hum, like the chanting of OM, solemn and continuous.

This ritual was ancient in pedigree, a precursor of all dances. It honored the elements, the things buried in the earth and latent in the air. Its cadence and continuous movement mimicked the passing of time.

Behind the men, the mist curled up in shifting, ethereal forms, and I thought of Dad, Sammy, Aunt Judy, even Simon Croft. Memories of them poured through me.

Farther out beyond the burning and the dancing, the old river flowed, the brush, trees and hills reared up darkly, and the moon and the stars made the ether resemble a heavy canvas that covered a very bright presence, which was visible only in pieces through a million tiny holes.

Something good was going to happen. Hell, good was happening right now. A lot of good had already happened.

ABOUT THE AUTHOR

Bill Vernon served in the United States Marine Corps as an infantryman (three years) and a Short Airfield For Tactical Support (SATS) technician. He then studied at the University of Dayton and Miami University (Ohio), and during this time began teaching English composition and literature, a career that included short stints at the University of Dayton and Wilberforce University before a long stay at Sinclair Community College, where he devised a highly successful course on the Vietnam War.

While teaching, he also wrote poetry, short fiction, novels and some nonfiction prose, mostly book reviews. Samisdat Press published three short collections of his poems in the chapbooks *To a Friend . . . ; Praising the Sand;* and *Cleaning the Bones.* Alms House Press published his *Boating on the Ohio* as the winner of its 1993 annual poetry chapbook competition.

His poems have also appeared in journals such as *Yankee, Albany Review, Cincinnati Review, Blue Unicorn, The Archer, Grasslands Review, Arete: the Journal of Sport Literature, West Branch, The Mickle Street Review, Southern Humanities Review, The Formalist, Hellas, The Runner, Hemlocks and Balsams,* and *Passages North.* His short fiction has appeared in literary journals, and most recently in on-line magazines such as *Fables, Spaceways Weekly, Mocha Memoirs, Alternate Realities, Fantasy, Folklore & Fairytales, Blue Murder Magazine, Foxfire, The A-List,* and *Rogue Worlds.* Anthologies containing some of his work are

Poetry Ohio: Special Issue of The Cornfield Review, Nemeton, Wetting Our Lines Together, The Runner's Literary Companion, and *The Sporting Life.* Additionally, he was a Major Contributing Editor of *Those Who Were There,* a bibliographical study of Vietnam War literature.

Bill grew up in the Appalachian foothills and the farm country of southern Ohio, played baseball and other sports, ran marathons, and lifted weights. Now he folk dances and hikes, works out daily one way or another. A lover of the outdoors, he finds urban sprawl's destruction of the once-beautiful fields and forests of his native region, its biota and its history, worse than disheartening.